*"I'll give you a thousand dollars
if you can make my sister
believe that you're my fiancée."*

Samantha couldn't believe what Jack Remington was telling her. "Do you like to play jokes on your sister."

"No, I like to make her happy. That's why I need a fiancée. Just for tonight."

"Don't you have a *real* fiancée?"

"I did, but we had a . . . misunderstanding. Look, my sister has never met her. She doesn't know what she looks like. You're an actress . . . "

"But you forget, I've never played anything but a corpse. On top of that, I've never been to a ball. And you don't understand. I have nothing to wear."

His gaze trailed deliberately over her body, then slowly moved to her eyes.

And that's when Samantha knew she'd say yes.

Other Avon Contemporary Romances by
Patti Berg

IF I CAN'T HAVE YOU
LOOKING FOR A HERO
TILL THE END OF TIME
WISHES COME TRUE

PATTI BERG

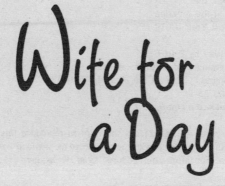

Wife for a Day

AVON BOOKS NEW YORK

AVON BOOKS, INC.
1350 Avenue of the Americas
New York, New York 10019

Copyright © 1999 by Patti Berg
Published by arrangement with the author
Library of Congress Catalog Card Number: 99-94776
ISBN: 0-380-80735-1
www.avonbooks.com/romance

First Avon Books Printing: August 1999

AVON TRADEMARK REG. U.S. PAT. OFF. AND IN OTHER COUNTRIES, MARCA REGISTRADA, HECHO EN U.S.A.

Printed in the U.S.A.

WCD   10   9   8   7   6   5   4   3   2   1

one

You will do foolish things, but do them with enthusiasm.

Colette

Samantha Jones' beat-up Volkswagen Bug was one perfect place to cry. It was small, confining, and with all her worldly possessions packed inside, it hugged her like a warm pair of grandmotherly arms.

She should have known Mr. Antonio would fire her if he caught her napping in the back room at Antonio's For Men. But she'd been so tired—tired of sleeping in the bug, tired of working too many hours for people who didn't appreciate her, tired of trying to earn enough money to pay off Johnnie Russo—so tired that she hadn't cared if she got caught. All she'd wanted to do was sleep.

Sam sniffed back a tear as she concentrated

1

on the blurry, palm tree-lined road and the cars whizzing by her slow-moving bug. She willed herself not to think about being unemployed. She didn't want to think about Johnnie, the money she owed him, or the fact that "Jaws," as Johnnie was affectionately known in loan-shark circles, had painted her a very vivid picture of what would happen if she didn't abide by the terms of their contract, which expired in four weeks and two days.

She didn't want to relive all that had happened five months ago. She needed to watch the road, to think about what she was doing now, but the memories flooded her thoughts. In the space of six horrid days, she'd lost everything: years of savings, her pride, and the most cherished person in her life—her mama.

How easily she could see Mama lying in the hospital, her cheeks sunken, dark circles surrounding her eyes. Sam remembered holding her mother's frail fingers, wishing some of her own energy for life could seep through her mother's skin; but she'd already lost the will to go on.

The doctors at the county hospital, where the poor and downtrodden were treated, said they'd done all they could possibly do. Surgery had repaired her internal injuries, but the chaplain told Sam the doctors couldn't do anything for an injured soul.

Sam had refused to listen. She'd already used her savings looking for a doctor who'd give her some positive news, so she'd gone to Graham Welles, an acquaintance who'd once said he'd move the sun and the moon for her. But Graham had added an addendum when Sam needed him most: he'd give her anything, but he wanted her in return.

Sam remembered the rage in Graham's eyes just before she'd run away from his home. She fingered the scar on her jaw, remembering the flash of his diamond ring when he'd struck her across the face. She'd nearly sold her soul to Graham Welles, but at the last moment she'd realized that wouldn't save her mama. Nothing could bring back the life that had been wasting away for years.

Later that night, the chaplain came again. The somber man walked into the hospital room not too long after Mama had died. He'd offered a prayer for Mama's soul, telling God that Felicity Jones might have been a prostitute—his voice lowering to a whisper when he uttered the word—but she'd had a heart of gold. He'd put a comforting hand on Sam's shoulder, and then he'd talked with her about options, emphasizing cremation because it was the cheapest way to go.

Sam could remember the look of shock on the minister's face, when she laughed and told him, "My mama's entire life has been scattered on the wind. I don't care how much it costs. I don't even care how I get the money, but my mama's going to have a place where she can put down roots, a place she can live forever, even if her final home is nothing more than a few square feet of dirt and grass."

That's when Johnnie Russo had come into the picture.

She stopped at an intersection when the light turned red and wiped a tear from her eye. *Johnnie Russo.* She shook her head at her foolishness. She was too street-smart to go to a man with a reputation like Johnnie's, but she'd tried borrowing from the bank, from friends, from high-rate loan companies, and heard the same refrains everywhere she turned: your credit's not good enough; you have no assets; sorry, Sam, but I'm just as broke as you are. Johnnie hadn't cared about assets. He said he trusted her, and she'd fallen for his sympathetic line, which shifted dramatically right after the funeral, when he'd told her the initial payment was due in a month. The first late charge would be a broken arm.

She'd stayed in Southern California long enough to make the first installment on the loan, and then she'd run away from Hollywood, from an acting career that had gone nowhere, from friends who'd been nothing more than acquaintances, from memories of her mother's tragic death. She thought she could start again in West Palm Beach, the town where she'd grown up.

But she'd finally destroyed any chance for a new life when she'd stolen the sewing machine from Mr. Antonio a few minutes ago.

A horn blared behind her, and Sam shifted into first and the bug crept up the road. She wished she could shift thoughts as easily, but the sewing machine was in plain view, and her guilt couldn't be pushed aside. She hadn't planned to steal it, but the opportunity had jumped at her when she was heading out of Antonio's For Men with the last of her belongings. She shouldn't have answered the phone— that was Mr. Antonio's job. She shouldn't have told the concierge from the Breakers that Antonio's would be honored to provide a tux for Jack Remington, the wealthy owner of the Remington Steakhouses. She'd planned to give Mr. Antonio the message, but when she'd interrupted him and the client he was working with, he'd made it perfectly clear he never wanted to hear from her again.

Stealing had been foolish—*and* wrong. But she'd promised the concierge that the job would be done and done right, and he'd assured her that Mr. Remington would be generous with his tip—a tip she desperately needed. Her justification for turning into a thief was skewed, but what was done was done.

She sighed, glancing down at the sewing machine sitting on the floorboards. Hopefully, Mr. Antonio wouldn't notice it was missing before she had a chance to return it. Hopefully, he wouldn't notice the credit-card receipt for the Armani tux she'd sold until it was too late. Hopefully, he wouldn't find out that she'd gone to the Breakers to alter that tux, because he'd told her time and time again that special jobs could only be handled by an expert—himself.

Well, she was an expert, too. Mama had taught her how to hand-stitch doll clothes when she was a child, and Sam had fashioned outfits from scraps of fabric the Salvation Army volunteers had given her when she and Mama had gone to the shelter for meals. She'd thought she was a pretty good seamstress until she met Sydney Bowes, the flamboyant drag queen she and Mama had lived with for nearly a year. He'd taught her the fine art of alteration, something he'd mastered to make his six-foot-one frame look stunning in size twelve sequined gowns.

Mama had taught her about love and trust, the importance of proper manners and being good, while Syd taught her practical things like which thrift stores stocked the fanciest clothes and how to dicker with the owners to get the best deal. He'd told her that diamonds might be a girl's best friend, but a stunning pair of shoes and confidence are *the* most important fashion accessories.

"You can be anything you want to be, as long as you have confidence," Syd had told her, and Mama had often echoed his words.

Sam was twelve when Syd came into her life and fourteen when he died of AIDS. He was the closest thing she'd ever had to a father, and she'd loved him nearly as much as she'd loved Mama.

Sam laughed, thinking about Mama and Syd. They were misfits living in a world that shunned their lifestyles. They were bold, daring, and claimed they didn't care that people laughed behind their backs. But Sam knew better because she was like them in so many ways. On the outside she was confidence personified; on the inside, beneath the bravado, was an insecure, lonely woman who'd been looking for a place to belong, but so far had fit in nowhere.

She already knew she didn't fit in at the Breakers. She'd been thrown out at the age of ten, when she'd crashed a wedding reception just to see how the rich people lived. Getting kicked out again was something she couldn't afford.

Pulling over to the side of the road, she tilted down the rearview mirror and took a good look at flushed cheeks and dark circles under her tear-reddened eyes. She felt like a two-bit crook *and* looked like a bedraggled waif. She'd be lucky to make it into the lobby, and even if she did get that far, she was bound to scare away Mr. Remington before she had the chance to earn a tip.

She licked the tissue in her hand and wiped away the smudged mascara and eyeliner, then dug in her tote bag for a compact and applied powder that was a shade too dark. It had been perfect in California, when she'd had the time to play in the sun. Here in Florida, where she'd worked all day and part of the nights in Mr. Antonio's sweatshop, it wasn't right at all. Still, it covered up the circles.

Lipstick came next. Cherry red wasn't her most becoming color, but the samples had been free, and she'd run out of her own shade two weeks ago. She fluffed her hair, doing the best she could with her curls, then reached over the seat to grab the black Versace sandals—lethal four-inch stilettos—that she'd found hidden behind a pile of Hush Puppies at How Tacky, a thrift store in West Palm Beach. They were perfect with her lacy white Kmart camisole and her How Tacky Donna Karan suit, things she'd bought because Mr. Antonio had insisted she wear fine, well-tailored clothing at work.

Mama and Syd had always told her that she should look her best, no matter what. And right now she needed to look like a million bucks. She was strong. She was going to get her desperately needed tip, and she wasn't about to let the Johnnie Russos and Mr. Antonios of this world knock her down.

Adjusting the mirror so she could once again see the oncoming traffic, she put the car into gear, and the VW sputtered up Royal Poinciana Way, passed the golf course and lush gardens, and came to a dead stop in front of *the* hotel on Breakers Row.

"You don't belong here."

The voice came from out of her past, the voice of the man who'd ushered her out of the hotel years ago, but she shoved it aside. *You do belong*, she told herself. *You can be anything you want to be.*

Right now, she wanted to be Cinderella. She wished her fairy godmother would appear, wave her wand, and turn her Kmart camisole and her How Tacky rich-lady ensemble into something casually elegant, so she'd at least *look* like she belonged at the exquisite hotel. She wished the magic wand would wave over her orange VW bug and turn it into a gold Ferrari, too, because at the moment it looked like a battered pumpkin.

And . . . she wished the valet leaning toward her open window would wipe the grin off his face. "Good afternoon. You must be from Antonio's," he said, glancing at the sewing machine on the floor. "The concierge told us to expect you."

Oh, good. Now they're going to send me to the delivery entrance. Well, she wasn't going to wait for something that humiliating to happen. She pulled a few precious dollar bills from her tote bag and slipped them into the young man's hand. "I won't be here long," she said hastily. "If you'll help me get my things out of the car and tell me how to get to the Flagler Club, you can park the car."

There. Direct, assertive, and confident. She took a deep breath and pretended she had just as much right to be here as anyone else.

Within seconds a bellman had the black garment bag and the gray-plastic carrying case that contained the portable sewing machine out of the car, the valet ground the gears as he drove away in her bug, and she looked like every other rich person walking into the grand and imposing lobby.

The bellman escorted her to the elevator, but she insisted on going the rest of the way alone. She wanted to soak in the opulence, to feel, for just a little while, like she was one of the millionaires who were as plentiful as sand in Palm Beach.

Of course, Jack Remington, the man whose tux she'd come to alter, wasn't your run-of-the-mill Palm Beach millionaire. She'd read about him once and knew he was a big-time rancher somewhere out west, that he owned a string of steak houses that served Remington beef, fine wine, and rich desserts, and that he had a much-married socialite sister who lived in Palm Beach and owned a big old mansion on South Ocean Boulevard.

She'd never seen a picture of Jack Remington, but rancher, to her, conjured the image of a tobacco-chewing cowboy with dusty clothes and a sweat-stained hat. She couldn't envision him wearing the tux she was going to fit on him or, she thought cynically, tipping any more generously than Max Stuyvessant or Chip Chasen, who'd ignored her yesterday afternoon when they'd left Antonio's with their perfectly tailored ensembles.

Still, she remained hopeful.

The bell chimed, and the elevator doors slid open. An arrangement of lilies nearly as big as the room she worked in at Antonio's greeted her. Shrugging the garment bag high on her shoulder, she gripped the handle of her sewing-machine case and confidently stepped into the Flagler Club. The concierge had been expecting her. He smiled, as if she were a real person—not a servant—and following his explicit instructions, she headed straight for Jack Remington's suite.

Raising her hand to knock, her knuckles stopped a few inches from the door when she heard a deep, irritated voice rumbling inside the room.

"Damn it, Arabella. Couldn't you have waited another week to call it quits?"

She could hear someone pacing. Jack Remington, more than likely, and he sounded like a bull ready to charge.

"I'm not going to argue with you," he said, his voice calming somewhat. "I know we haven't talked much in the past month, but—"

His words were cut short, and silence permeated the room. Sam held her breath, afraid the man on the other side of the door would know she was lurking outside. Finally, he spoke again. "Keep the ring," he said abruptly. "Keep the fur and the Jag. If I'm half the son of a bitch you claim I am, you deserve a hell of a lot more." His voice trailed off, and then he laughed. "Your timing couldn't have been better, Arabella. You knew my promise to Lauren. You knew this would break my sister's heart, and you knew hurting her was the only way you could hurt me."

Another pause. Sam's nerves were jarred by the sound of a slamming phone. She thought about leaving, but the weight of the tux she needed to deliver pulled on her shoulder, and the hope of collecting a good-sized, much-needed tip made her stay.

Sam swallowed and knocked lightly.

No answer.

She knocked a little harder.

The door flew open, and a man the size of John Wayne filled the doorway. "What do you want?"

Of all the . . . *Stay calm*, she told herself, as his words rumbled around her. *Remember the tip. Remember what's going to happen to you in four weeks and two days.*

"I'm from Antonio's," Sam said through a forced smile.

It seemed to take a good ten seconds for her words to penetrate his skull. He eyed her up and down, probably the same way he would analyze a heifer. "Right. The tux." He looked at his watch. "You're late, but what the hell. Nothing else has gone right today." He turned away, walking back into the room, where he removed the stopper from a crystal decanter and poured an inch of liquor into a sparkling tumbler.

He hadn't invited her in. In fact, he hadn't said one civil word since he'd opened the door. She might have grown up on the wrong side of the tracks, but she'd been taught that no matter what your station in life, good manners were the true sign of impeccable breeding.

Jack Remington swigged down half the booze and turned. A ray of light glanced off his light brown hair. It was shot full of gold, and the hair in his sideburns was turning white. *He works too hard,* she told herself, sizing him up. *Probably spends his days and nights bossing people around.*

As if he'd heard her thoughts, he stared at her with his sun-bleached brows knit together. "I haven't got all day. Are you going to stand in the hall or come in?"

"I'm not going to do either," Sam said, the words slipping over the end of her tongue before she could catch them.

"You're what?"

"You heard me." Sam's better judgment had just flown down the hallway and caught the express elevator out of the hotel.

She pushed the garment bag from her shoulder and let it slide to the floor. Already today she'd kissed her much-needed job good-bye and now she was saying so long to this tip.

Stalking toward her, Jack Remington stopped mere inches away. He was tall. Real tall, but she was no slouch herself and in four-inch killer heels, she came close to staring straight into his heated blue eyes.

"What the hell are you doing?" he asked.

"Leaving." She looked down at the garment bag lying in a heap between them. "That's your tux, Mr. Remington. If it doesn't fit, go naked."

She didn't bother waiting for a response. She just turned, headed back to the elevator, and stabbed two fingertips at the down arrow, hitting instead the rock-solid hand that had just slid over the button.

"I was led to believe that you'd alter the tux if it didn't fit," he said.

"And I was led to believe that rich people have manners."

He raised an eyebrow. "My apologies."

As if his curt repentance was enough, Jack Remington grabbed the sewing machine from her hand and strode back to his suite, leaving Sam standing at the elevator, watching his back.

A nice back, she had to admit. There was a strong possibility that his body—not to mention his good looks—were the only nice things about him. Still . . . she studied him. She'd never been keen on men who dressed like they belonged onstage at the Grand Ole Opry, but she admired the way his white cowboy shirt stretched tightly across wide shoulders. His slacks were charcoal, not too tight across the butt, not too loose. In fact, they were impeccably tailored, as if she'd done the fitting herself. He wore cowboy boots. Not the hundred-dollar variety with cow dung crusted on the soles, but a pair that must have cost a good thousand or more, and it looked as if he'd just left the hotel's shoeshine stand because the black leather glimmered when he walked.

For all his riches, Jack Remington wasn't wearing Gianfranco Ferre or Messori, not even tropical menswear like some others she'd seen at the Breakers. In fact, Jack Remington didn't look like he belonged in this hotel any more than she did.

"Are you coming?" he asked bluntly.

She knew she should keep her lips buttoned, but she looked into his frowning blue eyes and smiled her sweetest, most innocent smile. "Say please."

His eyebrow rose again, then he swept the garment bag up from the floor and waited silently for her beside the door. She strolled back to the room, thinking about asking him again to say please, then decided that she'd pushed about as far as she could at the moment. She might have salvaged her tip. No need to court trouble again.

Besides, she could push confidence and bravado just so far.

The inside of the main room was ... well, it was beyond compare. The apartment she'd rented in West Hollywood hadn't been much bigger than this living room, and it definitely hadn't been as well put together.

Scattered about the room were lavish arrangements of roses, lilies, and orchids, and Sam could detect the scent of gardenia coming from somewhere in the suite. She'd never seen anything so luxurious, but she wasn't going to let Mr. Remington think she was impressed.

When she heard the door close behind her, she did a slow turn to inspect the room, then looked at the cowboy millionaire and pretended she had as much right to be demanding as he did. She pointed to the farside of the room. "That desk over there will be perfect for the sewing machine."

Obviously, he hadn't heard her, because an arm that felt like granite brushed against her shoulder as he walked into the connecting room. "I prefer the bedroom."

"The lighting's perfect out here. I think—"

"*I* think we'll use the bedroom," he said,

and Sam didn't bother to argue as she followed him.

He tossed the garment bag on the bed and set the sewing machine on the vanity near one of the windows. "I'm in a hurry." He looked again at his watch. "I've got an engagement party in two hours, and I can't be late."

"Yours?"

"My what?"

"*Your* engagement party?"

He laughed, and the first hint of a smile touched his lips. "No," he said flatly. "My sister's."

"Oh, that's right," Sam said, unzipping the bag. "I read all about her and the polo player. What's his name?"

"Peter Leighton."

Ice could have formed on his words, and Sam decided to steer away from the subject of Australian polo players getting engaged to Palm Beach socialites, and said the first thing that came to mind. "I would have thought someone like you would already own a tuxedo."

Jack Remington raised the lid on a humidor and pulled out a cigar. He rolled it just beneath his nose, cut off the tip, then stuck it in his mouth while she took a pair of highly polished black shoes and all the pieces to the tux out of the bag.

Fire shot out of the silver lighter in his hand, and she could hear it sizzle as he held it close to the cigar and puffed. She could see his eyes studying her through the swirling smoke. "Are you always so inquisitive?" he asked.

"When the situation warrants it, I suppose." She lifted the trousers from the bed and slid open the zipper. "So, why don't you tell me what happened to your tux?"

"Why don't we just fit the one you brought?"

"I can listen and work at the same time."

"An admirable trait."

"Quite. Now take off your clothes."

Jack had never encountered a woman like the redhead. She wasn't just inquisitive, she was bossy, too. It was a rare occasion when he gave in to a woman, but he didn't have time to argue. There wasn't time to send her from the room while he changed, wasn't time to find a tailor who concentrated more on the clothes than on him or worked instead of talked.

And, Jack decided, even if he found a tailor with those qualifications, he'd never find one as easy on the eye.

Sitting in an armchair, he leaned over to remove his boots. Seconds later a pair of sky-high heels came into view, along with ten toes that seemed to tap to unheard music. He looked up, following the long length of her legs. She reached out and for a moment he thought she was going to help him pull off his boots. Instead, she plucked the hand-rolled Montecristo from his lips.

"This is in the way, Mr. Remington." She held the cigar gingerly between the tips of her index finger and thumb. "I can't do my job with you puffing nonstop, so I'll just stick it in the ashtray for safekeeping."

She walked across the room, her hips swaying provocatively. On some other woman the action might have seemed forced, but a natural seductiveness emanated from the redhead. She could probably bewitch him if he were in any mood to be seduced.

But he wasn't. Not at the moment, at least. Arabella Fleming had seduced him once with an exquisite smile and with hands that slid over his body like those of a highly skilled masseuse. She was smart, sexy, and a month ago he thought she'd be the perfect wife, but she'd dumped him over the phone—he looked at his watch—twenty-two minutes ago. They were never, ever going to get back together, a fact Arabella had made perfectly clear.

That meant he could look at the redhead all he wanted.

She set the Montecristo in the ashtray and turned. Her mass of flaming curls spun about her, almost in slow motion. She was one hell of a good-looking specimen.

He tossed one boot then another across the room, as the redhead moved toward him. He stood, unbuttoned his trousers, and slid open the zipper while the woman appraised his entire body in much the same way he would a prizewinning stallion. The only difference: her face didn't show any emotion. No pleasure. No excitement. No nothing!

"I thought you were in a hurry," she said, standing in front of him with her arms folded under sumptuous breasts. "We'll be here all night if you don't take off your clothes."

He started to shove down the trousers. *Damn!* He was wearing the black-silk thong Arabella had sent him a week ago and made him promise to wear when they flew to Florida. Her note tucked into the gift box had said something about fooling around at fifty-one thousand feet, with the other passengers just a few feet away from the action. He hadn't been thinking straight when he'd put the damned thing on this morning.

"Is there a problem?" the redhead asked.

Jack refocused his thoughts on her inquisitive brown eyes. "No."

"Well, there's no need to be modest. I may be a woman, but I'm also the finest tailor you'll find in Palm Beach. I've seen it all," she said, moving closer. Long, slender fingers captured the top button on his shirt and worked their way down, releasing each one as if she'd unbuttoned men's shirts a million times before. He could smell the dizzying scent of her perfume, could almost feel the heat of her skin, and taste the sweetness of the bright red lipstick on her mouth.

"You know," she said softly, "Mr. Antonio had a customer once who wanted me to personally tailor his underwear." She peeled the shirt away from his body, her eyes casually skimming his chest and arms. "He had this purple silk thong that just didn't fit right. I made a little tuck here, a little tuck there, and *voilà!* it was perfect. Even his boyfriend approved."

"I'm not the least interested in having my underwear tailored," Jack said, his hand still positioned over his zipper.

"It doesn't look like you want these trousers tailored either. Funny thing about tailoring, you can't do it unless your client is willing to put on the item you're planning to alter."

Her eyes trailed to his fingers, then back again to his face. "Would you like me to leave the room while you change?"

He'd never been afraid of anything in his life, and he wasn't about to turn coward in front of the redhead. He dropped his slacks and stood in front of her, all six feet four inches, 230 pounds of him, clad only in a thong.

The woman had the nerve to put a thoughtful finger over her lips and aim her eyes directly at the damned black silk. "You know, Mr. Remington, you look awfully good in that thong but, personally, I prefer boxers."

"Have you ever worn a thong?"

"Once or twice. I'm not crazy about the feel. But, we all have our own personal tastes."

She walked away, as if she'd lost all interest in the discussion and his body, and lifted the trousers from the bed. Turning them inside out, she dangled them in front of her.

Jack snatched the slacks from her hands. "I don't like wearing a tux any more than I like wearing a thong," he announced. "But since the airline seems to have lost all my luggage, since you were the only tailor the concierge was able to find on a Friday night, and since I'm in a hurry, could you just get this damn thing fitted so I can get to my sister's engagement party?"

A smile formed on a pair of picture-perfect lips as he slid into the trousers, struggled with the wrong-side-out zipper, and finally fastened the button.

"Are you a big tipper, Mr. Remington?"

"Only when I'm pleased with the service."

"You'll be pleased. I'm sure of it."

She went to work immediately, running her fingers around his waistband, over his hips, down the outside of each leg, his thighs and calves. "You could have modeled for these trousers," she said. "They're almost a perfect fit."

"Good. Then why don't we move on to the jacket?"

"All in good time. I need to check a few spots on the trousers." She placed one hand close to his crotch, and he gritted his teeth, fighting the natural instincts of his body. Never again would he allow a woman tailor to alter his clothes.

"There's a little problem with the fit here, Mr. Remington."

"Problem? What kind of problem?"

"It's not that *big* a problem." Her smile widened as she looked up at him through dark, thick lashes. "I just need to know which side you dress on."

The way she'd been running her hand over his body, she should have known by now. "The left."

"That's what I thought, but it never hurts to double check." She concentrated again on his zipper, and he tilted his chin and stared at wavy hair on top her head. "I have to make a few small adjustments. Won't take long." She pulled a pin from the black-velvet cushion fastened around her wrist.

She aimed the sharp steel head straight at his . . .

"Be careful with that."

"Relax. I know perfectly well what I'm doing."

Relax? Hell!

"You know, Mr. Remington—"

"*Jack!* Just call me Jack, will you?"

"So, *Jack*, how come a guy with all your money took a commercial flight from . . . Where is it you're from?"

"Wyoming."

"That's right. I've read about your ranch . . . and you. Anyway, I would have thought a millionaire like you would have his own Concorde or Lear."

"I own horses and cows, not jets."

"Too bad. If you'd flown here in your own plane, you wouldn't have lost your tux, and you wouldn't have been stuck here with me."

"As I said, this day hasn't gone according to—*damn it!*"

"I'm sorry, Jack." She looked up at him with a worried smile that he knew, without a doubt, was false. "It was just one little prick. I promise it won't happen again."

He glared at her. Her eyes had refocused on the straight pins she was jabbing into his pants, and she was trying like hell not to laugh.

Little prick? Ha!

He shook his head as he studied the woman kneeling in front of him. She had a wildness about her. A fiery exuberance that came damn close to making him smile, and it had been a hell of a long time since mere conversation with a woman had made him smile.

two

If the tailor had been a man instead of a pretty woman, Jack might have slipped into the terry-cloth robe the hotel provided. Instead, he'd completely redressed, found a comfortable place in the bedroom, and pored over a stack of restaurant-related papers.

The redhead and the way she hummed as she worked distracted him. He unbuttoned his cuffs and rolled up the sleeves on his shirt as his eyes drifted from the contract in his lap to the toes of her left foot, which kept perfect time with her tune. In contrast, her right foot pressed against the lever on the floor, making the needle thrum as it moved up and down, in and out of the trousers she guided through her sewing machine.

Damn if there wasn't something intensely erotic about what she was doing.

He leaned back on the bedroom sofa, forgetting the legalese before him. Lifting his cigar from the ashtray, he clenched it between his teeth, savoring the taste, and watched her through the pungent smoke. She'd removed her coat nearly half an hour ago and settled down at the table to sew. He'd watched her long, slender fingers nimbly work with the fabric, plucking out old thread, snipping the material with small silver scissors, and adjusting seams.

Arabella had once tossed a white cashmere sweater into the trash because a button had popped off. "I don't have the faintest idea how to sew," she'd told him. He'd offered to sew it on for her; she'd asked him to buy her a new one instead. Had that incident been the start of their relationship's demise? he wondered, or had they been doomed from the start?

He looked back at the contract, refocusing on the paragraph he'd read two or three times before. Arabella would have devoured the legal document in minutes. She would have offered opinions, made suggestions, and rewritten language she didn't find quite right. They would have talked for hours about mergers and acquisitions, the stock market, and the fiscal aspects of his ranch and restaurant chain. Business conversation came easy, their sex life was great, and he'd put a ring on her finger because he thought she'd be the perfect partner.

Somehow he'd forgotten about the personal side, their likes and dislikes. He'd forgotten all about love.

He laughed at his oversight.

The redhead glanced up from her sewing and tilted her head toward him. She swept a curl behind her ear, smiled softly, and when he smiled in return, she went back to work.

He doubted the tailor would ever throw away a cashmere sweater. In fact, he found himself wondering if she'd ever owned one. He tried picturing her in pearls, a classy business suit, and black pumps, her wild hair pulled back in a tight bun, but that was Arabella's style. He could more easily picture the redhead in blue jeans, which was the way he'd wanted to see Arabella. But ranch living wasn't her style.

Arabella loved the opera and ballet, which he despised. She wanted to take vacations on the Costa del Sol or the Riviera; he preferred a tent in the mountains. He wanted two or three children; her work was the only baby she wanted to nurture. And even though she'd grown up on her father's sprawling Colorado ranch, she loved the city and had no intention of living or even visiting the Wyoming outback.

Never again would he ask a woman to marry him without being damn sure that she'd fit in at the ranch. Hell, he didn't want to think about marriage again. A sense of relief had washed over him when Arabella had ended their relationship. Right now, he planned to take full advantage of being a free man.

And the woman who interested him most was sitting in his bedroom. He had an eye for beautiful women—and this one was gorgeous, from her toenails—painted fire-engine red—to the long flaming hair that hung halfway down her back in a hundred springing corkscrews.

She was tall, slender, and had breasts that were every man's fantasy come to life.

But there was more to her than that. Sitting in front of the sewing machine like a symphony pianist caught up in her recital, was a woman with circles under her eyes. She'd tried covering the darkened skin with makeup, but hadn't succeeded. Her cheeks were a little too hollow, as if she didn't eat often or enough, and her jaw bore the traces of a small, jagged scar.

What had happened to her? he wondered. And why?

Shoving the contract into his briefcase, he walked across the room and leaned against the wall in a place where he could see the concentration on her face. Her gaze lifted from her labor again, and her smile met his stare. One flick from those hot green eyes could set a prairie on fire, he thought, or reduce a man to cinders if he didn't stay on guard.

As if she'd heard his thoughts and knew it was time to turn off her smile, she focused once more on the trousers.

He knew he should go back to his work, knew he should ignore the tailor, who was there to do a job and nothing more, but he was restless.

Arabella entered his thoughts again, an ounce of remorse flowing through him. Maybe he should have tried to meet her halfway, but he didn't want to live in Denver any more than she wanted to live in Wyoming. He didn't want to spend any more time with her society friends than she wanted to spend with his ranch hands, the people who were his extended family.

In the past few weeks, their conversations about the future had ceased. Long phone calls became a rush to see who could come up with the best excuse for hanging up. Their engagement had been a mistake, and he knew it.

The only one who thought it was wonderful was his sister Lauren. Over the years she'd introduced him to one socialite after another, hoping her big brother would find a wife.

She'd been ecstatic when Jack had found the perfect wife-to-be all on his own, and she'd been anxiously awaiting their first meeting tonight.

How on earth could he tell Lauren that his engagement was over?

Poor Lauren. Her mother and father had a bad habit of disappointing her, and now he was going to do it, too. He sighed, letting out some of his frustration.

"Is something bothering you?" the redhead asked. She'd stopped sewing. Her head tilted toward him again and all he could see were luminous freckles bridging her nose and soft, warm eyes that were the color of good whiskey. "You may not believe this, but I can listen as well as I can talk."

"I don't make a habit of sharing my troubles."

"Too bad. My mama always told me that storing trouble makes you feel all constipated inside."

"I take it your mama's a pretty wise lady."

"She was," she said fondly. "She used to laugh at trouble, and believe you me, she used to laugh a lot."

"What about you?"

She smiled, and Jack could swear the room brightened. "I've been constipated a time or two."

The phone rang, interrupting the first light-hearted moment in his day. He answered on the second ring. "Remington."

"Thought for sure I'd miss you." It was Mike Flynn, his ranch manager. A call from Mike, when he was away from the ranch, could only mean trouble.

"Something wrong?" Jack asked.

"I suppose that's something you have to decide."

"Don't beat around the bush, Mike. You wouldn't have called if there wasn't a problem."

Silence stretched between them. Finally, Mike cleared his throat. "Beau is here."

The name hit Jack like a bull kicking him in the gut. He'd seen his son only once in sixteen years. He'd given up all hope of ever getting to know the boy, and now he was at the ranch.

"Are you okay?" Mike asked but didn't stop talking long enough for Jack to answer "no." "I hated to spring it on you so suddenly, but I didn't know what to say."

Jack didn't know what to say, either. "Are you sure it's him?"

"Positive."

"Is he alone?"

"Yeah."

Jack plowed his fingers through his hair. "How'd he get there? Hell, how'd he find out about me? There's no way his grandparents told him."

"He found his mother's diary, saw your name in it, and put two and two together. Then he hitched all the way from LA."

"Hitched? Damn it! He could have gotten lost. Killed."

"He's safe, Jack. He just wants to see you."

Jack crossed the room, poured a glass full of whiskey, then ignored the drink. "Why didn't he call first?"

"I didn't ask, but my guess is he was afraid you wouldn't want to see him."

"I would have seen him every day for the past sixteen years if his grandparents hadn't told me to stay the hell away!"

And he had stayed away—for Beau's sake. The boy's grandparents had taken good care of him, he wouldn't dispute that. But he'd stayed away only because they'd promised a messy custody battle when Jack turned eighteen and asked for his child. He had enough money to fight for his rights, but there was no way he was going to drag his son through the courts and the press.

He didn't regret that decision; he only regretted giving up his son in the first place.

"Jack," Mike said, his voice low, solemn, "the past is over and done. This is your chance to make up for all that happened."

"How much time do you think his grand-parents are going to give me? A day? Two?"

"Talk to them."

"I tried that years ago. They ignored my phone calls. They sent back every penny of support money, every birthday card. They love Beau. They've given him the best of everything, but they don't want me interfering in his life. You know damn good and well they won't listen to me now."

"Try again. He's your son, Jack. If you don't do something about it now, you'll lose him for good."

He couldn't lose him. Not again.

Jack looked across the room. The seamstress was watching him, her eyes narrowed to a frown. He could imagine the same kind of frown on Mike's face. Preaching on Sunday wasn't enough for Mike. He had a habit of doing it all week long, and Jack was the one he tar-geted most. He had the feeling the tailor would do it, too, if she had any idea what was going on.

He turned away from the redhead and ended the silence between himself and Mike. "Tell Beau I'll be home tomorrow afternoon."

"Anything else?" Mike asked.

"Yeah, tell him there's a lot we need to talk about."

Jack could picture the smile of satisfaction on Mike's face. "I'll tell him."

"And make sure Crosby doesn't run Beau off with one of his lousy dinners," Jack said, forcing himself to laugh.

After hanging up, he went back to the sofa and his contract, but he thought about Beau instead. Did he look like his mother, Beth, who'd been pretty and petite, or was he tall and skinny like he'd been at sixteen? Was he just as much trouble?

What could he possibly say to a teenage boy, especially the son he hadn't seen since he was one month old? Could they build a friendship? Could he actually be a father to the boy? Where could he begin? So many doubts filled his mind. He'd failed at far too many relationships, but, for his son's sake, he had to make this one work.

Tomorrow, when he returned to the ranch, he'd start a new life with his son. Tonight— Hell! Tonight he was faced with disappointing his sister. He'd spent a lifetime trying to make Lauren happy, endeavoring to make up for their mother's forgetfulness, thoughtlessness, and genuine disinterest in being a mom.

It wasn't his fault that Lauren had gone with their mother after the divorce, while he'd remained with his father on the ranch. But he'd felt awfully guilty staying with a dad who doted on him, when his sister was stuck in Florida being raised by nannies and servants.

He'd always felt the need to make things right.

Tonight was no exception.

The redhead's humming, her movements, were the perfect distraction from thoughts that were weighing heavy on his mind. She'd gotten up from the sewing machine and stood beside the ironing board that had been delivered earlier. He watched her find the creases at the front and back of each trouser leg and smooth the pants out on top of the board.

"Have you always been a tailor?" he asked, leaning back on the sofa, once more enjoying his cigar and the view.

"Not always. A few months ago I was a waitress. Five months ago a Hollywood actress. Variety's the spice of life, or so I've been told."

"Which do you prefer? Taking orders from hungry people, nipping and tucking men's clothes, or acting."

"They all have their plusses, but acting's what I always wanted to do."

"Why'd you give it up?"

She pressed the iron to the trousers, focusing on her work. "Hollywood and I didn't see eye to eye. Most people thought I did my best work lying on a dinner-theater floor playing a corpse." She looked up, her radiant smile giving no hint at all about how she truly felt about leaving Hollywood. "Dead actors don't make much money," she said. "I was penniless when I got to Hollywood and in the hole when I left. Right now I'm trying to dig my way out of the mess I got myself into."

"I take it you make good money doing this?"

"Depends."

"On what?"

"How big a tip I get." Her smile was infectious.

"That's the second or third subtle hint you've dropped."

"There's nothing subtle about me, Mr. Remington."

He'd already noticed and might have told her he didn't like subtlety in people, but the phone rang again.

"You're a popular guy," she said. "You've had more calls in the last half hour than I had in my entire Hollywood career."

"I don't like ringing phones. They bring nothing but trouble."

But his sister's voice on the other end of the line was the welcome exception. Rich women, especially those who'd been married and divorced twice, weren't always bundles of joy. Lauren defied all the rules.

"Thank goodness you're in town," she said. "I watched the Weather Channel and saw nothing but white over the eastern half of Wyoming. I was sure you wouldn't be able to get a flight."

"Wild horses couldn't keep me away."

"That's not true, and you know it. I've watched you tame a dozen wild stallions. It's an obsession that used to keep you from eating, from drinking, and even from women."

"My days of taming wild horses are over. We're supposed to whisper to them now." He watched the redhead's wild eyes peeking up at him through her lashes. She seemed the kind of woman no man could tame, the kind of woman no man in his right mind would want to tame. The kind of woman he had no business thinking about taming.

"There won't be any horses, wild or otherwise, at the party tonight," Lauren admitted. "I hope it won't be too boring for you."

"Stick a glass of whiskey in my hand, and I'll be fine. Dance with me a time or two, and I'll be even better."

"You'll be here on time, won't you?"

"Of course."

"If you'd stayed here with me, I wouldn't have had to call you to make sure. I would have gotten to see you sooner, too."

"I would have, but—"

"You don't have to make any excuses, Jack. I know how much you hate servants hovering around, how much you love your privacy, and

I know you can't get that here. Peter's the complete opposite. That's why we're perfect for each other. You're going to love him. I know it."

That was doubtful, but Jack would never let his sister know his concerns. She loved Peter Leighton, and even now she was ticking off each of his virtues.

Jack didn't see many virtuous qualities in Peter. He might be a top-notch polo player. He might have a love of horses, but he was a playboy, and Jack didn't trust him any more than he'd trusted Lauren's first two husbands. Yet the background check he'd ordered had found nothing more than a string of former lovers, with the emphasis on former, who'd raved about the man and his assorted charms. If Peter loved Lauren as much as he professed, Jack could bring himself to overlook his fear that the investigation had left some stone unturned and that his sister would be hurt yet again.

"I hope Arabella had a good trip."

Jack's attention was drawn back to the conversation at Lauren's mention of his ex-fiancée's name.

"You did tell her how much I'm looking forward to meeting her tonight, didn't you?"

Of course he had, but Lauren's feelings hadn't ranked high on Arabella's list of reasons not to kiss him and their engagement good-bye.

"Lauren," he said, pausing as he sought the right words to tell his sister that there was going to be someone missing at her engagement party. "There's something I need—"

"Just a minute, Jack," Lauren interrupted. He could hear someone talking excitedly in the background.

"I've got to go," she told him in a rush of words. "Apparently the ice sculptor was drunk when he carved the statue—one of the lovers has a very distinct penis—and I'm afraid the caterer is on the verge of having a coronary."

"Before you go, there's something I've got to tell you."

"Tell me later, please. I want tonight to be perfect, and if I don't assure the caterer that everything's all right, there's no telling what will happen."

He wanted the night to be perfect for her, too. He'd do anything to make his little sister happy. Hopefully, she would understand when he arrived at the party alone.

"Before I hang up, Jack, I want to thank you."

"For what?"

"For finally settling down with someone

you love. You'll never know how happy that's made me."

What could he say? She was happy now. Breaking her heart in two hours would be soon enough.

"I love you, Lauren," he said. "I'd do anything for you."

"Sometimes you do too much, Jack. But that makes me love you all the more." He could hear her blowing a kiss to him through the line, then the click at the other end just before he hung up.

"Feeling a bit constipated?" the redhead asked, a grin touching her face as she laid the trousers out on the bed.

"You could say that."

"My mama used to say—"

"Your mama's wisdom's not going to help me a whole hell of a lot."

"No, I suppose it won't. It didn't keep me out of trouble, either."

She came toward him, holding the altered shirt in her hand. "Why don't you try this on. As soon as I know everything fits, I'll get out of your hair and let you deal with your problems all on your own."

Jack took the shirt from her fingers, wondering why he didn't like the fact that she'd soon be gone. He didn't know her and didn't have the time to get to know her.

He picked the trousers up from the bed and went to the bathroom, this time making sure she wouldn't stare. "I won't be a minute. Make yourself comfortable."

Sam sighed with relief when Jack Remington closed the door. He'd been watching her for nearly an hour, even when he was on the phone. He'd never know how nervous she'd been with his eyes focused on her every move. She could feel him staring and spent too much time wondering if or when he was going to pounce. She knew how to take care of herself. A self-defense class had taught her all the important moves, and she'd use every one if the wrong man approached. But Jack Remington didn't seem wrong at all. Right now he seemed nice, something she never would have expected from the gruff, ill-mannered man she'd met at the start.

She swept away the scraps of fabric and loose threads scattered on the table and carpet and boxed up the sewing machine. Then she waited, listening to the water running in the bath. He was doing much more than trying on the tux. She'd heard an electric shaver, something the hotel must have provided since all his other belongings had gone to places unknown.

Well, she wasn't going to leave until she made sure the tux was perfect. She'd done a good job; she hoped for a good tip.

Prowling the room, she trailed her fingers over the rich wood furniture and fine upholstery. She sat on the sofa and rested her hand on the leather briefcase, tracing the initials JR embossed in amber cowhide. All the trappings in this room screamed *millionaire*, yet she sensed something down-to-earth inside Jack Remington.

She'd heard passion and warmth in his voice when he'd talked on the phone, and interest when he'd talked with her. It was amazing how something so simple could make her like a man she'd thought she would despise.

Crossing her legs, she leaned back on the couch and closed her eyes, letting herself dream that she belonged in Jack Remington's world. She'd never pictured herself in such a lofty place, but she had dreamed of someday living in an upper-middle-class neighborhood where families were presided over by a mom and dad, not a hooker and a drag queen. That's what her goal had been before her mama had died. Now her goal was to pay off Johnnie Russo. When that objective was met, she'd start saving again, start dreaming of better things, and hope someday to meet a man who didn't care about her past, who'd want her to be part of his future.

For now, or at least until she knew the tuxedo fit, she'd dream she was part of Jack Remington's universe. She was just imagining someone handing her a snifter of brandy when she heard Jack clearing his throat. Her eyes opened with a snap.

"Sleeping on the job?" he asked, a smile tilting his lips.

"Dozing. The couch was comfortable, and you were gone an awfully long time. Hope you don't mind."

He shook his head, as he fastened the top button on his shirt. His cuffs still needed to be clasped with the gold cuff links she'd brought, but the crisp white fabric smoothed perfectly over the rock-hard stomach she'd admired earlier. She slowly perused every inch of him, and she liked what she saw, from the light brown, perfectly trimmed hair that had turned nearly white at his temples, to broad shoulders and narrow hips, to long, muscular legs encased in black trousers.

His feet were bare, and he walked toward her.

Her heart beat hard, fast, and she felt the blood rise in her cheeks. She waited for him to speak, but all he did was watch her, his gaze settling on her eyes, her nose, her breasts. Finally, he found her eyes again, and a slow, tentative smile touched his mouth.

It was impossible to draw her eyes from his

freshly shaved face, or to keep from inhaling the muskiness of his aftershave. She wanted to touch him, to see if his skin burned with the same intensity as hers.

"There's something I need to ask you," he said.

Anything, her insides responded, but her sanity stepped in and rescued her. "Ask away."

But he didn't speak. He frowned, shook his head as if filled with doubt. He went to the bed, lifted the coat she'd altered, and tried it on. *Perfect*.

"You do nice work," he told her.

"Thank you."

He went to the window, as if he'd forgotten she was there. It seemed her job was over, that it was time to go, but she couldn't leave. He still had a question to pose. "I thought there was something you wanted to ask me."

"I changed my mind."

"Then I suppose you don't need me any longer."

"No."

Reality surfaced. *Stick with your dream of a middle-class world*, she told herself. *Jack's universe is too far above you.*

She got up from the sofa and walked toward the sewing machine, found her jacket, and slipped it on. He didn't look at her. Instead, he stared out the window at the first stars of twilight, as if deep in thought. She wanted to catch one last long look at his eyes, wanted to hear his voice again. But he'd retreated to his world, and she'd soon be back in hers.

Gripping the handle of the sewing machine, she slipped the strap of her tote over her shoulder and walked to the door.

"Hope your problems go away soon," she said, trying to sound unaffected by his stance and silence. She opened the door and stepped into the hallway. Soon she'd be back in West Palm Beach, looking for a safe place to park her VW and to curl up in the passenger seat to sleep.

That was her world.

Peering over her shoulder, Sam took one last look at Jack Remington's back. She waited, hoping he'd turn around and smile. When he didn't, she closed the door behind her. The short walk to the elevator seemed to last an eternity. She pressed the DOWN button, heard the chime and watched the doors open.

"Wait."

Relief rushed through her. She turned as Jack came down the hall.

"You forgot your tip."

She laughed. She'd forgotten her much-needed money in addition to her senses. A foolish thing to do, something she wouldn't let happen again. "I was beginning to think my hints were a little too subtle."

"There's nothing subtle about you."

She watched him pull a hundred-dollar bill from his money clip. He took her hand and pressed it into her open palm. His fingers slid over hers, and wrapped around them. He didn't let go. Uncertainty clouded his eyes. "There's something I need to ask you," he said once more. "Something personal."

"You're not going to change your mind again, are you?"

"I should, but . . . no. Would you mind coming back to the room?"

"You can't ask me here?"

He shook his head. "Like I said, it's personal." He took the sewing machine from her hand and walked at her side, holding the door open for her to enter. He set the case on the floor, and suddenly silence filled the suite as he walked away and paced the room in his bare feet.

A clock ticked somewhere, and she realized it was her own watch ticking off one minute, then two.

Finally, he stopped in front of her. "Remember that problem of mine?"

She nodded.

"I thought of a way to solve it."

"Great, but why are you telling me?"

"You're the solution."

"Me?"

"You." He stripped another bill from his clip, followed by another and another until she'd counted out a thousand dollars. "I need a woman tonight."

"*You what?*"

He frowned, as if she had no reason to be shocked. "It's a simple enough request."

She laughed. "I'm a tailor, not a whore." She slapped the hundred-dollar tip she'd earned against his chest and watched the bill flutter to the floor. "Go to hell, Mr. Remington. That's where you and every other rich man like you belong."

She grabbed her sewing machine, threw open the door, and heard it bang against the wall as she rushed down the hall.

A big hand gripped her arm and pulled her to a halt. She tried to slap him, but he had her in too tight a hold. "Stop your struggling and give me a chance to explain."

"What's to explain? I heard your request loud and clear."

"But you put the wrong spin on it. I don't want a prostitute."

"Then what do you want?"

"A fiancée."

The rich definitely had a unique way of looking at things. "Is that what they call it in your world?"

"That's what they call a woman who's engaged to a man. I want to hire you to *act* as my fiancée—just for tonight."

"Are you out of your mind?"

An elderly couple walked by, their eyes wide at the exchange. The diamond bracelets on the woman's wrist jangled as she gave Sam's arm a consoling touch. "Do you need some help?"

"No, thank you." She tried to calm down, tried to digest Jack's statement.

"Could we talk about this privately?" he asked.

"I don't know if that's such a good idea."

His jaw tightened. "Please."

She drew in a deep breath and let it out slowly. "If you hadn't said please the answer would have been a flat out no. Since you did say please, I'll give you five minutes and no more to explain why someone like you needs to *buy* a fiancée."

The elderly man's jaw dropped. The woman beside him grinned, and Sam smiled in their direction. "It's a little game we play," she told them, shrugging lightly. "It's the only way to get him excited."

Jack grabbed her arm and the sewing machine and dragged her toward his suite, slamming the door behind him after he dumped the sewing machine on the floor. "This isn't a game, and it sure as hell isn't foreplay."

"What is it then?"

"It's the only thing I can think of to keep from ruining my sister's party."

"You're not making any sense."

"Then let me explain."

"Please do. I like a good story."

She wanted to appear calm. She was anything but.

"I'll give you a thousand dollars if you can make my sister believe you're my fiancée."

"Do you like to play jokes on your sister?"

"No, I like to make her happy. That's why I need a fiancée. Just for tonight."

"Do you have a *real* fiancée?"

"I did."

Sam sat on the sofa, crossed her legs, and dangled one shoe from the toes of her foot. "What happened to your real fiancée?"

"We had a misunderstanding."

"She isn't by any chance the person you were talking to right before I knocked on your door? The one who thinks you're a son of a bitch?"

"You heard that?"

"I imagine everyone on this floor heard it."

"Look, my sister has never met Arabella. She doesn't know what she looks like. You're an actress—"

"But you forget, I've never played anything but a corpse. On top of that, I've never been to a ball, never socialized with rich people."

"You can do it. Rich people aren't any better than anyone else."

That's an understatement, Sam thought.

"Why don't you just tell your sister that Arabella dumped you?"

"I can't. Lauren's happy for the first time in years. She's excited about meeting Arabella, and I don't want to do anything to spoil tonight."

"What if someone recognizes me?"

"Have you been to any Palm Beach parties lately? Do you play polo or go yachting?"

She shrugged. "Not recently."

His brow rose. "Ever?"

"No."

"Well, Arabella certainly hasn't either, so I don't think there's anything to worry about."

She sighed, not feeling the least bit comfortable with his proposition. She went to the window, looking at the big round moon shining on the dark gray water. This was her chance to act—really and truly to act. On top of that, this was her opportunity to see how the rich and famous lived. Plus, she could make some desperately needed money. But . . . She faced him. "I can't do it."

"Why?"

"I'm not rich."

"I told you that doesn't matter."

"You don't understand. I have nothing to wear."

His gaze trailed deliberately over her body. Heated eyes settled on her lips, then slowly moved to her eyes. "Is that all that's bothering you?"

"That and the fact that I don't feel comfortable deceiving your sister."

He smiled, a true, deep smile that eased her fear about the masquerade she was embarking on.

"Thank you," he said.

"For what?"

"For caring about my sister's feelings." He reached into his pocket and pulled out the stack of bills he'd offered her before. "I'll explain everything to my sister in a few days. She won't hold it against you. I promise."

She stared at the money in his hand. It seemed wrong to take it, wrong to lie to his sister. Still, a thousand dollars would help get Johnnie off her back. He might even extend the loan.

"Okay, I'll do it," she said, plucking the bills from his palm. "But you'd better tell your sister the truth soon—tomorrow even. Playing your fiancée for a night is one thing, but I don't want you calling me next week and asking me to be your wife for a day."

His laughter filled the room. "Trust me. That's not about to happen."

She bit her lip, frowning at the grin on his face. "There's still the problem of what to wear."

"That's the least of your problems."

He checked his watch, then lifted the phone. "In less than an hour you'll look like a princess. Think you can act like a pampered socialite, too?"

Doubt clenched at her stomach, but there was no reason to let Jack see her anxiety. "As you said, I'm an actress, Jack. Just give me a few directions, and I'll do the rest."

three

"I can't do that," Sam said, sitting in the back of the limousine, staring at Jack Remington, who'd turned from something close to Prince Charming to a detestable frog in the space of five minutes.

"It's a simple request."

"I'm not going to spy on your sister's fiancé. Pretending I'm Arabella Fleming is bad enough, but trying to find out if Peter Leighton has some hidden agenda is out of the question."

"He doesn't deserve her."

"Do you have any concrete proof of that?"

Jack smiled, leaned forward, and took hold of her fingers. "I have no proof at all. I even had the man investigated and came up with nothing. But I do have a gut feeling."

"Your sister's in love with him, for heaven's

sake! If you don't have any proof, leave it alone."

She pulled her fingers from his grasp. "You know what, Jack?"

"What?"

"My mama wouldn't have liked you."

"Why?"

"You're rich, for one, and she didn't like rich men. Neither do I, for that matter. Number two, you're devious. She used to tell me that I should stay away from devious men because they have a tendency to lead good girls astray."

"I've been open and aboveboard in everything I've asked of you. There's nothing devious there. As for being rich, I can't help what I am."

He leaned back in the soft black leather and folded his arms across his chest. "All you have to do is dance with him, ask him a few questions, and maybe bat your eyelashes a time or two."

"No."

"I'll give you a thousand more."

The money was tempting, but she couldn't. She shook her head.

"Two thousand."

"I'm not a spy. Please don't ask me—"

"Five."

Her heart seemed to stop. She could pay off

most of what she owed Johnnie with five thousand dollars. It wasn't right, but she was desperate. "All right. Five."

"You drive a hard bargain."

"No," Sam said. "Sometimes I sell my services a little too easily. I always regret it in the end."

He leaned forward again, and lifted her hand. His felt warm; hers was freezing. "You asked me earlier if something was bothering me, and now I'm going to ask you. Are you in trouble? Something I might be able to help you with?"

She didn't know Jack Remington well enough to tell him her troubles. Besides, her foolishness was all too humiliating to talk about. Five months ago she'd confided in a rich man, she'd even asked for his help. In the end, she'd ended up with black eyes and a scar on her jaw. She didn't like the thought of Jack Remington seeing her as a greedy, moneygrubbing con, but she wouldn't be seeing him after tonight. His disdain was something she could live with.

"Thanks for asking," she said, pulling her hand away, "but I don't have a care in the world."

Lauren Remington Chasen Lancaster looked radiant. Sam picked her out the moment she and Jack walked through the massive double doors that led into a pink-and-white marble entry. With a devastatingly handsome fiancé at her side, she'd stood at the far end of the room greeting guests, dressed in a gold-colored gown covered with thousands of shimmering amber beads. A Paris original, Sam imagined. More than likely Christian Lacroix. She must have been close to six feet tall and looked more like a voluptuous Amazon princess than a willowy Palm Beach socialite. When she saw Jack, her face lit up like she'd just won a Vegas jackpot.

She threw her arms around Jack's neck, and he lifted her off the floor, spun her around, and every guest in the room stared, as if showing real, honest emotion was unrefined. Peter Leighton frowned, then instantly wiped the look of discontent from his face and put on a smile.

Too late, Sam thought. She considered herself a good judge of character, and Peter Leighton was definitely a man to be watched. Her feelings about Jack and his gut instinct rose a notch.

Jack caught Sam's arm and drew her toward his sister. "Lauren, I'd like you to meet my fiancée, Arabella Fleming."

Sam took a deep breath, as the charade began in earnest.

"I hope Jack told you how happy I am for both of you," Lauren said, "but if he hasn't, well, I'm just thrilled."

"Thank you," Sam said. She held out her hand, but suddenly found herself caught up in Lauren's sisterly embrace.

"You're perfect for Jack," Lauren whispered. "Of course, you don't look at all like he described you."

"What do you mean?" Jack said, obviously overhearing his sister. "She's exactly how I described her. Beautiful."

"Well, she is beautiful. But she's got red hair, not brown, you said something about her being average height when she's nearly as tall as me, and, oh, what does it matter. You're both here." The smile grew even brighter on Lauren's face as she linked her arm through Peter's, drawing him forward.

"Now it's my turn to introduce my fiancé. Peter Leighton, this is my brother, Jack Remington, and his wife-to-be, Arabella Fleming."

Peter was nothing but grace and charm. He was tall, slim, with slicked-back black hair that made him look more like a Latin lover than an Australian polo player. He had a heart-stopping smile, drop-dead gorgeous blue eyes, but his palm felt warm and damp when he took hold of Sam's, and her mama had always told her to beware of sweaty palms. She tried pulling away, but before he let her go, he squeezed her fingers and smiled one of those "we'll talk later" smiles she'd seen one too many times in Hollywood.

"It's a pleasure to have the two of you join us," Peter said. "Lauren has talked of nothing else all day."

"We wouldn't have missed tonight for the world," Sam said, slipping her hand around Jack's arm, looking at him with all the love she could muster.

"Mother said something similar," Lauren said. "Of course, she followed that statement with a *but* and told me she'd met an English lord who's to-die-for and they were going to spend the weekend at his country estate." Lauren laughed softly. "Actually, I'm rather glad she's not here. The lilies would have clashed with her gown, the champagne wouldn't have been the right year, and my dress, well, she'd tell me I should have gotten it in Milan instead of Paris because everyone, I mean *everyone*, is buying in Milan this season."

Jack laughed, the sound echoing around the room. Peter was restrained, typical of most everyone else at the party. He smiled, but the light Sam would have expected to see sparkling in the eyes of a man in love wasn't there.

"What about Dad?" Jack asked. "He's not

going to make an appearance, is he?"

"Are you kidding? In Palm Beach? He's worse than you, Jack. I doubt he'll ever leave Santa Fe. If the two of you would talk more than once or twice a year, you'd know he's got two or three girlfriends to keep happy and, in Dad's words, that's a full-time job."

Sam listened to Jack and Lauren talking about family and friends, about Pastor Mike, Jack's ranch manager and the minister who'd officiated at all of Lauren's weddings. Finally, Jack brought up the subject of Beau. She could feel the muscles tightening in his arm when he mentioned his son, but his words weren't strained. They were filled with a mixture of warmth, concern, and uncertainty.

Unconsciously, she found herself moving a little closer to his side, keeping her arm linked with his, and liking the feel of his fingers as they drew slow, lazy circles on the back of her hand.

And Lauren—without doing anything special—had made Sam feel like she belonged inside the big, fancy mansion. More importantly, she made her feel like she was a part of her family.

Belonging had never felt so good. Too bad it had to end.

*   *   *

The ballroom was crowded. Suddenly Jack knew how a mustang must feel when herded into the confines of a holding corral after spending a lifetime roaming wild and free on the plains. He never had enjoyed this life. The only thing that made him stay at the party now was the look of happiness he'd seen on Lauren's face when he'd introduced her to his *fiancée*—Arabella Fleming—and the obvious delight the two women had found in each other's company for nearly two hours.

On top of that, being there gave him the perfect opportunity to keep a watchful eye on Peter Leighton. The polo player had an innate charm. Either that, or he was as good an actor as the redheaded seamstress, who was doing a perfect job pretending to be Arabella.

She was lovely. Exquisite. The hotel beauty salon had done its job well. The circles below her eyes had been expertly camouflaged with makeup. Her red hair had been piled on top her head, but a few spiraling strands hung about her face and over her left shoulder. A trio of diamonds dripped from her ears, and a matching necklace rested just below the hollow of her throat. Her gown glistened like new-fallen snow dusted with morning sunlight, and it clung to every gentle curve.

And her smile. It was wide and infectious, and her laughter sang through the room. The nervousness he'd sensed in her while an army of workers fussed with her hair, her makeup, and her clothes had vanished. When they'd stepped out of the limousine and walked into Lauren's mansion, he thought she would high-tail it back to the car and order the driver to take her home. Instead, she'd taken a deep breath, whispered "break a leg" to herself, and gracefully floated over the threshold like she'd always belonged to high society.

She was worth every penny he'd paid her. Maybe even more.

He was about to cross the room and ask her to dance, when Peter Leighton stopped beside him, a glass of champagne in hand. "Beautiful woman, your fiancée."

"Yours, too," Jack said, not bothering to disguise the animosity in his voice. "Of course, I hear you've had a string of beautiful women in your life."

"In the past, but that's common knowledge in polo circles. Lauren is my life now—and forever. Too bad you can't accept that."

"I'm rather protective where my sister is concerned."

"Once she's my wife, you can stop worrying. I make a habit of protecting what belongs to me."

Jack took a glass of champagne from a tray. Taking a sip, he watched Peter over the crystal rim. He'd had a bad day, he didn't like Peter Leighton, and an old-fashioned fistfight, like the ones he'd gotten into as a kid, sounded good right about now. "Lauren's not chattel," he told his future brother-in-law. "You'll never *own* her."

Peter laughed. "You misunderstand, Jack."

"I hope so, but let me make something clear, just so you don't misunderstand me. Lauren's been hurt before, and I'll do anything in my power to keep her from being hurt again. For her sake, I'm going to make a big attempt at liking you, but if I hear even one word about you doing something to cause her the least amount of pain, I'll break you in two."

Jack saluted Peter with his champagne glass and walked away. His heart was beating dangerously fast, and he needed a way to let off steam. There weren't any bulls to rope in Palm Beach. There weren't any broncs to bust, but there was dancing, and he had a make-believe fiancée standing across the room looking like she needed to be rescued.

Sam laughed at the worst joke she'd heard all evening, then put her hand to her lips and stifled a yawn. Pretending to be rich, worldly, and part of the crowd was exhausting work. Lauren, however, made it look easy and fun. Sam assumed that was because she didn't pretend to be something she wasn't. Lauren was the most genuine person she'd ever met.

"Jack's coming," Lauren whispered, leaning close as if they were schoolgirls checking out the boys.

Sam turned, suddenly feeling wide-awake and happy to be at the ball. It wasn't hard to find Jack Remington in the crowd. He stood two or three inches taller than most of the other men and looked all-powerful, maybe even invincible. His jaw was set, his eyes heated, and he cut a path through the guests as he headed straight toward her.

"You've had my fiancée to yourself all evening," he said, flashing his sister a slightly off-kilter grin. "I want her now."

Lauren was genuine, Jack was . . . Well, Jack was Jack. Straightforward and no-nonsense. Nice qualities in a man, she decided.

Jack took her hand and led her from the ballroom to the terrace, where the air was warm, the humidity high. "Dance with me," he said, sliding one hand around her until it rested at the small of her back. He drew her tight against his chest, his hips, his thighs. She felt a little like clay, being molded to fit his need. Oddly enough, she liked the feeling.

The music wove through the windows and doors and surrounded them as they moved slow and easy.

"You're doing a good job," he said, his lips

close to her ear, his cheek brushing against
hers.

"I've had to wing it a few times. By the way,
what's an Andalusian?"

"A horse. Mostly for show. Why?"

"You didn't tell me Arabella's father breeds
them. If I'd known, I might have commented
on their silky coats or how much fun they are
to ride."

He angled his head to look at her. There
was a grin on his face as if he thought the
predicament had been funny. "I imagine you
carried your end of the conversation without
a hitch."

"I told them my father also raised rattlesnakes and sold their venom."

Jack's grin widened.

"I didn't have a clue what an Andalusian
was, but I figured it wasn't a rattlesnake, and
I was bound and determined to change the
subject."

"Do you know anything about rattlesnakes?"

"Enough. They give you a little advance
warning that danger's coming and then they
strike. You know what, Jack?"

"What?"

"With the exception of your sister and a few
others, I feel like I've been slithering around

with a bunch of rattlesnakes all night, and the one with the biggest rattle is your future brother-in-law."

"I take it spying on him hasn't been all that difficult?"

"I despised him right from the start."

"You danced with him, though. I watched you."

"I promised you I'd bat my eyelashes, and I did. You know what it got me?"

"What?"

"His hands on my butt when we were dancing. He also did some very slow maneuvering toward a palm tree and a dark corner of the room."

She felt Jack's fingers tighten around hers, saw the tensing of his jaw. "What did you do?"

"Told him I have a doctor friend who specializes in turning Australian playboys into eunuchs."

Jack laughed. "I told him I'd break him in two if he hurt Lauren."

"You could do it, too," she said, casually running one hand over the muscles in his arms, like a real fiancée would do with the man she loved. "Unfortunately, I think threats roll right off Peter's back. I don't like him. I don't like worrying that he's going to hurt

Lauren by doing something no one would ever expect."

"Why do you care what happens to her?"

"Oh, I don't know." She put her cheek next to his, enjoying the closeness. "She's different from what I imagined. All the things I've read about her being wild, about going to nude beaches with married men, about . . . well, you know, the tabloids say things that aren't very flattering. But she's not like that at all."

"Do you believe everything you read?"

"I read that you're worth close to a billion dollars. I could easily believe that."

"Believe it if you want. I don't make a habit of divulging my financial status to the tabloids or anyone else. I keep my private life secret, too. Lauren, on the other hand, hangs around with people who like having their names in the news. She can't control what they say about her, and she's given up caring. The only thing that's important is what her family believes about her."

"Want to know what I think?"

He nodded, his lips accidentally brushing over her cheek, an action that meant nothing, but made her toes tingle all the same.

She took a breath and attempted to swallow the anxious lump in her throat. "I think she's one of the nicest people I've ever met." Her heart fluttered as his lips trailed along her jaw, hesitating at her scar. He kissed the raised stretch of skin, and she nearly forgot what she'd wanted to say.

Don't pay attention to what he's doing, she told herself. *It's all an act. A charade.* "You know, Jack," she whispered, "if I was really your fiancée, I'd consider myself extremely fortunate to have Lauren as a sister-in-law."

He didn't respond, not in real words, but she heard some kind of muffled agreement vibrating against her neck, as his fingers moved along her spine, sliding over skin that the low-cut gown didn't cover. What she was wearing was far more daring than anything she ever would have picked, but right now, she liked the idea that she could feel the warmth of his hand on the small of her back, pulling her closer to his chest, so close she could feel the rhythm of his heart beating against hers. She couldn't remember the last time she'd felt so right in someone's arms.

She slid a hand across his shoulder, around his neck, and found herself playing with the ends of his hair. She inhaled the musky scent of his aftershave, surprised by the quiver that raced through her insides. She pressed her lips against the warmth of his neck, and heard him draw in a long, deep breath.

What on earth are you doing? she asked herself. *This is pretend, nothing more.*

Slowly, she drew her fingers away, resting them once more on his shoulder, the safest, sanest place to touch. She inched away, but he pulled her back.

"The music's slow and easy," he whispered, his breath soft against her ear. "And lovers are supposed to dance so close that a casual observer might think their bodies were fused together."

She swallowed, trying to retain some measure of sanity and confidence. "We're not lovers."

"Maybe not, but I'm thoroughly enjoying the masquerade."

Whispered words and warm breath turned to heated lips against her ear, moving ever so slowly along her jaw, to the corner of her mouth.

She was in trouble now, and she didn't care at all.

She closed her eyes and found herself opening up to him as he kissed her, holding her tight as he swayed with the sultry music.

How long they kissed was anyone's guess. She was too dizzy to keep track. They might have danced through one song. Maybe two, but the music had been little more than a blur. All she'd concentrated on was the fire in his kiss, the passion, the way his hand cradled her neck as his fingers teased the wisps of hair that had escaped the hairdresser's fancy coif, and the heat in his eyes when she'd braved a glimpse to see if he kissed with his eyes opened or closed.

They were definitely open, and they were gazing steadily at her face. He smiled, then whirled her around the room.

Pretending to be in love had never felt so right and so wrong at the same time. She'd been mad to go through with this charade. Foolish.

He did some kind of fancy dip, holding her tight as he bent over her, then pulled her back. Her breasts grazed over the silky tux, brushed the pearl buttons on his shirt, and desire like she'd never known in her entire life rippled through her insides.

Try as she might, she couldn't control the feelings. She didn't want to feel anything in his arms. Didn't want his kisses to turn her to mush. Didn't want to suffer when the night was over.

"Stop," she pleaded, backing away from his lips, from the touch of his beating heart.

He looked down at her, his eyes dark with hunger. "Don't pull away, Ara—" His hand pressed at her back, pulling her close again, and she found herself powerless in his arms. "I can't call you that. Not anymore. You don't look like Arabella, you don't act like her or feel like her." He swirled her around, across the terrace, to a place far away from anyone else.

They were behind a tall potted palm, and he backed her against a wall. The stone was cold against her skin, but the fingers he was tracing over her cheek were on fire. "Who are you?" he asked, his words slow, deep.

"An actress."

"Why all the mystery? You know my name. I want to know yours."

She swallowed the crazy knot of desire that had crept into her throat, and pretended his kiss, his eyes, his touch had no effect on her. She couldn't let him know that he'd stirred feelings in her. This was all an act, nothing more. If he called her by name, it would seem all too real—and she'd hurt even more when it was over. "There's no mystery, Jack. I can bluff my way through most situations, including calling someone by the wrong name. You, on the other hand, don't have a poker face. If you knew my real name, you might spill it in front of your sister and blow everything."

He kissed her cheekbones, gazing deep into her eyes. "Then I'll call you Whiskey."

"Whiskey?"

"Some men might call you Red, or Curly," he said, wrapping a spiraling strand of her hair around his finger. "Personally, I like your eyes, especially now, when they're warm and glowing. You've got eyes that could intoxicate a man."

"You aren't trying to butter me up so I'll help you out with some other foolish scheme, are you?"

"I'm not thinking about much of anything, except what's going on right now between you and me."

"There's nothing going on."

Again he kissed the corner of her mouth, and with every ounce of willpower she had, she fought the urge to give in to him.

"Jack, this isn't right."

"It might not be right, but it feels damn good."

"Stop, Jack. Please."

The moment she said stop, he drew back, and sighed. "What's wrong?"

"Don't pretend you care for me when it's only a farce. Don't—"

Sam's protest came to a skidding halt when a familiar man slipped into view.

"Am I interrupting something?"

Jack spun around, and Sam thought for sure her heart had skipped a beat when she recognized Chip Chasen standing behind Jack in a tux she'd altered for him earlier in the week. "Good evening, Jack," he said. "Good evening, Arabella. You're the talk of the party, and I've been anxious to meet you."

Forcing a smile, Sam held out her hand and Chip, one of Mr. Antonio's worst tippers, kissed her knuckles. He studied her with a frown on his face as if trying to remember where he'd seen her before.

"Arabella," Jack said, "I'd like you to meet Chip Chasen."

"I believe we've met somewhere else," Chip said.

"I don't think so," Sam tossed back, maybe a little too fast.

"She's firmly entrenched in Denver society, Chip," Jack said, coming to her rescue. "You're Cape Cod and Palm Beach."

"I've been to Denver a time or two. Do you know—"

"It's a big city," Jack interrupted firmly, then changed the subject. "What are you doing at Lauren's party? I didn't think the two of you were on speaking terms."

Chip took a swallow of his drink. "We made up years ago. I loved her once, she loved me, and even though she took me for half of what I'm worth, divorce didn't wipe out all the old feelings."

"You and Lauren were married?" Sam asked.

"For six not-so-blissful months. I might as well tell you the honest truth, before Jack puts his own spin on things. I liked to bet on the horses. In fact, I preferred horses to marriage—then, and now. Statistics-wise, I'm husband number one. Number two was killed in a boating accident a week after their divorce, and"—he leaned close to Sam, and she could smell the whiskey on his breath—"from the gossip I've heard tonight, number three might die at the hands of Jack Remington, even before the wedding takes place. Lauren's hell on husbands."

He was drunk. His words were slurred, his eyes red, and the face Sam had once thought was semihandsome now looked tired and old.

Chip continued to stare at her, and then his eyes widened. "I've got it. You look like the woman who altered a suit for me this week. Odd coincidence, isn't it? Of course, you couldn't be her, could you?"

"I could." Sam said with a confident smile. "if I was a good enough actress." She felt Jack's fingers tighten around her arm, and she quickly gave him a wink.

Chip took a drink of whiskey. "You'd have to be one hell of an actress, because those people from West Palm Beach just don't fit in here."

"*Those* people?" she asked. "Who exactly are *those* people?"

"I assume you have them in Denver, too.

Poor people, illiterate people, ones without much education."

"Oh, you mean the ones who cook your food, clean your house, wash your clothes and tailor them, too, because you've never learned the simple, basic skills of taking care of yourself?"

Chip laughed. "Sounds like you have an affinity for *those* people."

"I've known a few of those people in my life. Strip away the money you were fortunate enough to be born with and your pompous arrogance, and you could fit in quite nicely. No, I take that back. You'd still be a wimp unable to take care of himself, which means you wouldn't last more than a week or two on the other side of the bridge. You'd be pulp, Mr. Chasen. Dog meat. Now, if you don't mind," she said, clutching the skirt of her gown so she could make a hasty retreat, "I need some fresh air, and I'm not going to find it here."

She rushed down the marble steps and across the lawn toward the beach. Tears spilled from her eyes, and for once she didn't try to hold them back. She was one of *those* people, and she always would be. Going to the ball for one night didn't change anything. She could scratch and claw her way out of the hole her life had been since the time of her birth, but she'd always be one of *those* people. To-night, after getting an up-close glimpse of how crude and obnoxious some rich people could be, she finally realized that being one of *those* people was okay.

"Wait." Jack's voice hit her from behind, but she didn't stop until his hand wrapped around her arm.

"Where are you going?"

"Home. Back where I belong."

"You belong here. With me."

She jerked around. "Why, because you paid me to be here? If that's the reason, you can keep your money."

He shook his head, and smiled when he took hold of her hands. "No, because I don't know what you're going to say or do next. Because you're not a stereotype or a hanger-on. And, to be quite honest, because you make me feel good."

"Well, maybe I make you feel good, but you don't make me feel anything but anger. You didn't even stick up for me back there."

"You were doing fine on your own. It's not every day someone puts Chip Chasen in his place." He wiped away one of her tears with his thumb. "You know what, Whiskey?"

"What?"

"It was a sheer pleasure watching you at

work. Seems to me those Hollywood people underestimated your talent."

"I wasn't acting. That was me, the real me, impulsive and quick-tempered. I'd say I'm sorry, but I'm not."

"I'd be disappointed if you were." He touched her cheek, and for the first time she noticed his fingers weren't soft and smooth, but callused, used to hard work. "Come on back," he urged.

She shook her head. "It's been a long day, and Chip's right. People like me don't belong here. If it's all the same to you, I'd rather go home."

"Then *I'll* take you."

She started to say no, but he put a finger to her lips and silenced her.

"Do me a favor, Whiskey. Just this once, don't argue with me."

four

Jack's suite seemed different now. Personal, filled with many special reminders of the man who'd turned her into a princess for a few hours. As he closed the door behind them, Sam walked about the room, absorbing the scents of gardenia, tobacco, and the musky aftershave he wore, which had smelled so wonderful as they'd danced cheek to cheek. She swept her fingers over the exquisite fabrics that covered the backs of chairs and sofas, capturing a few additional memories of the night she went to the ball. Slowly, she turned around and looked at Jack. He was the best part of the entire evening.

A man she would always remember.

He'd been silent on the short ride to the hotel, as they walked through the lobby and rode the elevator to his floor. Even his eyes had been silent, betraying none of his thoughts.

She wished the things going through his mind mirrored her own. She wanted more time with him. She wanted to get to know him better. She wanted to dance together again, and kiss while they were doing it. But she didn't hold any hope that he wanted more than just one night.

The kisses, the gentleness of his touch, so many of the things that had made the evening perfect were all part of the charade. After all, a handsome, society-loving millionaire could never be interested in one of *those* people Chip Chasen had talked about.

Mama had fallen for a man from Palm Beach once. He went to her street corner every Thursday night for nearly two months, and he'd told her she was worth far more than he paid her. He'd made promises, too, about taking her home to meet his family, about taking her out on his yacht with his friends.

Mama had tried to laugh—she had known all along he was lying to her. But Sam remembered her tears. She'd been hurt anyway; Sam didn't want to suffer the same fate with Jack Remington.

"Would you like a drink?" Jack asked, capturing her attention again. He loosened his tie, looking casually elegant as he went to the bar and removed the stopper from a crystal decanter.

"No, I'm fine. Thanks."

"You missed Lauren's dinner. I could order something from room service."

She shook her head. Part of her told her to accept his offer, but that would only prolong the agony of saying good-bye. "You've got a party to get back to, and I should change clothes and head for home."

He returned the stopper, his hand resting on top the crystal knob. "Lauren knows I'm with you. She'll understand if I don't go back."

"The charade is over, Jack. You're with *me*—the woman who altered your tux—not with Arabella. Had you forgotten?"

"I haven't forgotten a thing," he said, his eyes hot, enflaming her skin as they blazed over her body. "I told you before that you're not at all like Arabella. And she's not the one I want right now."

She was foolish to listen to his words. Crazy to think he meant anything more than that he wanted her just for tonight. She turned away, yet she didn't run. Instead, she watched his reflection in the picture window as he moved toward her and cupped her shoulders in his hands. His head tilted toward her. His lips were warm, teasing, as they trailed the length of her neck, over her shoulder. He fingered the thin straps on her gown, and she dragged in a deep breath, trying to remain calm when his touch was making her anything but.

"You're beautiful," he whispered, slowly sliding the straps over her shoulders. "I couldn't have asked for a more perfect accomplice tonight."

The word *accomplice* brought her back to her senses, made her think of something sinister, made her remember that the night had only been a game, that she'd been paid to do a job. If they went any further tonight, she'd feel as if she'd been paid for that, too.

And she wasn't a whore. She'd loved her mama with all her heart, but she wasn't like her and never would be.

"Stop. Please." She pulled out of Jack's arms, pushed the straps back to her shoulders, and walked toward the bedroom. "I'm going to change. It's late, and I need to get home."

He didn't argue or try to coax her into something more. He'd never know how much she appreciated that, because if he'd given her any kind of excuse, she might have rushed back into his embrace. She already felt guilty about deceiving Jack's sister; she didn't want to feel shame and disgrace, too.

She could feel his heated gaze on her back long after she closed the door. She wondered if he might try to follow. She wanted him to; she didn't want him to. She wanted to go back out to him; she didn't want to.

She leaned against the door. *Oh, Mama. What should I do?*

The answer suddenly came into view. Sitting just inside the bedroom she saw Jack's luggage, two expensive leather bags that had been found in some other airport and returned to Palm Beach. The suitcases reminded her that he was rich, that he could afford anything he wanted—a last-minute tux, a rented fiancée, a temporary makeover for a girl from the wrong side of the tracks. It also served as another reminder that the past few hours had been nothing more than a one-night stand. It was over now. Time to pack up and go home.

Slowly, she locked the door to keep him out.

Jack heard the distinct click of the lock, answering the question he'd been asking ever since she pulled out of his arms: *does she want me to follow her?*

Hell, she didn't want him to follow. She didn't want him anywhere near. She'd been paid for a job, she'd performed her part to perfection, and she was ready to go home—his feelings, his needs be damned!

Stalking across the room, he took his checkbook from the inside pocket of the coat he'd worn on his flight from Wyoming. He still owed the redhead five thousand dollars for spying on Peter Leighton, and he didn't hold any hopes that she'd turn it down.

Arabella had liked his money. She'd never come right out and told him so, but she'd had a knack for spending one hell of a lot. The handful of women he'd dated before Arabella hadn't been much different. He'd never really cared about the money issue because he had plenty to spare.

But the redhead asked for money right off the bat. As far as she was concerned, he was a means to making big bucks fast and easy.

That annoyed the hell out of him.

He grabbed a pen from the desk and scribbled the date on the check, then hesitated at payee. Damn! He still didn't know her name.

He filled out the rest of the blanks, stuffed the check into the pocket of his tux, then went to the humidor and took out a cigar. Next he poured himself a swallow of whiskey and felt the burn in his throat as he swigged it down.

Staring at the bedroom door, he thought about knocking to find out what was taking her so long. Maybe she was changing her mind about staying. He didn't want to interrupt her thoughts if that was the case.

God, he didn't want her to go.

Not now.

Sam stood in front of the dresser in her How Tacky ensemble. She took the pins from her hair and let it fall, and pulled her own lipstick from her tote and painted her mouth cherry red. She almost felt like herself again, except for the diamonds.

She touched the earrings and necklace that she hadn't yet removed. They'd looked beautiful when she was all dressed up. Now they felt cold, impersonal, like almost everything tonight. Taking a deep breath, she took off the jewelry and set it on the dresser.

Slipping her tote bag over her shoulder, she grabbed the handle of the sewing-machine case and headed for the bedroom door, stopping for one last look at the shimmering white gown she'd worn tonight, at the diamonds the hotel's jewelry store had loaned Jack for the evening, at the rhinestone shoes that had sparkled when she'd stepped out of the limousine. Those things had made her feel all aglow as she'd walked and danced with Jack Remington.

That glow had now begun to fade. The night was nearly over.

So was the dream.

When she heard Jack's knock, she turned the knob.

He filled the doorway, looking so handsome in his tux, his perfectly cut hair disheveled now, with a light brown lock falling over his brow. The expression on his face betrayed none of his feelings, and then he gazed at her lips. She could easily see the rise and fall of his chest as he leaned a shoulder against the doorjamb.

He still wanted her. But he'd still be leaving in the morning.

"You didn't by any chance change your mind about staying while you were in there?"

She had no home to go to except her bug. No job to go to in the morning, only an apology to make to Mr. Antonio for taking his machine. Staying would be so easy, but she shook her head.

"You're sure?"

"Positive."

He studied her eyes for the longest time, as if waiting for her to show a sign that she'd changed her mind. But she didn't waver, and finally he said, "Come on. I'll walk you to your car."

He'd know she was living in her bug if he saw the clothes hanging in the back, the shoes on the floor, the boxes stacked on the backseat, and the pillow and blanket up front. He'd know she was down on her luck, and she didn't want him to know about her troubles.

She remembered the sneers, the leering eyes and taunts of people who'd chastised her mama for living on the streets, for not having a decent job. Mama hadn't cared what those

people thought, and Sam had held her head
high. But when they were alone she'd hear her
mama cry, while she was crying, too. That
wasn't the life she wanted.

It seemed as if she'd never get away from
her past, no matter how she tried. Right now,
the only good things she had in her life were
a shred of dignity and her pride. She'd already
put a damper on both by taking Jack's money
to play a part in his charade. If he knew more,
she'd jeopardize whatever she had left.

She hitched the strap on her tote bag higher
on her shoulder. "The evening was magical,
Jack. But why don't we just say good-bye
here?"

He touched her arm, and she impulsively
jerked away. She wanted to leave before she
got hurt, and if he touched her again, if he
made an attempt to kiss her, she'd fall into his
spell.

Laughing, he reached into his coat pocket
and pulled out a piece of paper. "You hadn't
planned on leaving without this, had you?"

She frowned, and then she knew what it
was. She'd nearly forgotten the five thousand
he owed her for spying on Peter Leighton. It
seemed an awful lot of money for such a simple job.

"Are you going to take it?" he asked, holding the check out to her.

Guilt ripped through her. She didn't want to take it, but over Jack's shoulder she could again see their reflections in the window, and lurking behind her was a vision of Johnnie Russo, laughing as he sliced an index finger across his throat.

As much as she wanted to tell Jack no, as much as she wanted to leave with a few shreds of self-respect intact, she took the check from his hand. Right now, money seemed far more important than dignity.

"That's not made out to anyone," he said, his gaze focusing on the check. "I still don't know your name."

What difference would it make if he knew her name or not? He'd never come looking for her, and she had nothing to hide, except the pitiful state of her life, even if he did. "Sam Jones," she told him.

His brow rose. "You expect me to believe that?"

"You asked for a name, I gave you one."

"Yeah, and you asked for money, and I gave it to you."

That made her mad. "Then we're even, aren't we?"

"If you can call it that," he said cynically. He walked across the room and opened the door. "Let's go find your car."

"I said I could go alone."

"It's late, and I'll be damned if I'm going to let you go to your car by yourself."

"You don't need to worry about me."

The phone rang, and he let out an exasperated sigh.

"I bet that's Lauren," Sam said. "She's probably wondering what happened to the two of us."

Jack stared at the tote hanging over her shoulder, at the sewing machine that was growing terribly heavy in her hand. The phone rang again.

"I'll just be a second." He started toward the phone, then twisted around to look at her. "Don't go. Promise."

She put one hand behind her and crossed her fingers. "Promise."

The minute his back was turned again, she rushed to the elevator. Saying good-bye would be too hard.

The elevator doors opened, and she stepped inside. When the wooden panels were sliding closed, she heard Jack's shouted plea from the hallway. "Wait, Whiskey. Please."

She stared at the STOP button, giving it a moment's consideration, but the doors shut tightly, and the elevator began its descent.

The fantasy had ended.

Jack Remington had disappeared from her life.

five

Jack caught a flight for home at eight the next morning. He didn't particularly care for flying. Solid earth beneath his feet felt better than clouds and thin air, and he preferred the wide-open spaces of the prairie to the confines of a first-class seat.

As the plane fought bad weather, he tried to concentrate on the contract he'd promised his business partner he'd review over the weekend, but his mind wandered far too much.

Thoughts of Beau—what they would talk about, what he would look like up close instead of in an impersonal school picture, how his voice would sound—captured his attention. He wasn't afraid to meet his son, but he *was* frightened over the uncertainty of their future. Jack knew full well that money could solve a lot of problems. But it couldn't fix sixteen years of being apart. That was something only words and actions could mend.

He didn't even know where to begin.

Thoughts of Beau led to thoughts of Lauren. She'd been radiantly happy last night, even though she was marrying a man Jack considered to be a jerk. He'd continued the charade long after Sam Jones had disappeared, fabricating a story as he talked with Lauren on the phone about Arabella having a terrible headache. Afterward he'd gone back to the party and attempted to have a good time, but something was missing.

The redhead.

She hadn't said good-bye, and even now that weighed heavily on his mind. She hadn't given him the chance to discover personal things about her, like where she lived, her age, her phone number, or whether or not her name really was Sam Jones.

That she'd run off while his back was turned was a less-than-subtle hint that she didn't want him knowing anything more about her. She'd made it perfectly clear that she didn't want to see him again. Of course, what she wanted and what he wanted were two different things.

When he was leaving the hotel that morning, he'd asked the concierge to send flowers to her at Antonio's. He took a chance having them addressed to Sam Jones, hoping she'd told him the truth about her name. On one of the Breakers' note cards he'd called her Whiskey, scribbled his phone number, and asked her to call him collect.

She made him feel good. Damn good. And he wanted to see her again. He'd even settle for hearing her voice—at least for now.

The plane arrived late in Denver, and the connecting flight touched down even later than it should have in Sheridan. From there it was a two-hour drive to the ranch. The weather was good, the evening sky cloudless, the moon full, and Jack used the time alone to run through the speech he planned to deliver to Beau.

I'm sorry, he'd tell him right at the start. *I'm glad you're here.* Then he'd tell his son about the accident, about his mother's death, about giving custody to Beth's folks because he'd thought they were better able to take care of a baby than a sixteen-year-old kid who lived with a bunch of cowboys.

God, how could he tell Beau those things when for sixteen years guilt and remorse had eaten away at his heart?

When he turned onto the road leading to the ranch house, Rufus barked as he ran through mud and patches of snow to greet the truck.

The dog jumped and twisted in circles, glad to see Jack even though he'd been gone less than two full days.

Pulling the pickup to a stop, he climbed out of the cab, ruffled the Border collie's fur, and headed toward the unfamiliar silhouette he saw sitting on the porch. A lump formed in his throat. Even if he'd been able to utter the words to his speech, the emotions that had welled up inside him—anxiety, fear, love— would have kept him silent.

That was just as well. Right now, he had no idea what to talk about. They were strangers— a father, a son, who had nothing in common except their genes.

He mounted the steps, with Rufus right on his heel, tossed his hat, upside down, into an empty chair, and pulled another up close to Beau and sat. The boy never once looked up. Instead, he stared at the knife and piece of wood he was whittling.

Jack took a cigar from his pocket, leaned back in the chair with his legs crossed, and watched the stars twinkling overhead. "Have you been waiting out here long?" he asked.

"Most of the afternoon."

He captured the sound of Beau's voice, imprinting the tone in his mind. It was the first memory he'd added since the boy was four, when he'd watched from afar as Beau played in the park with his friends.

That day he'd promised Beau's grandparents he'd stay away, that he wouldn't interfere. He'd kept his word, standing quietly in the shadows, his emotions rendering him speechless. Words weren't coming much easier now.

"It's awfully cold to do nothing but sit and wait," he said awkwardly.

"It's no big deal," Beau muttered. "I've been waiting for you for sixteen years. A few hours in the cold didn't seem so bad."

The statement hit him hard, but Jack knew he deserved every reproachful word.

Beau turned his head, and Jack saw the spitting image of himself at that age—square jaw, the first stubble of a beard, dark blond hair that had a mind of its own, and an angry, blue-eyed glare. Jack wasn't big on crying, but he could feel a whole lot of tears building up behind his eyes.

"Smoking can kill you," Beau said, staring at the cigar, and for one moment he allowed his eyes to take in the height and breadth of his dad before turning back to his whittling.

Jack stubbed out the cigar and tried his damnedest to think of something meaningful to say.

He leaned forward. With his legs spread

wide, he rested his elbows on his knees and tilted his head toward his son. "Did your Grandpa Morris teach you to whittle?"

"Yeah, when I was a kid. He had arthritis in his knees and back, so he wasn't big on sports. Whittling was about the most active thing he ever did."

"What about you? Do you play any sports?"

"Some basketball and football. A little baseball, when the mood strikes. I wanted to rodeo once. Even thought I'd like to be a cowboy, but I didn't have a horse." Beau's eyes flickered toward Jack, then back to the knife in his hand. "I wouldn't have had anyone to teach me to ride even if I did have one."

"I guess you deserve an apology."

Beau laughed cynically, digging the knife deep into the wood and shoveling out a chunk that flew across the porch. "If you were going to apologize, you would have done it before you sat down in that chair and started asking about sports."

Hurling the knife into the floor planks, Beau shoved up from the chair, and it skittered out from under him as he stormed from the porch and across the yard.

Jack watched him, seeing himself in every one of the boy's moves. The baseball cap he took from his coat pocket and pulled low on his brow and the blue-and-gold letterman's jacket he wore were a sure sign that sports weren't just a passing thing. That sure as hell wasn't something they could talk about. What Jack knew about sports could be written on the back of a baseball card. He knew cows, horses, how to rodeo and run a ranch.

As for teenage boys, he knew as much about them as he knew about women, and that wasn't saying much.

He left the porch, following Beau at a slower pace. He was making a mess of things, but he knew he couldn't fix sixteen years of wrong right away.

Beau straddled the top rail of one of the corrals. Jack rested his arms on top, staring at the moon rising in the distance.

"Do your grandparents know you're here?"

"Yeah. Pastor Mike made me call them last night."

"Are you planning on staying long?"

"Don't know yet."

Pecos, the gelding Jack had ridden since he was just a few years older than Beau, came toward him, looking for a handout. He didn't have carrots, an apple, or even a sugar cube. Instead, he rubbed the horse's jaw, wishing it would be that easy to smooth things over with Beau.

"I was sixteen," Jack said, "the same age as you are now, when you were born."

"So," Beau snapped. "I wouldn't give up my kid, no matter how young I was."

"I'm not saying what I did was right, but I can't change that now, and apologizing isn't going to make up for sixteen years of us being apart."

"I don't think anything can make up for all that time."

"If you felt that way, you wouldn't be here now."

Jack gave the boy a nudge with his arm. "By the way, I heard you hitchhiked all the way here. You can get killed out on the road. Don't do it again."

There was rage in Beau's eyes when he glared at Jack. "What gives you the right to tell me what I can and can't do?"

"I could tell you I'm your father, and you have to do what I say, but you know as well as I do that I gave up all my rights to you a long time ago."

"Pretty shitty thing to do to your kid, wasn't it?"

"Yeah, it was," Jack threw back. "But that's history. The way I see it now, we're starting from scratch. I've got to earn your respect, and you've got to earn mine. And don't think I'm going to coddle you, tell you something's right when it's wrong, or let you do whatever you want, just because you think I owe it to you."

"Maybe I should go back home."

"If that's what you want, go."

Hell! He didn't mean that, but it was too late to take it back now. He could already see the anger in Beau's face.

"Fine. I shouldn't have come in the first place." He jumped down from the corral and headed for the house, but Jack caught his arm and brought him to a halt. The boy struggled, but Jack didn't let go.

"Why did you come?" Jack asked.

"What does it matter?"

"If you came to tell me you hate me, go right ahead. You're more than justified."

"I don't hate you."

"Then why are you here?"

Tears built up in the corners of Beau's eyes, and he turned away, wiping them with the back of his hand. Jack watched the boy's shoulders rise and fall as he took a deep breath. Slowly, he looked back. "I just wanted a chance to see you, to find out what you were like."

Jack swallowed the hard, heavy lump that had formed in his throat. "I'm not an easy man to know."

"Well, guess what. I'm not an easy kid to like."

*   *   *

The television blared through the house when Jack walked inside. It was Saturday night, and that meant Mike and Crosby had a date in front of the TV. Ever since Mike's wife had passed away four years ago, he'd come up to the house in the evenings. In the beginning he'd done it to fight off the loneliness. After a year or so he said he came in an attempt to save Crosby's ornery soul, but when those efforts failed, he'd settled into the comfortable routine of keeping the old man company.

Jack liked having him around. Mike had been his friend for thirty-two years. They'd grown up together on the ranch, been taught in a one-room schoolhouse together, and gotten in trouble together when they were young. They'd taken separate paths when they'd grown up. Jack wanted to make money; Mike wanted to be a minister. Six years earlier, when Jack's dad left the ranch for Santa Fe, Mike's folks, who'd spent a lifetime working with and for Reece Remington, went with him. That's when Mike and his wife moved from town to the ranch, taking over the log home where Mike had been raised.

If he'd looked forever, Jack couldn't have found a better manager or a better friend. He'd been at Jack's side after Beth had died and when he'd given up his child. Jack had been at Mike's side through his wife's illness, through her death. As far as Jack was concerned, Mike was family—and he'd do anything for those he loved.

Mike was as devoted to Jack and the ranch as he was to his God. Jack liked the combination—although he didn't always like the preaching.

"How did it go?" Mike asked, catching sight of Jack and following him up the stairs and into his bedroom.

Jack slung his garment bag across the bed. He didn't want to talk but knew Mike would hound him until he did.

"I would have preferred getting thrown and gouged by a bull."

Mike leaned against the doorjamb. "It's not going to get any easier."

"Beau pretty much said the same thing." Jack unzipped the bag and pulled out his newest tux. "Did you know he got kicked out of school last year?"

"Is that what he told you?"

"Yeah."

"When I talked to Mrs. Morris last night, she told me Beau's had a three-point-nine average for the last two years, just made captain of the baseball team, and was thinking about being a doctor, like his grandpa."

Jack stopped unpacking. The kid had lied to

him, but Jack chalked that up to anger. What he didn't understand, though, was why the boy would give up so damn much to come to Wyoming, especially to find a man who'd never been a part of his life.

"Was coming here a surprise to his grandparents?" Jack asked. "Or had he been talking about it for a while?"

"A surprise. He didn't show up at school on Tuesday, and when they called to check up on him, Mrs. Morris found a note on his bed saying he was going to find his dad."

"Has he said much to you about his reasons for coming?"

"Not much. He's got a stubborn streak. Takes after you, I imagine."

Jack refused to comment. Mike was trying to make light of something that was resting far too heavy on his soul. "Any idea why he'd lie to me about school?"

"He's a teenager. How can anyone know what's going on inside his head. The way I see it, Jack, you're just gonna have to talk to the kid and find out."

"He's not big on talking."

"Neither are you."

Jack heard Crosby approaching long before he reached the room. He had a distinct, limping walk, and a habit of clearing his throat just before beginning a conversation. "You two havin' a party in here?"

"Just shooting the breeze," Mike stated, as Cros hobbled across the room and plopped down on the bed.

"Talkin' about that boy's more like it." He aimed his rheumy eyes at Jack. "Spittin' image of you when you was a kid. Sure in hell hope he don't have the same temperament, though. You was a piss-poor excuse for a man at that age."

"Thanks for the compliment." Jack unloaded a pair of shoes from the bag and tossed them into the closet, wondering why in the hell he couldn't get any privacy in his own home.

"You going to keep him around?" Crosby asked.

"Were you thinking I'd toss him out?"

Crosby scratched the stubble on his wrinkled face. "Your pa and I wanted to toss you out a time or two. If Mike's ma hadn't caterwauled about you being a good kid under all that hate you was carrying around, we might have."

Mike laughed, and Jack aimed a scowl in his direction. "Seems to me you were a pain in the butt when you were sixteen, and that you might have ended up in jail if you hadn't found God and a good wife." Jack ripped the second tux from the bag. "As for you, Cros, I've been thinking about replacing you. Lauren has a cook who fixes eggs Benedict for breakfast. That sure as hell sounds better than burned biscuits."

"Replace me and you'll lose the only sensible person on this spread."

Crosby pulled a woman's shoe from the garment bag and dangled it on a bent index finger. "What the hell is this? You cross-dressin' these days?"

Jack snatched the redhead's rhinestone shoe from Crosby's hand and tossed it back into the bag, but not before Crosby got his fingers around the silky white gown. "A dress, too? Your pa told me that Palm Beach was full of crackpots, but I never thought you was one of them."

"It's a long story, and you're the last man on earth I'd share it with. Besides, isn't it past your bedtime?"

"S'pose." Crosby struggled to rise. Neither Jack nor Mike helped. They both knew the old man didn't want any fuss. He was eighty-two going on a hundred and ten, but he wasn't ready to be put out to pasture—and Jack was in no hurry to have him go.

"You coming for breakfast in the morning?" Crosby asked Mike.

"Are you serving burned biscuits?"

"The best ones in eastern Wyoming."

"I'll be here then."

Jack waited to hear Crosby's boots on the stairs, then turned his head to Mike. "Okay, you saw the shoes and dress, so what questions are on *your* mind?"

"Why are they in your bag and not Arabella's?"

"There is no Arabella."

"Seems to me you were engaged yesterday morning. What happened?"

"In Arabella's words, I'm self-centered, I have very little class, and I don't have any idea how to treat a woman." Jack laughed for the first time since last night. He grabbed one of the rhinestone shoes and looked at Mike. "Arabella did have one more thing to say."

"What's that?"

"I'm a son of a bitch."

Mike grinned. "Did she tell you all that before or after Lauren's party last night?"

"Way before. She didn't go to Palm Beach."

Mike glanced at the shoe Jack was holding. "Then where did that come from?"

Jack collapsed in a chair at the far side of his room, took a cigar from the humidor, and aimed his eyes at Mike. "I have a story to tell you, and knowing what an upstanding, ethical, and righteous man you are, you're not going to like it."

SIX

Sam set the latte-to-go on the bar, counted the handful of change the customer dumped into her palm, and sorted it into the cash register. The work was easy, mindless, and that's pretty much what she needed this afternoon. For the past two weeks, ever since she'd gotten fired from Antonio's, she'd worked six hours a day at the Espresso Nook, and waited tables at Denny's from eight at night until four in the morning, taking on extra hours whenever she could get them. Today, she was bone tired.

Leaning against the counter, she watched her coworker, Maryanne, slice into a decadent, five-layer chocolate mousse cake and decided that's what she would have for lunch. The caffeine in the cake and the three or four mochas she'd drink during the day would help her get by until she could catch a bite of dinner at Denny's.

She was thinking about a well-done patty melt with extra cheese and grilled onions, when Maryanne started talking. "I went out with Sean last night." Maryanne slid the knife underneath the piece of cake. "Gorgeous guy. Great butt, nice mouth. He says he's a lawyer, but I've got my doubts. He's got a friend if you're interested."

"Not interested," Sam told her. Even if she was, how could she squeeze a date into her schedule?

Maryanne eyeballed the customers to make sure no one was looking and stuck her fingers in her mouth, licking off the whipped cream and dark chocolate after she put the piece of cake onto a plate. "Umm. This reminds me of last night. Let me tell you about Sean's mouth . . ."

Sam closed her eyes for a moment, listening to the soft purr of Maryanne's voice. When she opened them again, the plate of dessert was gone and Maryanne was glaring at her, her arms folded under her double-A breasts.

"Better not let the boss catch you napping." Maryanne smiled, shoved a cup of steaming coffee in Sam's hands, and stared at her again. "You look awful. How much sleep have you gotten in the past week?"

"Enough."

"One of these days you're going to collapse,

face first, into one of these desserts, and let me tell you, it's not going to be a pretty sight."

"If you see me falling, do me a favor. Point me in the direction of something chocolate."

They both laughed, and Sam went back to work, thinking there were worse ways to die, like falling asleep and drowning while she was cleaning one of the toilets at the KOA campground west of town.

That was another job she'd taken on, although she wasn't earning any money for her work. She'd made a deal with the managers. She'd clean the bathrooms every morning in exchange for a place to shower and change clothes, do her laundry, and park her car. She imagined they knew what else she was doing, but they never said a word, not even when they'd found her in the TV room sleeping through the *Today Show*. Twice she'd taken advantage of the swimming pool and once she'd joined a few vacationing families for a game of volleyball. Sleeping in the bug under the shade of some big old palms, or even dozing in the KOA's TV room, sure beat grabbing a nap in the back room of Antonio's.

With any luck, she'd have Johnnie Russo paid off in two weeks and two days. Of course, luck would have to come in the form of hundred-dollar bills raining down from the sky—thirty-seven of them to be exact. After sending Johnnie the sixty-one hundred she'd earned for her foolish night with Jack Remington, she thought the payoff on her contract was only two thousand. Unfortunately, Johnnie had a unique way of figuring interest, and she hadn't had the courage to argue when he'd hit her with the new figure over the phone last week.

Of course, two thousand dollars would be just as hard to come by as thirty-seven hundred, but worrying about it now wasn't going to keep her employed.

Noticing crumbs and spilled cocoa on the counter, she took a wet cloth and started wiping up the mess, moving to the front of the baked-goods display case to make sure the glass sparkled from the customer's point of view. When the bell over the door rang, she turned.

"Oh, my God!"

She jerked around, whipped off her apron, threw it and the washcloth at Maryanne, fluffed her hair, and whispered. "You don't know me."

Maryanne frowned. "What on earth?"

Sam put a silencing finger to her lips. "Please. Pretend I'm a customer."

Maryanne shrugged.

"I'll have a mocha, *please*," Sam said, emphasizing the last word and half-frowning, half-pleading for Maryanne to go along with her charade.

Maryanne leaned against the counter, getting close to Sam's face. "That makes three in the past two hours."

"I know," Sam said through gritted teeth. "But—"

"Arabella?"

Sam swallowed her anxiety, and turned slowly when she heard the familiar voice. She forced a smile to her nervous lips. "Lauren!"

A pair of arms flew around her. "Oh, my gosh. Never in my wildest dreams did I expect to see you again so soon. What on earth are you doing in Florida?"

"It's a long story. Why don't I tell you over a cup of coffee," Sam said in a rush of words. "My treat."

"I'd kill for a double iced mocha with whipped cream and chocolate shavings." Lauren studied the contents of the display case. "One of those éclairs would be nice, too. I've been shopping for hours, and you can't imagine how beat I am. Thought it would be nice to get off my feet for a bit."

"I know how exhausting shopping can be. As for me, well, I just got out of bed," Sam lied, coming up with a quick excuse to explain her sleepy-eyed appearance, while trying to think up some reason for being in West Palm

Beach instead of Denver, where the real Arabella belonged. "Why don't you grab a table? I'll get the coffee."

Lauren walked across the room, all grace and elegance packed into a curvaceous size sixteen. Sam watched her while she absently ordered the mochas and dessert, thinking Jack's sister looked like a zillion dollars in a sky-blue silk shantung pantsuit, not to mention the Richard Tyler beaded satin sandals. Sam made a mental note to check out How Tacky in two or three months—if Johnnie Russo hadn't disposed of her by then—to see if this latest fashion had made it from some rich lady's closet to the discard pile.

"Who's that?" Maryanne whispered, capturing Sam's attention. "And why is she calling you Arabella?"

"I can't explain right now. But please, *pleeeze*," she begged, "don't give me away."

"You're not doing anything illegal, are you?"

Sam shook her head rapidly. "Of course not. Now do me a favor and fix the mochas, okay? One other favor. Don't charge me for anything. *Please?*"

Maryanne went along with the game, and while she was working on the drinks, Sam took a deep breath and found a seat across from Lauren.

Her hair was perfect. Soft, light brown tresses hung just to her shoulder in the sleekest style Sam had ever seen outside a copy of *Vogue*. Her fingernails were perfect, not too long, not too short, and were painted a pastel pink. Her eye makeup was exquisite, her skin without flaw, and she was the last person on earth Sam had ever expected to walk into the Espresso Nook.

Tell her about the masquerade, Sam told herself. *If you don't, you're going to end up in one heck of a mess.* But she couldn't. If Jack hadn't told his sister the truth, he must have had a good reason. He'd paid her good money to play his fiancée. What could it possibly hurt to keep up the sham a little while longer?

Besides, she liked Lauren. The night of the party she'd made Sam feel comfortable in an uncomfortable situation. She'd treated her like a sister, and she'd always wanted a sister. She'd wanted close friends, too, but she and her mama had rarely settled in one place long enough to make lasting friendships. When she was older, people shied away when they knew her background or met her mother. She didn't hold any of that against her mama; she never would.

Right now, though, she wanted to take advantage of the situation. She wanted to sip coffee and gab with the woman sitting across from her, a woman who was one of the nicest people she'd ever met, a person she'd want for her sister if she had a choice.

She only hoped by doing so neither one of them would get hurt.

"So," Sam said, leaning back in the chair and crossing her legs, as if she hadn't a care in the world, "do you really want to know what I'm doing in West Palm Beach?"

"I have a pretty good idea already," Lauren told her. "Chip, my first husband, advised me—in strictèst confidence, of course—that you have friends in West Palm Beach. He also told me you were very outspoken in sticking up for *those* people." Lauren smiled warmly. "Chip's a snob. Always has been; always will be. He thinks the main reason we got divorced was because of his preoccupation with horse racing, but the biggest reason is that I got tired of his elitist attitude. What possessed me to marry him is anyone's guess. Where I come from we don't treat people that way, so I'm glad you attempted to put him in his place. Not many people would."

"It was a pleasure, I assure you."

"Now," Lauren said, "tell me why you haven't called."

Think fast, Sam told herself, almost letting out a sigh of relief when Maryanne approached, giving her a brief reprieve. For some reason, pretending to be Arabella didn't seem so easy today.

Maryanne put the mochas and dessert on the table, and Sam swallowed a hot gulp that burned her insides. She looked at Lauren through the steam. As sweet and special as she had been at the party, Lauren had pretty much faded from Sam's mind in the past two weeks. Jack—tall, hard-muscled, sexier-than-all-get-out and the best kisser on the face of the earth—she hadn't forgotten at all.

"I'd planned to call," Sam finally said, hoping she sounded sincere, hoping Lauren wouldn't hear the anxiety in her voice. "I flew in for just a couple of days, to visit my friend Maryanne. That's her behind the counter. We met in summer camp when we were kids, and we've stayed in touch ever since." She took a breath, then continued with her hastily made-up tale. "Last night we celebrated her twenty-fifth birthday, and, well, that's the reason I look the way I do right now. Not enough sleep, a little too much celebrating."

"Champagne?"

"Beer. To be perfectly honest, I prefer it to champagne," Sam said, although she rarely imbibed either. "I think sometimes Jack finds me a little too unsophisticated."

"I imagine that's why he fell in love with you. I've met some of his former girlfriends.

They were far too much like the Chip Chasens of this world."

"They were?"

"Hasn't he told you about any of them?"

"Well, no. I haven't told him much about *my* past, either."

"How odd." Lauren frowned. "Oh, well, I doubt Jack cares a thing about your past. I have to tell you, I was a little concerned when he first told me about you. I was expecting a gold digger, someone out to take Jack for half of what he's got—and believe you me, he's got a lot. But I watched the two of you together. So did Peter, and he was one hundred percent positive you were devoted to Jack. As for me, I've never seen my brother look at someone the way he looked at you."

"What way was that?"

Lauren took a bite of éclair, then slowly licked the chocolate from her lips. "Like you were sweet cream and he wanted to lap up every drop."

Sam felt a tremor of delight zinging around her insides. It was a fleeting moment of happiness, and then reality set in. Jack Remington had been her employer for a night. Nothing more. Right now, she was an actress, and she should pay attention to her role.

"I noticed Peter looking at you that way, too," she fibbed, remembering the flash of disdain she'd seen in Peter's eyes when he'd looked at his fiancée. If Lauren was a real, honest-to-goodness friend, she might tell her how she felt about Peter, but it wasn't her place.

Lauren's eyes reddened at Sam's comment, and she stared at her plate. Something was wrong in the relationship, Sam decided. But there was nothing she could do.

The pretty smile that seemed commonplace on Lauren's face returned slowly. "Peter was a little out of sorts the night you met him," she said. "We'd had a small argument before you and Jack arrived at the party, but . . ." She leaned across the table. "After everyone had gone, Peter gave me the most gorgeous emerald choker you have ever seen, and then he suggested I model it—and nothing else."

Lauren sat back in her chair and fanned her face. "None of my other husbands ever asked me to do something like that." She took another bite of éclair. "You know that Jack had Peter investigated, don't you?"

Sam looked away, feeling uncomfortable with the turn in the conversation. "He'd mentioned something, but only briefly."

"I could have murdered him. Can you imagine how horrid Peter felt? Maybe he was a playboy once upon a time, but I'm not exactly pure as the driven snow. Of course, Jack still acts like I'm ten years old and need his protection. He doesn't trust me to make right choices, and he definitely doesn't trust the men in my life." She stabbed the éclair and sighed. "I suppose I shouldn't be saying all this to you."

"I don't mind. I like hearing about Jack."

"Well, he hasn't trusted anyone since my mother and father got divorced. They promised us they wouldn't pull me and Jack apart, but they did. I went with Mother, he stayed with our dad. And then there was that horrible time when Beth died and her parents moved away and took Beau with them, but I'm sure you know all about that."

She didn't, and she wanted to know, but she couldn't ask about something so personal.

"And I can't forget the fact that his first steak-house partner embezzled a whole bunch of money."

Lauren took a deep breath, lifted her mocha to her lips, and looked over the top of the cup at Sam. "Suffice it to say, he isn't too trusting. Sometimes he makes me so mad I could scream. Of course, he's gone out of his way since we were kids to make sure I'm happy. My mother moved me from city to city as she moved from man to man. Jack stayed out west, but he made a point of calling me nearly every day to make sure I was okay. How could I possibly get upset with a brother like that?''

"It would be pretty hard."

"That's why I'm so happy he's found you. You're perfect for him, Arabella. Absolutely perfect." She cut into her éclair, but ignored the delectable concoction on her fork. "By the way, when do you go home?''

"Tomorrow." The moment Sam said tomorrow she regretted not saying today. "Very *early* tomorrow."

"Then you could go to another birthday party tonight—with Peter and me."

"I wish I could, but—''

"Let me guess, you haven't got anything to wear?''

"That's an understatement."

"You can't turn me down, Arabella. Not tonight. It's *my* birthday we're celebrating."

Sam toasted Lauren with her cup of coffee. "Happy birthday. If I'd known, I would have gotten you a present."

"Having you at the party would be the best present of all."

Not if you knew the truth, Sam thought, feeling awfully crummy for continuing the lie.

"I can't, Lauren. I didn't bring a single fancy thing with me. You know how it is—no clothes, no party." Sam hoped her statement would end the questioning.

"Nonsense. We could go shopping. Right now, as a matter of fact. My favorite boutique's on Worth Avenue. I'm sure we could find something perfect for you to wear tonight. I might even get something new, too."

"I'm not dressed for shopping. I'm a mess."

"Don't worry about any of that. I don't think you could ever look anything but beautiful." She lifted the fork to her mouth. "Jack's got an account at my favorite boutique. He orders all of my gifts from there. You can charge whatever you want to him."

"I couldn't do that."

Lauren frowned. "Why not?"

Think fast! "We plan on keeping separate accounts after we're married, and I don't expect him to buy things for me. Flowers, maybe. Dinner, of course. But not my clothes."

A small smile tilted Lauren's perfectly colored lips. "I honestly don't see what there is to worry about. If you don't want to put it on Jack's account, you could open one yourself, or charge something. I doubt an outfit for the evening will cost much more than two, three thousand."

"That would blow my entire budget." *For the rest of my life,* she thought.

Lauren laughed. "A budget? You're marrying my brother! If you don't mind me butting in a bit, I think the two of you need to do some serious talking about your likes and dislikes *and* about the future, not to mention the fact that you're on a budget—which is absolute nonsense. This afternoon I'm going to show you *how* to be the wife of a very rich man, and trust me, Jack won't even blink an eye."

Sam felt a sickly green color rising up her neck and tingeing her cheeks.

"Wouldn't you and Peter like to celebrate alone?"

"We'll do that *after* dinner." A hint of desire gleamed in her eyes. "Peter has a special gift for me, something he wants to give me in private. Which reminds me, I should buy myself something for *after* dinner." Lauren reached across the table and gently squeezed Sam's hand. "Go shopping with me, Arabella. We didn't have much time to talk at my engagement party, and there's so much I want to know about you."

Going anywhere with Lauren would be fun, but doing so was out of the question. "I'll have to take a rain check. Besides having nothing to wear, Maryanne and I have plans tonight."

"She could join us."

"I don't think so. She's more a billiards kind of girl."

"Now *you're* sounding like a snob." Lauren laughed, refusing to take no for an answer. She pushed back in her chair. "Don't worry about a thing. I'll talk to Maryanne."

A bad case of anxiety ripped through Sam's body. Her stomach churned, rumbled. She could feel sweat beading on the back of her neck even though the air conditioner was cranked down to sixty-eight.

Lauren was chatting animatedly with Maryanne, and when she headed back to the table, Maryanne grinned, as if the whole thing was some big joke, and she was thrilled to play along.

"It's all set," Lauren said. "You and I are going shopping right now. We'll have another mocha at the boutique. Some wine, too, if that sounds good to you."

"It sounds terrific," she lied, "but what about my plans with Maryanne?"

"You were right. She *is* a billiards kind of girl and wasn't the least bit interested in joining us at the country club. What a sweetheart she is. I can see why the two of you are such good friends. When I explained that we're going to be sisters-in-law, and that we'd never had any time alone together, just to talk, she understood perfectly. I promised I'd have you back at her place by ten, and I always keep my promises. Now, come on. We're going to have a ball."

A ball? Right. Sam mentally calculated the number of parking tickets she'd have on her car when she got back to the coffee shop that night. She tried to think of a place she could reasonably picture as Maryanne's home so she'd know where to have Lauren drop her off at ten. And she was wondering if she'd ever find a moment alone so she could find someone to take the first few hours of her shift at Denny's.

Lauren chattered all the way to the zippy red Mercedes two-seater parked in front of a battered orange bug, but Sam didn't hear a word she said. Instead, all she could hear was the constant refrain singing through her head: *"What have I gotten myself into now?"*

seven

Jack hunched over the ledger on his desk, making note of the number of cows he and Mike had counted on the home range in the past week. The winter had been brutal, yet healthy newborn calves were spilling right and left. It was shaping up to be a record year for shipping in the fall.

Behind him he heard the ring of the fax. He was expecting his business partner—the creative genius behind the Remington steak houses—to send him a proposal for next year's advertising budget. Jack didn't know the first thing about running a restaurant. Hell, he couldn't even grill a steak, but he knew how to make money. He left the day-to-day operation of the restaurants up to Ben Richman, but he kept an eye on income and expense. Where money was concerned, he trusted his own judgment and no one else's.

He pushed back the heavy oak chair and went to the fax, laughing when he saw the name of a familiar Palm Beach boutique on the invoice that came through. Over the years, he'd ordered dozens of gifts for his sister from Michel's, and rarely a week went by that she didn't purchase another trinket or two and send the bill to Jack. Lauren had more money than she knew what to do with, but she still got a kick out of spending *his* money on frivolous things.

Tearing his gaze from the invoice, he stood at the window and watched Beau practicing his roping skills on a fence post and anything that walked by. Poor old Rufus seemed to get the brunt of it, but the dog kept going back for more.

In the two weeks Beau had been at the ranch, Jack had taught his son how to ride everything from a swayback, aging mare, to a cantankerous stallion, how to rope almost like a pro, and how to handle a Stetson. The boy was a natural at everything. He listened. He learned. But he didn't say much. Jack didn't either. The relationship was strained, at best, and Jack didn't have any idea how to make it better.

Maybe he should take up shopping, he thought. Hell, his sister seemed to take comfort in buying unnecessary frills. He tore the invoice from the fax machine. What had she purchased now? Emanuel Ungaro dress: $3,850; Gucci shoes and purse: $972; Voyage bra and panties: $320.

Jack ran a hand through his hair, shaking his head—$320 for underwear. Damn! He ordered boxers from JC Penney's, and he could wear a new pair nearly every day for the next three months and still not pay as much as she had for a few skimpy pieces of silk.

He sure as hell hoped she wasn't buying them to please Peter—but that was her business, not his.

The price of the earrings and bracelet she'd purchased were a blur as his mind turned back to the cost of running a ranch. He tossed the invoice on his desk and set his newly acquired paperweight—one lone shoe, size 9-1/2, that was nothing more than rhinestone straps affixed to a sole and four-inch heels—on top the other bills he needed to pay.

For a moment he allowed himself to think about red ringlets, the soft curve of a woman's spine, whiskey-colored eyes, and a sweet, luscious mouth. Two weeks had gone by, yet he could still taste the champagne on her lips, and feel hard nipples and soft, full breasts burning through his shirt as he held her against his chest.

Damn, if his life hadn't gotten complicated.

He lusted after a woman who hadn't called after receiving the roses he'd sent and his heartfelt note telling her he'd like to talk and get to know her better. On top of all that, he had a son he couldn't talk to and a sister in Palm Beach who thought he was engaged to a beautiful redhead when, in truth, he was engaged to no one. The blasted shoe he was using as a paperweight served as a reminder to call Lauren and tell her the truth, and never again to pay a stranger to be his fiancée.

He picked up the phone. He was distracted now. He couldn't think, which meant he couldn't work, so he figured he might as well call his sister, wish her a happy birthday, and break the news.

What would she think of what he'd done? Would she cry? God, she'd cried so damn much when she was little, when their mother would go off on one of her escapades to Europe or South America, and leave Lauren with the servants. He remembered their long-distance phone conversations over the years. She always put up a front, trying to sound brave, but he could hear her fighting back sniffles and tears. She'd ask him what he was doing. She'd ask about Dad and Mike and Crosby. She'd even ask about the cows and horses, and at the end of every conversation tell him that she loved him, that she knew she could always rely on him, that she knew he'd never hurt her.

He'd blown it this time!

None of this would have happened if he'd told her the truth the night of her engagement party. But he'd been too damn worried about making her cry. Those tears would probably come tenfold now.

His grip had tightened on the receiver as he listened to the ring. Finally, the butler answered, and informed Jack that Mrs. Lancaster—her second husband's last name—was out to dinner "with Mr. Leighton and Miss Fleming."

Miss Fleming?

"She's what?" Jack asked incredulously.

"They're celebrating Mrs. Lancaster's twenty-eighth birthday, Mr. Remington. Surely you hadn't forgotten."

"I didn't forget her birthday. Who did you say she's out with?"

"Mr. Leighton and Miss Fleming, your fiancée, sir."

"Oh, hell!"

"Is there an emergency?" the butler asked. "They've gone to the country club. I would be happy to get in touch with Mrs. Lancaster for you."

"No, that won't be necessary. Just tell her to call me as soon as she comes home."

"She and Mr. Leighton are leaving for London tonight, directly after dinner."

"Miss Fleming isn't going, too, is she?"

"I don't believe so, sir. I believe Mrs. Lancaster said Miss Fleming would be returning to Denver early tomorrow morning."

She would, would she?

"Thanks, Charles," Jack said. "Next time you talk with my sister, tell her I called to wish her a happy birthday."

"I'd be happy to tell her, sir."

Jack hung up the phone and stared at the rhinestone shoe. What the hell was the redhead up to? he wondered. She'd easily taken his sixty-one hundred dollars. Was she now trying to get money from his sister?

He grabbed the phone again and called information. When he had the number for Antonio's, he stabbed at the buttons on the phone while absently scanning the invoice again. He listened to the constant ring as he stared at the total: $7,857 and some change. When he realized it was after 9 P.M. in Palm Beach, he hung up the phone, but his eyes didn't leave the invoice. Instead, they concentrated on the name carefully written at the bottom. *Arabella Fleming.*

"Damn her!" He ripped the invoice from under the shoe. Arabella signed her name in a flamboyant script. The redhead might be wild and engaging, but her handwriting was shaky and unrefined, and he planned to tell her, up close and personal, that he'd hog-tie her and brand her a con artist if she got within ten miles of his sister ever again.

Except for the black tux, Jack thought that Mr. Antonio looked more like a snake-oil salesman than the proprietor of a fine men's store. He greeted Jack with one hand tucked in his pocket, the other extended flamboyantly in front of him.

"Good afternoon. I'm Mr. Antonio."

Jack was in no mood for pleasantries, especially after the long flight to Palm Beach. "I need to speak with one of your employees."

"Is there a problem, sir?"

"No. Not at the moment, anyway."

"Messrs. Erickson and Hansen are with clients. Perhaps I could help you."

"I'm looking for a woman."

"I'm sorry, Mr.—"

"Remington. Jack Remington."

"The restaurateur?"

Answering someone else's question was the last thing Jack wanted to do, but he managed to nod.

"It's an honor to meet you, Mr. Remington. I've had the pleasure of eating in your Boca Raton steak house many times. The food is superb." Mr. Antonio kissed his fingers and flung them into the air.

Jack wanted to punch his lights out.

"You have a redhead working for you. A female tailor named . . . Sam Jones."

"Ah, yes. Miss Samantha Jones. I'll apologize now for any grief she may have caused you a few weeks ago. But let me assure you, Mr. Remington, Antonio's always stands behind its merchandise. If there's any problem with your tux—"

"I don't give a damn about the tux. I need to talk to Sam Jones."

"She is no longer in my employ."

"Then where can I find her?"

"I'm afraid Miss Jones was not the kind of woman I associated with; therefore, I was not inclined to keep an account of her whereabouts. She stole a sewing machine from me. Oh, she returned it the next day, and I was kind enough not to turn her in to the authorities, but I couldn't have someone of her ilk working in my establishment."

"Look," Jack said, tired of Mr. Antonio and his attempts to cover his ass. "I need to find her, and in an establishment such as this, I'm sure you keep records on your employees. Social Security number? An address where you can send a W-2? A phone number for someone to call in case of emergency?"

"Perhaps." The man fussed nervously with one of his cuff links. "Would you like some wine while I look?"

"No!"

Beads of sweat had built up along Mr. Antonio's hairline. "I'll see what I can find," he said, his voice faint, almost strangled.

Jack followed the weasel of a man to an ornate, highly polished table at the farside of the room. He took a key from his pocket, opened a drawer, and pulled out a gray index file. "Let me see. Jones. Jones. Ah, here it is. Samantha Jones." The man's eyes flicked up toward Jack. "A Social Security number and post office box, nothing more. No phone number, either, but that doesn't surprise me."

"Why?" Jack asked, jotting the information down on a pad of paper he'd grabbed off Antonio's desk.

"I fired her, in part, for spending her nights in the sewing room and bathing in the restroom sink. Can you imagine?"

Jack glared at the man. "You're telling me she lived here? That she might not have had anyplace else to stay?"

"I never asked. She had certain talents where tailoring was concerned. My clients never complained about her work, and I do not pry into the lives of my employees."

"What about your other employees? Do you

think any of them pried, or even took the time
to get to know her?"

"Mr. Hansen, possibly."

"Where's he? In the back?"

"He's with a client right now. I could ask
him and get in touch—"

"*I'll* ask him."

Jack stalked across the room, through the
swinging doors that led to a hallway lined
with dressing rooms. He knocked on the first
closed door but didn't bother waiting for an
answer. "Are you Mr. Hansen?" he asked,
barging in and frightening the bald-headed
man who had straight pins protruding from
his mouth.

"Yes. May I help you?"

"Do you know where I can find Samantha
Jones?"

The tailor stood slowly, pulling one pin
from between his lips and then another. "No."

"Do you know anything about her?"

"I haven't seen or heard from her since she
left a few weeks ago. Nice lady. A little down
on her luck. She'd been living in her bug before she came here to work."

"Her bug?"

"A battered orange Volkswagen."

Jack stuck his hand in his pocket, pulled a
hundred-dollar bill from his money clip, and
slipped it into the tailor's hand. "Thanks."

Mr. Antonio was hot on his heels when he walked toward the front door. "Perhaps I could interest you in a new suit while you're here, Mr. Remington. Why, just this morning I received a Tombolini that would look perfect on you."

"Not interested," Jack barked, then slammed through the glass door and headed for his rented Lincoln. The only thing he was interested in right now was finding Samantha Jones—thief, con artist, and . . . Hell! Homeless person.

The post office refused to give Jack any information. They wouldn't even verify if the box number he'd given them did, in fact, belong to Samantha Jones. He wasn't going to give up, though. How many orange VW bugs could there possibly be in West Palm Beach?

He'd picked up a map from the Chamber of Commerce and started his search, driving up one street and down another, the wheel in one hand and a cigar in the other. After an hour of searching, he took his cell phone and electronic address book from his briefcase and punched in the number for Wes Haskins, the same investigator he'd hired to check out Peter Leighton.

"I need you to find out everything you can

about someone," he told Wes. "Her name's Samantha Jones."

"You're gonna have to give me more info than that."

"Red hair. Five-nine, maybe five-ten. Slender."

"What did she do? Break your heart?"

"Why I want to find her is no one's business but my own. She used to be an actress in Hollywood. Played in some kind of dinner theater."

"What else do you know about her?"

Not enough, Jack thought, *and more bad stuff than I ever wanted to know.* "She's around twenty-five. Drives a beat-up orange VW bug and might be living in it now, somewhere around West Palm Beach."

Jack gave Wes Samantha's Social Security number, her post office box address, and all the other details he could remember, little things they'd talked about while she'd altered his tux, sat across from him in a limousine, danced in his arms. He had no idea what an investigation might turn up. Was she on the run from the law? Was Samantha Jones her real name? Was she married?

That last thought bothered him the most.

Deep inside, he hoped Wes would come up empty-handed. He'd spent a lifetime not trusting people, but for some reason, he didn't want to believe the worst of Samantha Jones.

Eight hours later he was still driving the streets. He thought he had checked out every parking lot, every back alley, and every surface street in West Palm Beach. He'd counted twenty-three bugs. Five of them were the new models, the remaining seventeen were in various stages of decay or had been souped up with wide tires and bright paint—but not the color he was searching for.

There didn't seem to be an orange bug anywhere in West Palm Beach.

At 1:00 A.M. he drove through the parking lot of Denny's. He thought about stopping to get a cup of coffee, but he was tired and ready to head to the Breakers and catch a few hours' sleep.

The lot was well lit and more cars than he'd expected at that hour filled the spaces. He was just about ready to pull back onto the street when he caught sight of a round headlight in his rearview mirror. He turned, and partially hidden behind a Dumpster at the back of the lot was an orange VW.

Backing up, Jack pulled the Lincoln close, got out, and checked the inside of the car. Half a dozen wire hangers holding an assortment of clothes were suspended from a rod mounted over the cramped backseat. A jumble of shoes rested on the floor. A pillow and folded blanket sat on the passenger seat, and on top of the bedding was a gold-and-black shopping bag marked Michel—a boutique in Palm Beach that was all too familiar to Jack.

Pay dirt.

Jack locked the Lincoln and headed for the coffee shop.

"Just one?" the hostess asked when he walked through the door.

Jack nodded. "Is there a Samantha Jones working here?"

"Sam? Sure," the young girl answered. "Would you like to sit at her table?"

He nodded again, checking out the two women behind the counter with their backs to him. Sam was easy to pick out. She stood a good head taller than her coworker, and her flaming red hair could be seen a mile away.

"Is this okay?" The hostess set a menu on the table and smiled.

"It's fine. Thanks."

He slid into the booth, hung one arm over the back of the seat, and got comfortable. He wanted a clean view of Samantha Jones as she headed for his table.

She had a coffeepot in one hand and a glass of ice water in the other when she stepped out from behind the counter. The water sloshed onto the floor when their eyes connected.

"Evenin', Sam."

She let out a sigh, and he could easily see

the rise and fall of her breasts beneath the white shirt and Denny's tie. "I was wondering if you'd come looking for me."

"You weren't easy to find."

Her hand was shaking when she set the glass of water on the table. "Coffee?"

"I'd prefer answers."

She leaned across the table and turned over the mug. "The coffee's good, and I'm busy." Steam rose from the cup as she poured. He could tell she was trying to concentrate on the coffee, but her eyes peeked at him through thick lashes. "Have you had time to look at the menu?"

"I'm not hungry."

"You can't sit here if you're only going to have coffee. We need the tables for customers who want to eat."

"Then give me a hamburger with fries."

"How do you want it cooked?"

"Medium-well."

"Onions?"

"No."

"Would you like a salad, too?" she asked, scribbling down his order.

He stilled her hand. "What I want is to talk."

She pulled away. "I can't. It's busy tonight, and I've got other customers to take care of."

"When do you get off?"

"Four."

He lounged back in the seat and lifted his cup of coffee. "I'm in no hurry."

The skirt she wore was short and tight, and he couldn't miss the provocative swing of her hips as she walked away. A thick braid hung down her back, and just then he wanted to pretend it was a rope and pull her back to his booth.

All in good time, he decided.

She must have walked by three or four times, clearing tables, delivering an armful of plates to another, not slowing down a moment. She didn't take time to count the tips she shoved into her pocket, or to glare at him as he watched every sensual step she took.

Ten minutes later she delivered his plate.

He wasn't interested in the food—only in her. "Looks good," he said, watching the way she stared at the table instead of him.

"Thanks. More coffee?"

He put a contemplative finger to his lips, making her wait for an answer. "Do you have any apple pie to go with it?"

She rolled her eyes. "We had a run on apple earlier tonight. Is peach okay?"

He lifted the burger and held it close to his mouth, watching the way her pretty lips pursed in annoyance while she waited. Let her get angry. She'd made him angry when she'd walked out of his hotel room without saying good-bye. Let her see how it felt to be totally annoyed.

"I'm waiting for an answer, Jack. Do you want peach pie?"

"Do you have berry?"

"Only peach."

"Well, I prefer apple, but I suppose peach will do."

Again she filled his cup, but this time she didn't bother watching what she was doing. Instead, she stared him right in the eye. "Are you going to make my life miserable all night?"

"That's my plan."

"Couldn't you wait outside until four?"

"I prefer the view in here. If it's a tip you're worried about, don't."

"I don't want a tip from you."

"What about money for services rendered? What about clothes and jewelry?"

"I don't want anything."

"That's a switch."

She straightened, looking away as if she couldn't face the animosity he knew was in his eyes. "I deserved that," she whispered.

"Hey, miss," a burly man called to her from two booths away. "Could I have some more coffee."

"Be right there."

Jack wasn't hungry, but he managed to choke down the hamburger and fries as he watched every one of Sam's moves. He didn't know if she'd bolt, but he wanted to be ready to go after her if she did.

When Sam came back to the table, she slid a jumbo slice of peach pie in front of him. He hadn't asked for ice cream, but there were two scoops on the side.

"Look, I'll return the clothes," she said, putting the glass coffeepot on the table and sliding into the seat across from him. "I'll pay back every penny you paid me. It might take me a while, but—"

"Am I supposed to believe you?"

"Why shouldn't you?"

"You promised you wouldn't leave without me that night in Palm Beach, but you did."

She laughed lightly. "And that makes me untrustworthy?"

"That and a whole series of things."

"Such as?"

"Stealing a sewing machine."

"I borrowed without asking. I don't know how you found out about that, but obviously the person who told you left out the fact that I returned it the next day. I might be one step away from the poorhouse, but I don't steal."

"Then what do you call buying nearly eight thousand dollars worth of clothing and jewelry, including lingerie that must have been made out of gold, and charging all of it to me? And while we're at it, what do you call going to the country club with my sister and pretending to be Arabella Fleming?"

"I call it saving your miserable ass."

Jack couldn't help but laugh. "Now that's an excuse I don't hear every day."

Her pretty eyes narrowed into a frown. "Didn't Lauren call you?"

"Why should she?"

"Because, Mr. Remington, your sister accidentally turned up at the espresso shop where I work when I'm not working here. It was her birthday, and she asked me to go shopping and have dinner with her. I said no, but she insisted. I don't know how well you know your sister, but let me tell you, *Jack*, she doesn't believe in the word *no*."

"That doesn't explain the clothes."

"Miss," someone at another table called, "could I have an ice tea?"

"One second," she tossed over her shoulder, and leaned close. "Your sister insisted I buy the clothes and charge them to *my* fiancé. It was pretty obvious to me that you never told her the truth. What was I supposed to do? Screw up your little charade by telling her I don't have a fiancé *or* the proper clothes to wear to a country club?"

She didn't wait for him to respond. Instead, she slid out of the booth and walked away.

He watched her as she worked. She didn't look the type who would perpetrate some clever scam, yet she'd fallen so damn easily into playing a role when he'd asked her to, and she'd picked it up again without missing a beat. She'd seemed hesitant about taking his money, so hesitant she'd made him think she was a troubled woman, then she'd plucked the money right out of his hands.

But, hell, when he was around her most all his anger drained out of him. She had a smile that warmed him and a way with words that made him want to spend every minute in her company.

She might be a con artist, then again she might not, but he found himself wanting to be the victim of any one of her schemes.

Fifteen minutes later she was back, and she slipped into the booth again. "I've got a ten-minute break. If you think you can be civil, I'll keep you company."

He pushed his cup of coffee toward her. "Want some?"

She took the cup in both hands and held it to her lips. "I thought you were going to tell Lauren the truth."

"I couldn't bring myself to do it. I've spent

most of my life trying to make her happy."

"She told me. She also said you sometimes do too much."

"Old habits are hard to break. I tried calling her last night to tell her, but she'd already gone to London. I know I should have told her sooner, but I had other things on my mind."

"What could have been more important than telling your sister about the crazy scheme you concocted?"

"A troubled son."

She smiled softly, and damn if that smile didn't come close to melting his heart. "I'm sorry."

"Your mama didn't by any chance have any sage advice about teenage boys, did she?"

"Only to stay away from them."

"Good advice for a teenage girl, not good advice for a dad."

Sam picked a cold french fry from his plate, swirled it in the catsup, and stuck it in her mouth. Her cheeks had filled out some since he'd seen her last. Working as a waitress instead of a tailor had obviously provided her with steady meals. Still, the dark circles beneath her eyes were far more visible than they'd been before, and he couldn't help but wonder why.

"Have I answered all your questions?" she

asked, before putting a second fry in her mouth.

"There's only a few more."

"Then ask away."

"Why didn't you call me?"

She frowned in puzzlement. "I didn't have your phone number."

"It was in the note with the roses."

The frown deepened. "Did you send me roses?"

He nodded. "To Antonio's. A few days after you ran out on me."

She bit her lip, looking a little contrite, as if all that had happened weighed heavy on her mind. "I didn't get any roses. They must have come after I quit."

"*Quit?* I heard a different story. Something about being fired because of the sewing machine."

"The sewing machine wasn't the reason. I took that *after* I was fired."

He put an elbow on the table and rested his chin on his knuckles. He couldn't help but grin. "Care to tell me the *whole* story?"

"It's long. My break's not."

"Then give me the condensed version."

She took a sip of his water and stared at the table as she spoke. She told him about getting fired, about taking the sewing machine, about needing a tip to tide her over until she could get another job. He could sense her embarrassment, but he felt nothing but compassion for her and her troubles, and concern that there was much more to the story, things he wished she would share.

When she finished, he reached across the table, sliding his fingers over hers. "What are you doing when you get off work?"

"Going home."

"You don't have far to go, do you? I saw the Volkswagen in the parking lot, Sam. I know where you live."

Discomfort was plainly written on her face, and he knew her living conditions were another cause for embarrassment. Still, she offered him a smile. "It's cozy."

"So is my room at the Breakers. You could curl up there and sleep. Maybe have dinner with me later in the day."

"I'm not into one-night stands. I don't like one-day stands, either. Besides, we don't have anything in common."

"I thought we had a lot in common."

"Such as?"

The cowboy part of him that had a tendency to fade when he stepped on Palm Beach soil kicked in. "You fit right nice in my arms when we're dancing."

"An inflatable doll would, too."

"I've never tried kissing an inflatable doll,

but I doubt they holler 'stop' just when things are getting good."

"I hollered 'stop' because you were moving too fast."

"What if we started over? Moved a little more slow? Dinner really does mean just that—dinner. I won't do anything you don't want me to."

"It won't work, Jack. You don't trust me. More than likely you never will."

"I'll admit I'm not a trusting man, but I'll also admit that I've been wrong about people before. Maybe we should give each other a second chance?"

"I don't think so. We're from two different worlds, and I don't want to go somewhere that I don't fit in."

She reached into her pocket and pulled out a sapphire bracelet and earrings. "I've been carrying these around for two days now, scared to death someone would know I was carting around a few thousand dollars' worth of jewelry. Lauren insisted I buy them." Sam laughed, a sound that made him feel good, a sound he wanted to keep on hearing. "Your sister's got great taste, but they're not my style. I kind of go for plastic and thrift-store hand-me-downs, you know, things I can keep in my purse or the bug, things no one would bother to steal."

Jack slipped his hand over her upturned palm. "Keep them," he told her, but she shook her head as she pulled away, leaving only the sapphires in his grasp.

Pushing back the cuff on his shirt, she looked at his watch, and the simple brush of her fingers over the hair on his arms made him ache.

"My break's over," she said in a rush. "I've got to get back to work."

"Dinner's not a long-term commitment, Sam. Are you sure you won't reconsider?"

"No."

Rising, she took the check from her apron pocket and set it on the table.

"Waitress!"

She shrugged her shoulders. "Looks like duty calls."

Her words rang with finality, but he wasn't ready to give up. "You can push me away, Sam, but I'll come back. I let someone important get away from me once. I won't let it happen so easily this time."

"Those are pretty words, Jack. But they're only words. Actions speak so much louder. If you want to impress me, I need something more."

"Such as?"

She laughed, and blew him a parting kiss. "For starters, you could leave a big tip."

eight

"**H**ey, Sam, there's a phone call for you."

"Be there in a minute," Sam grumbled, when Tyrone called out to her from the kitchen. She cleared the table where Jack had been sitting a few minutes before, slapped down four new place settings, and stormed behind the counter, ready to do battle with anyone who got in her way.

What a fool she'd been! For the first time in her whole entire life a good man, someone downright decent—even though he'd inconveniently forgotten to leave a tip—had been interested in getting to know her better, and she'd pushed him away.

You're crazy, Sam! Absolutely out of your mind.

She dumped Jack's dirty dishes in a nearly full tub and stared at the peach pie he'd barely touched.

Maybe she wasn't so crazy. She remem-

147

bered her mama and the rich man who'd promised her fancy things. She also remembered her mama saying that women from the wrong side of the tracks were the forbidden fruit rich men craved. They'd take one bite, maybe two, then drop the remains in the gutter and go away.

Jack Remington might have wanted more than a one-night stand. He might have treated her to three or four nights of his time, maybe even days, but in the end, he'd go back to his mansion in Wyoming and she'd still be waiting tables at Denny's.

She didn't want to be the girl he loved and left behind. She didn't want to get hurt by the only man who'd ever made the soles of her feet tingle. Her heart had wanted more, but self-preservation had won out in the end.

"Are you ever gonna take this call?" Tyrone growled.

She pushed through the swinging kitchen doors and grabbed the phone out of his hand, tossing him an apologetic smile. "Hello."

"Good morning, Samantha."

Johnnie Russo had picked the wrong moment to call. She'd made a habit of being polite and obedient to Johnnie in the past five and a half months. This morning, tired, cranky, and totally confused about her feelings for Jack Remington, she couldn't be bothered with

Johnnie and one of his all-too-frequent calls.

"What do you want?"

"Is that any way to talk to your benefactor?"

"It's late, I'm exhausted, a millionaire just stiffed me on a tip, and no, I don't have any money to send you."

"You're running out of time, sweetheart."

"Don't you think I know it? I told you I needed a few more weeks."

"And I told you when you signed the contract that I don't give extensions, no matter what the reason."

"I'm working two jobs. I'm living in my car."

"I know all that. I know about the Espresso Nook. I know about Denny's. And I know about the KOA. By the way, I hear you play a mean game of volleyball."

Sam leaned against the wall, almost ready to give in to defeat. She'd thought that putting three thousand miles between herself and Johnnie would keep her safe until the contract expired. Obviously, she'd thought wrong. "Are you having me followed?"

Johnnie sounded like a hyena when he laughed. "Just keeping tabs on you."

"I'm not going anywhere. I told you I'd pay you back, and I meant it. So why don't you get off my case."

"Actually, all I want to do right now is deliver a message from an old friend of yours."

Sam didn't have to ask who. She knew perfectly well.

"Graham Welles said to tell you hello. He also said he'd be willing to pay off the contract if you'd be willing to come back to Hollywood."

The mere thought of seeing either Graham Welles or Johnnie Russo again sickened her. "Tell him to go take a flying leap off the Hollywood sign."

"He won't be pleased."

"I'm not worried about pleasing him, I'm worried about paying you. Now, if you don't mind, I can't make money if I'm talking on the phone."

She hung up. Her insides began to shake as she started to think of the mistakes she'd made five months ago. She'd sought out Graham Welles when she should have known better. Mama had told her not to trust him, not to believe any rich man who promised the world. Yet she'd gone to him when her mama needed help. Gone to him and pleaded for his aid, only to have him ask for her body first. She'd made a promise to herself that she'd never sell her soul, and she'd come so close that night. So very close. But she couldn't—not even for her mother.

She'd trusted Johnnie Russo, too. During a

time of desperation she'd let down her defenses, fallen for big talk and a fancy smile, and gotten herself so deeply in debt to him that she now feared that in two weeks he'd claim her life as the balance she still owed.

And now Jack. There was a possibility that he might be more ruthless than either Graham or Johnnie. Jack Remington could easily steal her heart and, when he was through with it, toss it away.

Of all the worries in her life, that one seemed to bother her most.

"You got a problem?" Tyrone asked, staring at her as he cleaned the grill.

"Several," she tossed back, trying to hide her fears behind a smile. "Thanks for asking."

"Anything I can do to help?"

Tyrone stood a good six-foot-six. He must have weighed close to three hundred pounds and had arms the size of palm trees, but he was a pussycat at heart, and Johnnie Russo's goons would chop him down in no time at all if he got in their way. Jack Remington might not appreciate his interference, either.

"It's sweet of you to ask, Tyrone, but unless you have thirty-seven hundred dollars you can lend me, I guess I'll have to take a rain check." She grinned as she shoved away from the wall and left Tyrone's kitchen.

By 3:30 the restaurant was virtually empty.

This was the time of morning she usually asked Tyrone to fix her a big plate of biscuits and gravy, but she wasn't hungry.

Grabbing the vacuum cleaner from the back room, she plugged it in and mindlessly pushed it over the carpet. She touched the scar on her jaw, and thought of Graham Welles. He'd ripped her blouse the night she'd gone to him, asking for money to help save her mama's life. He'd laughed at her and called her a bitch. He'd hit her, and told Sam a whore like her mother was better off dead.

Graham's opinions didn't matter. Felicity Jones never talked about what drove her to the life she'd lived, and Sam had never asked. She'd never talked of the man who'd gotten her pregnant. She'd never complained about her lot in life. She'd just lived it.

And she'd loved her daughter.

Sam couldn't have asked for a better mother, and her opinion was the only one that mattered.

She'd given her mother the finest funeral money could buy. She'd given her a granite headstone that would last an eternity and a plot of ground Felicity Jones could always claim as her own.

Going to Johnnie Russo for money had been foolish; he'd even told her so after the funeral. But she didn't regret it at all.

Foolishness seemed to be part of her life.

Pushing Jack Remington away might have been her most foolish mistake so far.

Don't think about it, she told herself. *What's done is done, so move on.*

She continued to vacuum, moving chairs and tables, and pouring an occasional cup of coffee for the one or two people who straggled in and out.

At five till four she put the vacuum cleaner away. She was so darn tired, but she still had to go to the KOA and clean bathrooms. Taking her tote bag from her locker, she said goodbye to Tyrone, to the other waitress crazy enough to work this shift, and headed for the door.

It was dark outside. At the far end of the parking lot, right next to her bug, she could see someone rummaging through the Dumpster, and she waited in the light of the Denny's sign for the man with the shopping cart to disappear.

She hated being out in the middle of the night. It made her feel vulnerable and alone.

A white van pulled to a stop in front of her, and the man behind the wheel stuck his head out the window. "Are you Samantha Jones?"

She grabbed the handle of the door and started to go back inside. She still had two weeks to pay off her loan, but maybe Johnnie had decided not to wait.

"Hey, don't run away. You look like the lady I was told to deliver something to."

As if that was supposed to make her feel better.

The guy looked at a white piece of paper fastened to a clipboard. "You *are* Samantha Jones, aren't you?"

"Yes," she said hesitantly.

"I thought so." He climbed out of the van and slid open the side door. "I was told to deliver these to you and you only. The guy who bought them said you had long red hair and a killer body. You fit the bill."

"Thanks," she said, feeling a sudden blush touching her cheeks as she wondered who, besides Johnnie Russo, would send an unmarked delivery van out in the middle of the night with a driver who'd been ordered to give her something.

The man, who'd been leaning into the van, faced her, holding a bottle of Chivas Regal and a bouquet of roses. "These are for you. I told the guy he was crazy sending flowers and a bottle of booze at four in the morning, but he told me actions speak louder than words. Personally, I think he might have been drunk."

Sam's throat tightened as she took the whiskey and flowers. She made a valiant attempt to smile, but tears were already threatening.

"There's a card, too." The deliveryman dug an envelope out of his shirt pocket, handed it to Sam, then stuck the clipboard in front of her. "Could you sign this. I need to show I delivered everything."

Sam's fingers trembled as she set the gifts on the concrete. She kept the card clutched in one hand, and with the young man holding the board, signed her name.

He checked out the signature. "That ought to do it." He climbed into the cab and slammed the door. "That cowboy sure went to a lot of trouble to have this delivered to you. Enjoy," he said through the open window, and drove away.

With shaking fingers she drew a plain white note card from the envelope. A piece of paper was folded inside, and she opened it. One of Jack's checks stared up at her. She angled it so she could see the writing in the light from the streetlamp. Her name was plainly written on the check, and a tear slid down her cheek when she saw *one thousand dollars* on the line below.

Her vision was blurred by the buildup of tears in her eyes, but she managed to read the note.

Sam,

Actions do speak louder than words. Yours send mixed messages, Whiskey, so I'll have to check them out again.

For now, I hope you didn't think I'd forgotten your tip.

Jack

She sat down on the pavement next to the whiskey and flowers, not bothering to hold back her tears. They dripped right off her face and splattered on Jack's note. He'd given her two dozen beautiful roses. He'd given her the finest Scotch whiskey. He'd given her a thousand dollars.

Best of all, he'd given her hope that she'd see him again.

And he hadn't asked for anything in return.

nine

Jack sat in the saddle, hands folded on the horn, and watched his son mend a stretch of downed barbed wire. A Norther had blown in after he'd gotten home from Florida last night, and he turned the collar up on his jacket to keep the icy air from hitting the back of his neck. Beau didn't have the luxury of a jacket, but it was his own damn fault, and Jack wasn't going to coddle him now.

They'd been riding fence all morning, and the boy's knuckles and palms were raw, bleeding from too many scrapes. He was shivering and wet, but Jack wasn't going to bend. He'd reminded the kid once to take a jacket and gloves, but his words had gone in one ear and out the other. Damn, if he wasn't exactly like Jack himself had been at that age.

"Can I borrow your gloves?" Beau had asked a few hours ago.

157

"What about yours?"

"I forgot them."

Jack remembered shaking his head at the boy's irresponsibility. He remembered pulling on the finger of one of his gloves so he could give them to Beau, then he stopped. "I won't always be around to loan you a pair of gloves," he'd said. "See how it feels to stretch that wire with your bare hands. Maybe you'll remember the next time."

The kid had struggled with the wire, stretching, twisting, doing exactly what Jack had shown him when they'd come across the first section of downed fence. The job wasn't easy. Nothing out here was easy, but in Jack's opinion it was the best life a man could have.

He wanted Beau to love being a cowboy for what it was, not because he was attracted to some romantic vision of home on the range.

They checked a few more miles of fence. If Jack was alone, he'd probably ride till sundown instead of noon, but he'd watched Beau shiver, watched the way his face twisted in pain when he stretched the last piece of wire. Heading for home seemed a wise idea. He'd always considered himself a hard man. But he was human, too.

They rode in near silence back to the ranch. Jack couldn't think of anything to say, and Beau looked as if he were in too much agony to speak. Maybe he'd gone overboard teaching him a lesson.

"Your hands hurt?" Jack asked.

"Some."

"Crosby's got a cure for just about everything that could ever ail a man. He'll take care of them when we get back."

"Did Crosby take care of you when you were growing up?"

"Sometimes. Most of the time my dad did."

The boy looked at him sideways. "Must have been nice having a dad who cared about you."

"Yeah."

"You don't like having me around, do you?"

"What makes you say that?"

Beau shrugged. "Doesn't matter." He put his spurs into the gelding's flanks and took off at a gallop. Jack would have stopped him, but the kid needed to let off steam, and Jack needed to think about the question.

Did he like having Beau around? Hell, he felt like a mustang being saddled for the first time. The only difference, a mustang kicked and jumped until the saddle started feeling comfortable.

Beau didn't feel comfortable, and Jack didn't know if he ever would. But that didn't keep those damned lumps from forming in his throat every time he thought of the boy, didn't keep his chest from expanding with pride every time his son learned something new.

Beau was walking Diablo around the yard when Jack rode in. The boy had learned quickly that he couldn't run his horse and not cool it off afterward. The horse came first; his wounds came second. He didn't complain, and he did his job.

His grandparents had raised him well. Letting them take Beau after Beth was killed in the car accident had probably been the best thing after all. Jack could have fought for custody. His dad could have hired a dozen lawyers and spent endless amounts of money so Jack could keep his child, but he'd felt so damn guilty after Beth's death that he'd signed away all his rights.

One impulsive act on his part had changed so many lives, had hurt so many people. He shouldn't have begged Beth to run away with him that night. No one in his right mind would have married two sixteen-year-olds, but they were in love. They wanted to raise their baby together.

The accident had ended their dreams, had torn the girl he'd loved away from him forever—and he hadn't been able really to love anyone since.

Until Beau. But hell if he knew how to show him.

Sam had wisely said that actions speak louder than words. He, unfortunately, was failing miserably at both.

Rufus barked at the boy, nipping at his heels, wanting nothing more than to have Beau reach down and ruffle his fur, but the boy ignored him, in much the same way Jack had been with Beau most of the day.

He swung down from his mount, removed the saddle, blanket, and bridle, took hold of the lead rein and matched his steps with Beau's.

"Are you getting tired of being a cowboy?" he asked.

"No."

"Mending fences is a big part of the job."

"You think I can't handle it?"

"I think you can handle anything, if you put your mind to it."

Beau shrugged, refusing to cut Jack any slack. He'd been a pretty poor excuse for a man sixteen years ago, and figured a cold shoulder was a small price to pay.

When the silence didn't end, he asked Beau about school. "How do you like your math and English tutor?"

"She's okay."

"Home school's not quite the same as going

to classes with a bunch of other kids."

"I don't mind." Beau frowned, and angled his head toward Jack. "If I'm still here during the summer, I was thinking it might be fun to have a friend come up and visit."

"I think that could be arranged. What's his name?"

"Sean. We grew up together."

God, he'd missed so much. He didn't even know his son's friends.

Beau shifted the lead rein from one hand to the other, and Jack watched him wince.

"Want me to doctor those hands for you?" he asked.

Beau glanced at Jack, a questioning frown narrowing his eyes. "I thought you wanted Crosby to do it."

"No need to disturb him."

They turned the horses loose in the corral and walked silently toward the house. Rufus, tired of being ignored, had curled up on the back porch, and out of the corner of his eye, Jack caught Beau reaching down to scratch the top of the dog's head with swollen and scraped fingertips.

A smile touched Jack's lips, and something reached inside him and squeezed his heart.

"Get the water good and hot," Jack said, when they entered the kitchen, "and wash up with lots of soap."

While the boy was at the sink, Jack rummaged through the cabinet where they kept bandages and other first-aid supplies, pulled out antiseptic, some of Crosby's special salve, a pair of scissors, cotton balls, and bandages, and set everything on the table.

"Want a Coke?" he asked Beau.

"Could I have a beer?"

"No."

"I figure I did a man's work today."

"You did, but that doesn't have anything to do with beer."

He set a Coke on the table, popped the top, then twisted the cap off his Bud and took a swallow.

Beau pulled a chair out with his boot and sat, then picked up the Coke and took a drink.

Without speaking, Jack lifted the boy's empty hand, inspected the abrasions on his knuckles, the blisters on his palms, and the cuts that seemed to appear in every fold of skin. Then he poured the antiseptic on a cotton ball and went to work.

"I heard you were made captain of the baseball team right before you left home," Jack said, keeping his eyes on the wounds.

"No big deal."

"You told me you'd been kicked out of school."

"Seemed like a good thing to say at the time."

"Why's that?"

"I figured if I was a failure, it would make you feel guilty about never being part of my life."

"I carry around my own guilt," Jack said, glancing at his son. "Your statement didn't add much to it."

Jack put a bandage around Beau's thumb, then took a swallow of his beer. Setting the bottle back on the table, he pushed it toward Beau. "I suppose a swallow or two wouldn't hurt. Just don't go telling Mike. He doesn't approve of cussing, drinking, or smoking. Hell if I know how we ever became friends."

Beau laughed, and God it sounded good.

Beau picked up the beer with the hand Jack had cleaned and bandaged. "Did you ever play baseball?" he asked, holding the bottle to his mouth.

Jack looked up from the palm he held. "We didn't have a baseball team where I went to school."

"Why not?"

"There were only three guys and two girls in the school, and we ranged in age from six to seventeen. Would have made a pretty sorry team."

"Was my mother one of the girls in the school?"

"No."

Beau took another sip of beer and handed it back to Jack. "Where'd you meet her?"

"At a rodeo in Sheridan. I was fifteen and got thrown from a bronc. Broke my shoulder, and her dad—your grandpa—patched me up."

"I don't think my grandfather liked you much."

Jack lifted his eyes from Beau's hands. The boy was staring at him, looking for answers Jack didn't want to give.

He'd stretched the last bandage over Beau's palm. Pushing up from his chair, he grabbed his beer, and went to the window. "You've got schoolwork to do. Might as well get busy."

"You ever going to tell me about you and my mom?"

"Nothing much to tell."

He needed fresh air, needed to get out of the house and away from Beau. He dumped the rest of the beer down the sink and went outside.

The past was crowding in on him, and he didn't like it at all.

Rufus followed him across the yard, his tail wagging, his nose turned up waiting for a friendly pat, a chance to nuzzle. But Jack wasn't in the mood.

"Go on back to the house," he told the dog, and Jack watched Rufus turn around and run. Beau was waiting for him, kneeling just outside the kitchen door, staring at Jack with way too many questions in his eyes.

When he reached the old cottonwood, he stopped, leaned against the tree, and pulled a cigar and lighter from his pocket. He'd quit smoking in front of Beau. He'd given up the quiet of his home, the sheer pleasure of riding out alone whenever he wanted, and his peace of mind. He'd be damned if he'd give up the cigars entirely.

He'd forgotten his coat, and it was getting cold. The wind blew the cigar smoke away before he could enjoy the smell, and it shook the old wooden swing that hung by ancient rope. Seventeen years ago he'd pushed Beth in that swing. He'd had only one good arm at the time, but she was as light as the summer breeze, and he'd pushed and pushed, listening to her laugh as she soared high into the sky.

When she settled down on earth, he'd wrapped his arm around her and kissed her. It was early summer. Wildflowers were blooming, and they'd smelled so damn good mixed with her perfume. They'd found a spot near the stream where the grass was high and the ground was smooth. Man could never have made such a perfect bed.

Beth· was the first girl he'd ever loved—emotionally as well as physically. And Beau was right. Her father had despised him. He was a spoiled, wild kid who got whatever he wanted. And that day, down by the river, he'd wanted Beth.

The sound of a car coming up the road tore his attention from the past, from one of the best days in his life, from the memory of the girl he'd loved.

He pushed away from the tree, shaded his eyes with his hand, and looked off to the west. The rear wheels of a blue Explorer kicked up mud. The unfamiliar vehicle swerved and slid on the slick dirt road, as if someone was in a hurry to get to the ranch.

Jack took a puff on the cigar as he headed down the slope, taking his time getting back to the house. At the pace he was going, he'd get there about the same time as the speeding car.

He pictured Beth at his side, walking hand in hand over the grassy slope. He heard her laughter, realizing that Beau's laugh had sounded just the same. He remembered that day over sixteen years ago when she'd lovingly held a newborn in her arms, then held him out to Jack. He'd been scared to death of that little bundle, but had felt damn proud holding the child he'd helped create. He remembered touching the tiny hand, running the tip of his callused finger over the soft pink palm.

He'd walked around the hospital room, telling his son about the pony he'd get him when he turned two. He'd talked about fishing together, going hunting, and riding the property that would someday be his.

But all his hopes and dreams had been shattered three weeks later—when Beth died, when he'd allowed Beau's grandparents to take him away.

He hadn't seen that little palm grow and mature into the hand he'd doctored this afternoon. He hadn't seen the boy take his first steps, hadn't held him when he fell down and scraped his knees. He'd missed so much—and he had no one to blame but himself.

How could he make Beau believe that even though he hadn't been part of his life, not one day had gone by when he hadn't thought about his son—or loved him?

For a man who'd easily turned a million-dollar ranch into a nearly billion-dollar empire, he'd sure made a mess of his personal life. First Beth. Now Beau. And, of course, there was Sam.

He thought about her smile, her laugh. He

detested Florida, especially the superficially rich trappings of Palm Beach, but he wanted to hop a plane right now and see Sam again.

The timing was all wrong, though. He had to focus on Beau, to build something strong and lasting between them. When that was accomplished, he'd go after the redhead. Maybe she'd know what she wanted by then, maybe she wouldn't push him away.

He stubbed the cigar out in the dirt just before he reached the house. Beau was sitting on the front porch, his boots perched on the railing. Mike was walking out of the barn with two of the hands who lived a few miles up the road, and the screen door slammed as Crosby hobbled out the front door.

"Someone's in a gall-darned hurry."

The Explorer turned off the road, swerved to miss a mudhole, then skidded to a stop right in the middle of the yard.

"Well, I'll be," Crosby muttered. "If it ain't little miss Lauren."

"Who's Lauren?" Beau asked his dad.

"My sister . . . your aunt."

Jack walked toward the car, totally baffled by Lauren's sudden and uncommon visit. He opened the door, and a sobbing Lauren threw her arms around him.

"Oh, Jack," she cried. "I've just had the

worst two days of my entire life, and I never, ever thought I'd get here."

Jack smoothed damp strands of hair from her cheeks and tried to calm her down, but he knew from experience—and from memories of her two divorces—that he was in for several long rounds of tears.

"Did Peter do something to hurt you?" Jack could feel anger seething inside. He'd told Peter he'd break him in half, and he'd meant every word.

Lauren looked stricken when she raised her head and nodded. Her already-red face turned blotchy, and she started to cry even harder.

Sliding a comforting arm around her waist, he led her up the stairs, but she stopped before they reached the threshold. She sniffed back her tears, applied a lacy white handkerchief to her nose, and aimed her eyes at the befuddled kid sitting on the porch.

"Oh, Beau!" She threw her arms around the boy. "I am *so* happy to finally meet you." She pushed him out to arm's length. "You look exactly like your dad when he was sixteen. *Exactly*. It's wonderful to have you here."

Lauren twisted around, smiling as she looked at Jack, at Crosby who was scratching his whiskers, at Mike walking toward the house, his arms laden with three suitcases, probably only a tenth of the gear she'd brought with her.

She kissed Crosby's cheek before he limped into the house shaking his head. When Mike got close, she threw her arms around him and her lips started to tremble. "You don't have to go to Florida," she blubbered. "Peter and I . . . Oh, it's so awful. We're not going to get married."

"Want to talk about it?" Mike asked gently, his ministerial side pushing the ranch-manager part of him clean out of sight.

"There's nothing to talk about. It's over. Finished. Forever."

Mike set the luggage on the porch and slipped an arm around Lauren's shoulders. "Come on inside. We'll have some coffee and try to sort all this out."

Jack gladly let Mike take over. He was a hell of a lot better at solving problems. He had a special calling, something that had completely eluded Jack.

"Does she always cry like that?" Beau asked after Mike and Lauren disappeared inside.

"Only when she gets a divorce or loses another love of her life. Usually about every two or three years."

"That often?"

"Unfortunately."

"Who's Peter?"

"A rattlesnake."

"Are you thinking about murdering him?"

Jack unconsciously hung an arm around his son's shoulder. For a moment he thought about pulling it away, but he left it there instead. Just like hearing Beau's earlier laugh, holding the boy made him feel good.

"What do you think would be just punishment for a man who'd tampered with a woman's affections?"

Beau shrugged. "I don't know. String him up by his balls?"

Jack laughed and, feeling a natural bond with his son, even though they'd always been separated, pulled him closer. "That's exactly what I was thinking."

Beau looked at him and smiled, the first true smile he'd seen on the boy's face. Jack dragged the baseball cap from Beau's head and looked at it. "You know, I've got a Stetson upstairs that I've never gotten around to breakin' in. Think you might like to try it on for size?"

"Yeah." Beau tilted his head, looking at Jack's hand on his shoulder, then turned back, a grin on his face. "Maybe I could wear it to church on Sunday. There's this girl. Tynna. Prettiest thing I've ever laid eyes on."

Jack's throat tightened. His son had gone from newborn to girl-crazy in the blink of an eye. He'd missed so much, so damn much.

Those sixteen years were lost to him—but the future was still ahead, and it was starting to look a hell of a lot brighter.

Two hours later Jack still had no idea what had happened between Lauren and Peter. "Everything was fine at dinner the other night." She sniffed, and looked up at Jack through tear-dampened lashes.

Jack sat on the coffee table facing her, his elbows planted on widespread knees. Mike sat beside her, fingering the cross hanging around his neck. He'd been silent for a long time, but that was okay. Lauren was spilling her guts about everything and nothing. She needed to talk. Didn't matter to Jack if she said anything constructive. All he wanted was for her to get stuff off her chest. He wanted, *needed* for her to be happy again.

"Did I tell you that Arabella helped me celebrate my birthday? We had such a wonderful time, before . . . before . . ." Another tear slid down her face.

Jack pulled a clean red-plaid handkerchief from his pocket and held it out to her, wishing she hadn't brought up the subject of Arabella. He should have told her the truth long before. Telling her now would be a disaster.

"Did she tell you we went shopping together?" Lauren asked, taking the handkerchief from his fingers and daintily touching the skin beneath her eyes.

"She told me."

"She's got terrible taste in clothes, Jack. Oh, my gosh, you should have seen the outfit she wanted to buy for the country club. It was so totally wrong, but, you know what?"

"What?"

"You couldn't have fallen in love with anyone more perfect."

"Who's Arabella?" Beau asked, grabbing one of Crosby's half-charred oatmeal cookies.

"Your father's fiancée." Lauren looked from Beau to Jack, her brow wrinkling into a frown. "Don't tell me you haven't told Beau about your fiancée."

"He ain't told me, neither," Crosby stated. "When did you get yourself a fiancée?"

Mike leaned back on the couch. He crossed one boot over his knee and grinned at Jack. He was the only one who knew the truth, and now he was going to enjoy watching Jack sweat.

"You know I don't talk much about my personal life."

"You ain't never had a personal life, but I sure as hell figured you'd tell me if you got one," Crosby muttered.

"Oh, Jack, I can't believe you haven't wanted to tell the world." Lauren looked at the four men surrounding her. "Arabella's wonderful." She aimed her eyes at Beau. "She's not all that much older than you, but you're going to love having her as a mother."

Jack stared down at the floor. If he looked up, he knew he'd be forced to face eight glaring eyes.

"You aren't getting married soon, are you?" Beau asked, and Jack could hear a hint of anger in his voice.

Jack tilted his head and looked at the boy. "Haven't made any plans yet."

"That's exactly what Arabella told me," Lauren stated. "You know me, I don't believe in long engagements, and I told her so. Spring weddings are always the nicest." She took a sip of the coffee Crosby had made. "I love planning weddings, Jack. I hope you and Arabella will let me help."

Hell! He'd sure gotten himself into a mess this time.

"When the time comes, I'm sure she'd like your help. But that could be years from now. We're not in any hurry."

"That's nonsense, Jack. You need to be together. Just like . . . Just like . . ." She started to cry again, and Jack lifted her hands into his. He hated to see her cry, but at least with her thinking about Peter, she wasn't focusing on the dangerous topic of Arabella.

"Do you feel like talking about what happened in London?" he asked. "Maybe you'd feel better if you got it all out in the open."

"I can't talk to you. *Any* of you." She drew in a shaky breath. "It's one of those woman things that you couldn't possibly understand. Oh, I wish Arabella was here."

Lauren blew her nose on Jack's handkerchief, then looked at him with tear-filled blue eyes. "Would you call her, Jack?"

"Why?"

"I need her. She'll understand what I'm going through."

Hell! "She's busy, Lauren. I can't ask her to drop what she's doing and come up here."

"Please."

Tell her the truth, he told himself. *Tell her now and get it over.*

"There's something I need to tell you."

She sniffed and attempted to dry her eyes. "Please don't tell me something I don't want to hear. I just don't think I could take it right now."

Jack smiled, and wiped a tear from her cheek. "All I wanted to say is—" Ah, hell! "It might take me a while to get in touch with her, but I'm sure she'll come."

He hoped.

ten

Sam sat in the VW and watched the blur of traffic flying by in front of Denny's. It was two in the morning, and she was taking a ten-minute break. She'd dealt with one too many frustrated diners tonight, Tyrone had had a fight with his lady before coming in to work and snapped at every special request or substitution, and she was so darn tired she could easily grab her pillow, put her head down, and go to sleep.

Instead she thought about Jack, the same thing she'd done ever since he'd sent the gift. She'd FedEx'd the thousand dollars off to Johnnie, the whiskey she'd wrapped in a few brown paper bags and tucked away in her trunk for a special occasion, and the flowers she'd carried with her from her car, to the KOA bathrooms, to the Espresso Nook, and to the salad station at Denny's.

The roses had opened fully, and every chance she got she inhaled their fragrance, remembering the scents of the many bouquets in Jack's suite. She held the vase in front of her now, closed her eyes, and wished for Jack to appear.

Like a child, she cracked open one eyelid and peeked to see' if he might have miraculously shown up. He hadn't, but that didn't keep her from hoping. She'd blown it the other night when she'd pushed him away, and wanted nothing more than another chance—and time together—to see if anything could develop between them.

Mama would have told her she was silly to have such a far-fetched dream, would have reminded her that men—especially rich ones—had a bad habit of hurting women.

"Sorry, Mama," she whispered. "I'd have to ignore you if you said those things. Jack might hurt me, but that's a risk I have to take."

There was something special about Jack Remington. More than anyone in her entire life, he made her feel good inside. It had nothing to do with words *or* actions, because all he had to do was appear, and she felt a strange, uncontrollable tug on her heart.

Even now, just thinking about him, she felt the powerful pull deep inside her. She laughed, feeling so darn wonderful even as her break time came to an end.

When she returned to the restaurant, she scooped up a tip from one of her tables, stopped and asked two diners how they were doing, then went behind the counter and started to make a double chocolate malt for Tyrone, hoping it would put him in a better frame of mind.

She heard the phone in the kitchen ring but ignored it. She'd only gotten one call since she'd started working at Denny's, and that was from Johnnie Russo. She remembered Jack Remington telling her their first night together that phone calls had a nasty habit of bringing bad news. Well, she'd had enough bad news in her lifetime—and she didn't want anything spoiling the wonderful mood she was in right now.

"Hey, Sam. It's for you," Tyrone yelled over the pickup counter.

She looked up from the tub of vanilla ice cream. "Me?"

"You know anyone else named Sam?"

"Not around here." She wiped her hands on a towel and went into the kitchen.

"You're getting to be awfully popular around here," Tyrone barked, flipping two hamburger patties on the grill while holding the dingy white phone out to her.

Her eyes trailed from Tyrone's disgruntled
face, to the receiver, then back to Tyrone. "It
isn't a man, is it?" she whispered.

Tyrone nodded.

"Does it sound like the same guy who called
a few days ago?"

Tyrone shoved the mouthpiece against his
hard, rotund stomach and glared at her like
she'd gone mad. "I ain't no secretary. You
want to know who it is, you ask."

"Thanks loads!"

She grabbed the phone from his meaty fist.
The last person she wanted to talk with was
Johnnie Russo. She'd called him yesterday,
right after she'd shipped off a thousand-dollar
cashier's check. Again she'd asked him for an
extension, and again he'd given her a flat-out
no. Now she had the feeling he was calling to
tell her that he'd refigured her balance, and
found out that she owed him more than
twenty-seven hundred dollars.

That thought wasn't too pleasing. Maybe
she should attempt to be courteous. Friendly
even. "Hello."

"Evenin', Whiskey."

The deep, familiar voice vibrated her insides. A smile touched her lips, and the giddy
feeling slid all the way down to her toes.
"Hello, Jack."

"Surprised to hear from me?"

"I'm *thrilled* to hear from you." She inhaled deeply, hoping she might be able to pick up the scent of his cigars and cologne and picture him standing in front of her. Just like in the car, he didn't appear, but she could see him plain as day. A lock of light brown hair hung over his brow. He had a hand tucked into his trouser pocket, and the tie to his tuxedo was loose about his neck. He had a slightly off-kilter grin on his face, and lips that looked in desperate need of a kiss.

Too bad he was so far away.

"Thank you for the gifts . . . and the tip."

She could hear his laugh, and it sounded better than a theater full of applause. She was feeling kind of dreamy, kind of warm and tingly inside, waiting for Jack to speak again. Until a moment ago, she hadn't realized how much she liked the deep, resonating tone of his voice, sort of like Harrison Ford at his sexiest.

"How are you doing?" he asked, his question sounding strained, as if he'd been searching for something to say.

"Fine. How about you?"

"Good." She heard his long, drawn-out sigh. "Sam?" It seemed forever before he continued. "There's something I need to ask you."

"Okay."

He hesitated, just as he had their first night

together, right before he'd asked her to play his fiancée.

"Is something wrong, Jack?"

"No."

"Then what do you want to ask me?"

"Have you tried the whiskey I sent?"

She laughed, winding her finger around the cord, wishing it was Jack's hair, that he was close, that she could see what emotions were crossing his face, because she couldn't tell over the phone what was causing him so much uneasiness. "I'm saving the whiskey, Jack. I'd rather share it with someone—like you."

"Then come to Wyoming."

She straightened, trying to regain her senses, then walked away from the wall to a place where she could have an ounce of privacy, stretching the spiraling cord as far as it could go. "Would you repeat what you just said?"

"Come to Wyoming."

This was better than anything she'd hoped for, but all she could think to say was, "Why?"

"Lauren's here. She's broken up with Peter and . . . and I need you to be Arabella again."

Of all the . . . Sam walked across the room and without another word, slammed the phone on its hook.

He was supposed to tell Lauren the truth. He was supposed to have feelings for *her*, the *real* her, not some fake fiancée. He was supposed to have given her all those gifts without wanting anything in return.

And now this.

The phone rang again. Once. Twice.

On the third ring she shot an annoyed glance at Tyrone. "Would you get that?"

"No way. It's bound to be the guy you just hung up on, and I don't want to be the one who gets yelled at."

"What if it isn't him? What if it's the guy who wants money from me?"

"Just answer the damn thing!" Tyrone bellowed.

Sam jerked the phone off the wall, and took a deep breath. "Hello," she said sweetly.

"Sam? Is everything okay?"

"Is that you, Jack? You sound so far away."

"I *am* far away. What the hell's going on?"

"Nothing. We have a bad connection, and I couldn't hear you."

"Then answer me. Will you come to Wyoming? Lauren's been crying all evening and none of us can make her stop."

Jack didn't want her for himself. He only needed her help—for his sister. If he'd given her any other reason, she would have given him a flat-out no. But he'd asked for Lauren's sake, and Sam liked her too much to turn him down

"How soon do you want me to come?"

"Your flight's at eight in the morning. Be there no later than seven and pick up the ticket at United."

"You already bought the ticket?"

"I consider myself a good judge of character. I knew you'd come—for Lauren."

That hurt. She would have gone for him, too.

Definitely for him.

But now? She was so mad she could . . .

Jack might think he was a good judge of character, but his opinion of her was going to go downhill any moment now.

"Jack?" she said, in her most syrupy voice.

"What?"

"I'll need two thousand seven hundred dollars."

"You *what*?"

"Don't yell. If you want me to be Arabella again, you'll have to pay me."

"Where's the thousand I gave you two days ago?"

"That was a tip. That was free and clear with no strings attached—and I spent it."

"What did you do? Buy more bras?"

That did it!

"Yeah. But don't count on ever seeing any of them."

She could hear half a growl, half a sigh. "I suppose you need clothes, too?"

"Well, the way I hear it, sundresses and bikinis just won't cut it in Wyoming this time of year."

"You know what, Whiskey?"

"What?"

"You're going to be the death of me. Either that, or you're going to lead me straight to bankruptcy court."

"You could always tell Lauren the truth."

"I thought about that."

"So why didn't you?"

There was a long moment of silence, and then an even longer, agonized sigh. "Because for some damn reason I wanted to see you again, but hell if I can remember why."

eleven

The plane rattled around like a pocketful of marbles, and Sam knew for certain it planned to fall from the sky. She clenched the armrests, feeling rather foolish as she watched the other passengers casually reading newspapers and magazines or poring over documents they'd taken out of their briefcases.

Tyrone had told her that flying was a piece of cake. Tyrone, of course, was full of it. As far as she was concerned, plane travel was for people with a death wish. She preferred living, and once she landed in Sheridan she had every intention of staying firmly on the ground—for the rest of her life.

Leaning her head against the seat back, she willed herself to relax, but all she could think of was the jerking motion of the plane as the unexpected storm tossed it around.

And then there was the storm going on inside her.

How could she possibly fool Jack's son and his friends? How much longer could she fool Lauren? This wasn't just a one-night masquerade, this could stretch out for days.

But the real problem had nothing to do with whether she could pull the wool over their eyes, it had to do with the fact that she didn't want to deceive anyone. She wanted them to know the truth.

She wanted a real relationship with Jack, but he wanted something different. He wanted an actress; he wanted someone to make his sister happy. She imagined he'd sent her the whiskey, the flowers, and the big tip to appease her, just in case he needed her services again. Last night, he'd probably thrown in that line about wanting to see her again to take the sting off his invitation. Well, that hadn't worked. He'd hurt her.

She was an employee to him, an accomplice in his charade, nothing more.

But she was tired of acting, tired of pretending that life was perfect, tired of reaching out for something good and having it disappear when her fingers had merely touched the surface.

What was it her mama used to say? *"Be con-*

*tent with touching the clouds, honey. The stars are
too far beyond our reach."*

I want the stars this time, Mama, she thought.
The clouds just aren't good enough.

The plane hit another bump, and this time
even Sam's fellow passengers gripped the
arms of their seats. She stared out the window,
but there was nothing to see. They were flying
through a heavy blanket of ever-darkening
clouds that looked ominous and frightening,
kind of like the adventure ahead of her.

She pressed her forehead to the cool glass.
With all her heart, she wished she could blow
a hole through the clouds and at least catch
sight of the stars.

Jack could see the wind. It picked up the
powdery snow from the ground and blew it
across the runway. Anyone in his right mind
would hide at home on a day like this. But
Jack couldn't hide. He was waiting for a plane,
and the one coming in was doing a hell of a
lot of wobbling as it headed for earth.

Even from the terminal, Jack could hear the
tires screech as they bounced off the concrete,
then hit again. The muscles in his shoulders
and neck tensed as he watched the wing lights
dip toward the earth. The turboprop veered to
the right, then straightened, and finally slowed
as it headed for the tarmac.

"Thank God," he whispered.

He'd flown hundreds of times, sitting back and relaxing while the pilots did their job. He figured if the plane went down he'd die, and there wasn't too much he could do about it. That brand of worrying wasn't his style.

But this was different. Sam was on that plane, and the thought of never seeing her again ate at his insides. Somehow she'd wiggled her way into his thoughts and dreams. In a moment or two he'd see her again. It had been just a few days since he'd left her at Denny's, and it had been over two weeks since he'd kissed her good-bye. It seemed an eternity, yet he could still feel her softness, could taste her lips, could hear her voice.

In a few minutes she'd be real again, no longer just a memory.

For once he was glad Lauren was troubled, glad that she'd been crying and knew what— *who*—she needed to make her happy. Hell, he needed Sam, too.

The drifting snow piled up on the wings and against the wheels of the plane the moment it stopped. Jack tilted his hat low over his eyes and tucked his chin into the collar of his coat as he stepped out of the terminal and watched a string of warmly dressed passengers filing off the plane. They gripped coats and briefcases as the wind and snow tried to knock them from the steps, but within moments the last commuter rushed past him into the heated building. The only people left on the tarmac, even on the steps of the plane, were the maintenance and baggage crews.

Sam hadn't come. The knowledge hit him with the same force as the hoof of a crazed bronc. He shook his head, trying to deflect the image creeping into his mind of Sam Jones cashing in the tickets and taking off for parts unknown. He didn't give a damn about the money, but he did give a damn about the fact that he'd trusted her to be on that plane.

He should have called the airline to make sure she'd gotten on in West Palm Beach. Better yet, he should have hired a car to pick her up at Denny's and an escort to deliver her safely to the plane. Hell, he should have gone to Florida and escorted her himself.

He was just about to turn away when he caught a glimpse of a beautiful woman peering through a window. Finally, he smiled. He should have trusted her. In the future he'd know better.

Long red hair slapped against Sam's cheeks as she peeked around the doorway, and a hesitant foot, clad in a knee-high, black-leather boot with confoundedly high stiletto heels, moved to the top step. Jack laughed at the sight of her. She'd come to Wyoming dressed in nothing more than a tight black skirt that barely covered her thighs and a jacket that wouldn't protect her from a sea breeze let alone a prairie blizzard.

Damn fool woman. She was going to freeze her butt off, but hell if she wouldn't look good doing it!

Shoving through the gate, he raced toward the plane. Sam's eyes were wide with something that resembled fear, and her body shivered when she met him at the bottom of the stairs. "I don't like flying," she shouted at him over the sound of airplane engines and wind. "When it's time to go home, you'll have to drive me there."

He laughed, tore off his coat, and wrapped it around her. "One of these days I'll teach you how to ride a bull. You won't mind flying after that."

He drew her close as he led her across the asphalt and into the warmth of the terminal, far away from the doors that opened and closed letting in blasts of icy air. He stood back and looked at her. He'd thought she was gorgeous the night of Lauren's party, but now, with her cheeks reddened from the cold and her nose and hair sprinkled with snowflakes, she looked sweet and young and . . . Hell!

"Come here!" He wrapped one arm around her and pulled her hard against his chest, took off his Stetson, and held it behind her back. "I just remembered why I wanted to see you."

"Mind telling me?"

"Thought I might show you instead."

He kissed her, soft at first. Tentative. He felt her hands pushing against his chest, an ounce of protest before her lips parted and her fingers slid over his shoulders and wove together behind his neck.

She was perfect. From her curly hair to the tips of her toes. From her wild spirit and boldness to the beguiling innocence that often wrapped around her.

He watched her eyelids flutter, felt her lashes brush lightly over the bridge of his nose, and tasted the saltiness of peanuts on her tongue. He could have kissed her for hours, but she drew back.

With their lips touching just an infinitesimal amount, her eyes opened and she whispered. "Lauren isn't here by any chance, is she?"

"No. Why?"

"I just wanted to know if that was a pretend-you're-my-fiancée kiss, or an I'm-glad-to-see-you kiss."

"Guess I didn't get the point across."

He pulled her tight. He couldn't feel her body through the thickness of his coat, but he could easily remember gentle curves and lush breasts, and a fleeting image of her standing naked in his arms rushed through him as he captured her mouth.

She wasn't warm any longer. She was hot, and he was starting to burn. Her fingers slipped through his hair, cupping the base of his neck and holding him close. Her tongue slid over the back of his teeth, across the roof of his mouth. It danced with his, a sultry, exotic, body-rubbing dance that made him think he was in the tropics instead of standing just a few feet away from a blizzard.

He felt a slap on his shoulder, and all thoughts of a steamy island and Sam in a skimpy bikini came to a skidding halt.

"Afternoon, Jack."

The voice was far too familiar. He turned slowly. "Afternoon, John." He drew in a breath, trying to bring some semblance of reality into his mind. "Good to see you."

The man who owned the spread that butted up to Jack's on the west had a grin on his aging, ruddy-colored face. "I have the distinct feeling I've interrupted something."

Sam tried to move away, but Jack ran his hand beneath the coat she was wearing and wrapped it around her waist. He dragged her close to his side. "John Atkinson, this is my fiancée, Arabella Fleming."

A frown swept across Sam's face the moment he uttered Arabella's name, then disappeared into a smile as John stuck out a large, work-hardened hand and swallowed her slender one in its grasp. "Nice to meet you."

"You too," Sam said.

"You here to pick someone up?" Jack asked.

"Yeah. Fay's been in Southern California baby-sitting grandkids for a week. She's gonna be surprised to hear you're gettin' married. That's the kind of information she usually brings home from the beauty shop, but she never mentioned a word."

Hell! Jack hadn't thought about the gossip mill, and with Fay coming home, word about him getting married would be spread around Sheridan in less than twenty-four hours.

"We haven't been engaged all that long," Jack announced. "In fact, this is the first time Arabella's been to the ranch."

"You didn't pick the best time to visit our fair state," John told Sam. "Summer's the best; of course, that only lasts a month."

Sam slipped her arm around Jack's waist and looked into his eyes with so much love he felt like nominating her for an Oscar. "Jack can keep me warm the other eleven months."

"I imagine he can. I sure as hell miss Fay when she's gone. She's been warming me up for forty-two years. I hope the two of you have that many good years together."

"That's our plan," Sam quipped.

Plan? Hell! The only plan Jack had was to get Sam out of the airport before they ran into anyone else from town.

He stuck out his hand and shook John's once more. "We've got to get Arabella's luggage and head for home. Looks like a bad Norther blowing in."

"Fay and I are spending the night at the Holiday Inn. Why don't you and Arabella do the same. We could have dinner tonight."

"Wish we could, but I've got work to get back to."

"Well," John said, slapping Jack on the back again, "be careful on the road."

"Will do."

"Nice meetin' you," John said, smiling at Sam. "Don't forget to invite Fay and me to the wedding."

"You'll be right on top the list," Sam tossed back.

The moment John walked away, Jack dragged Sam in the opposite direction. He stopped behind a group of passengers waiting to claim their luggage. "What do you mean you'll invite him to the wedding?"

"What did you expect me to say? That we don't want him and his wife there."

"I didn't expect you to say anything. We're not getting married, and even if we were, it wouldn't be some big event where half the town comes."

"This is your little charade, Jack. I'm just trying to make it work."

She pulled out of his grasp. "That's my bag," she said, pointing to an old brown suitcase held together with duct tape. "I had to borrow it from a friend. Better not let anyone see it, or they're going to wonder why your rich and uppity fiancée doesn't travel in a little better style."

"To hell with the suitcase."

She folded her arms across her chest. "If something's bothering you, Jack, couldn't you just spit it out? This crazy mix of hostility and lust you're displaying is wearing me out."

He speared his fingers through his hair and shoved his Stetson back on his head. "I don't like being caught off guard. I don't like the thought of John knowing I'm engaged."

"You're not engaged."

"But he thinks I am, and pretty soon everyone else in this town's going to think so, too."

"Seems to me you've gotten yourself into a pretty big mess. Of course, none of this would have happened if you'd told Lauren the truth."

"Yeah, well, you wouldn't be here now if I *had* told her the truth."

Jack's reminder hit her like a bucket of ice

water. She'd made a huge mistake falling into his arms when she'd gotten off the plane. She'd been foolish to think there was something more than lust behind that kiss, especially when he'd easily pulled away from her lips and introduced her as Arabella.

Arabella. Imagine him calling her by some other name but her own. After that kiss!

She straightened her shoulders, and stared him right in the eyes. "You know, Jack, I could always turn around and go back home."

"You could, but you won't."

"Do you really believe that?"

"You want your money, don't you?"

His words hurt worse than a slap across the face, worse than calling her Arabella, but she deserved them. He hadn't offered her money to come to Wyoming. She'd *asked* for it, not just last night, but several times before. This was the final time, though. This last chunk of money would pay off Johnnie, and never again would she have to look like a moneygrubber in Jack's eyes.

"I *do* want the money," she told him, staring at his chin instead of his eyes because she didn't want to see the disgust. "Could I have it now?"

"Do you plan on telling me what you need it for?" He quickly looked her up and down, slowly checking out every inch of her How

Tacky boots. "You're obviously not spending it on yourself."

"Does it matter?"

"I'm persistent, Sam. I'm going to keep asking until you tell me."

"All right, I'll tell you. I'm paying off a debt," she told him, hoping that brief bit of an answer would suffice.

"What did you do?" He laughed sarcastically. "Borrow from a loan shark?"

"Of course not." She stared down at the floor, astonished that he unwittingly knew the truth. "I wouldn't do anything that crazy."

Jack gripped her arms, frowning as he studied her betraying eyes. "You did. Didn't you?"

"It's none of your business."

"I'm making it my business since you've obviously been using me and *my* money to pay him off."

"I haven't been using you. In fact, it's the other way around. You've been using me. And it's *my* money, Jack. I earned it—every single penny."

"Okay, then, how much more do you need to earn?"

She jerked away. How could she have made such a big mistake telling him about the debt? She should have known he'd put two and two together. Now he knew how foolish she'd been.

"Look at me, Sam."

Slowly, she tilted her head toward him. His smile was warm, concerned, and that look took her by surprise. Where she came from, no one looked at you that way. "How much more do you owe?"

"The exact amount I asked you for. Twenty-seven hundred."

"I should have known." He reached into his pocket, and handed her a check. "I could make this out for more, if you need it?"

"I don't want more, Jack. I feel bad enough taking this."

"Don't. You need money, I need to make my sister happy. Consider that check part of a business transaction—nothing more."

"Silly me." She kept her hurt and tears hidden behind her smile. "I'd almost forgotten."

He laughed again, as if all of this was a game to him. "Come on. Let's go home before the storm gets any worse."

He held Tyrone's duct-taped suitcase in one hand and her arm in the other, and led her outside into the cold.

I should have listened to you, Mama, she thought. *Men, especially rich ones, are all alike.*

twelve

Jack opened the driver's side door, and Sam slid across the seat of the old and battered truck, shivering when her nylon-clad legs touched the frigid Naugahyde. She'd expected him to drive a Mercedes or Cadillac or, at the very least, a brand new truck with rich leather upholstery. The old truck was about the same vintage as her bug, and the fact that he drove something that didn't jump out and say "I'm rich" made her like him even more.

Too bad he considered her just part of a business transaction.

After tossing her suitcase into the back, Jack climbed into the cab behind her, slammed the door, and shoved the keys in the ignition. "I'll have it warmed up in here in a minute." The engine roared to a start, and after revving the motor a time or two, he turned on the heat.

His chambray shirtsleeves and faded blue

jeans were dusted with snow and as the warm air trickled out of the dashboard it turned the flakes of white into damp spots all over his clothes. He rubbed his hands in front of the vents, and when the redness disappeared, he took hold of Sam's and massaged them between his palms.

Jack Remington might be her employer, he might be paying her to do something that wasn't on the up-and-up, but she had to admit he was the most considerate—not to mention the sexiest—boss she'd ever had.

That made it awfully hard to fight her attraction to him. But fight she would.

She worked her hands free of his grasp. "Thanks for lending me your coat."

"Any man would have done the same."

"I don't think so."

He turned toward her, the vinyl seat creaking beneath his bigger-than-life frame, and smoothed a strand of damp hair from her cheek. His eyes were hot, radiantly blue, and were doing a better job heating her up than the warming gust of air coming from the dash. "I think you've known the wrong men in your life."

She couldn't argue. She hadn't dated much, but the men she had gone out with were definitely all wrong. They didn't open car doors.

They certainly didn't offer a lady their coat to keep her from getting cold.

Then, again, they didn't ask her to play tricks on their family members, either.

Jack reached over the back of the seat, his arm brushing against her shoulder. There was nothing intentionally erotic about it, but the simple touch sent a tingle through her insides. She didn't want those feelings to hit her, but she didn't know how to combat something so powerful, something that came of its own accord.

"I got you a welcome-to-Wyoming present," he said, pulling a pale gold brushed leather coat with the same soft lambswool lining as his over the seat. "Thought you might need this."

She touched the leather as if it was priceless. Running her fingers over the off-white stitching, she forced back the tears that threatened. Gifts had been few and far between in her life. A Barbie doll from the Salvation Army. A pink feather boa from Syd. Kisses, hugs, and words of wisdom from her mama. She'd treasured every present, no matter how small.

The coat overwhelmed her.

Jack smiled when she looked up at him. "It's beautiful. Thank you."

"You're welcome." He nodded over the seat. "There's more in the back."

Sam twisted around. Beneath the tattered bag belonging to Tyrone, sat a pile of forest green-and-burgundy paisley suitcases.

"Those aren't for me, are they?"

"I figured you might be traveling a little lighter than the real Arabella, so I bought a few pieces of luggage and filled them with things you might need."

"I know I asked you for clothes, but you didn't have to buy so much. A sweater and a pair of jeans would have been enough."

His brow rose. "That might be enough for you, but not for Arabella."

"As far as I can tell, no one knows much about Arabella. Couldn't I just be me, dress like me, talk like me, and only be *called* Arabella?"

"You could, but I'd prefer that you start acting like money's no object. Lauren's already getting nosy about our relationship."

"Why?"

"She couldn't understand why you felt so damn uncomfortable spending my money."

"It's *your* money, Jack. Not mine."

"Then *pretend* it's your money."

"I *did* pretend, remember? And you got mad when I spent it."

"It wasn't the money that made me mad, and you know it," he snapped. "I fully expect the woman I marry to spend my money."

"Well, you're not marrying me, so don't feel obligated to give me another thing."

"Fine. I won't."

The sudden tap on the driver's window brought silence to the inside of the cab.

"Hey, Jack." John Atkinson and the woman standing beside him peered into the truck. "Are you having car troubles?"

"Ah, hell!" Jack sighed in frustration, then rolled the window down a mere three or four inches. "The truck's fine, John. We're just waiting for it to warm up."

"That's good," John stated. "Want to reconsider joining Fay and me at the Holiday Inn?"

"Not tonight."

A moment later, Fay's eyes came into view. "Hi, Jack." Her gaze trailed to Sam's face. "You must be Arabella."

Sam nodded. "It's nice to meet you, Fay. Did you have a nice trip to California?"

"Wonderful. I could show you pictures of my grandchildren if you'd join us for dinner."

"Can't," Jack barked. "We've gotta get home before the storm really kicks up. Seems to me the two of you should get in out of the weather."

"S'pose we should," John said, looking disappointed that his offer had been turned down.

Jack shoved the truck into drive and popped

the emergency brake. "Thanks again for the invitation. We'll take you up on it some other time."

"That would be lovely," Fay said, and turned her smile from Jack to Sam. "Make sure Jack drives carefully. I'd hate to see him getting into another accident."

"That's enough," John said, his hand clamping down on Fay's shoulder, pulling her back. "We'll see you around."

Anger radiated from Jack's eyes when he pulled on his seat belt, stepped on the gas, and headed away from the small airport. "You still want to go to the bank?" he asked gruffly.

"Yes, please," she answered. On the walk from the terminal to the truck, she'd asked Jack if he could take her to the bank and then to FedEx. The sooner she could get a final cashier's check and send it off to Johnnie, the better she'd feel.

Of course, she might be getting Johnnie off her back, but now she had Jack to contend with, and their heated words before John and Fay interrupted made her uneasy. "Could we call a truce, Jack?"

He looked at her out of the corner of his eye, then turned his gaze back to the road. "I didn't know we were at war."

Glossing over the problems between them wasn't a good idea. She wanted to clear the air, right here and now. Wanted him to know where she stood. "I'm not comfortable with this charade. I haven't been from the very beginning."

"I know."

"I've felt guilty taking every dollar you've given me—except the tips."

A grin tilted his lips, but he didn't comment.

"This is the last time I'm going to come to your rescue, Jack. I'll do my best to help Lauren get through this crisis with Peter, but I can stay only a few days, and then I have to get back to work. You've got to figure out how to tell her the truth because the next time she wants me, I'm not going to be around."

She could sense his anger in the way his jaw tightened, the way his eyes narrowed. Let him be mad. She wasn't about to let him go on thinking that she'd be available at his beck and call—not for his sister, not for anything.

The studded tires grabbed on to the icy roadway as they left town and headed for the ranch. Sam sat on the farside of the truck, her fingers gripping the edge of the seat, just as she'd done from the airport to the bank to FedEx. Jack sat behind the wheel, staring at the road, concentrating far too much on the words she'd uttered earlier.

She'd be leaving soon. He'd hated to hear

her say it, but he'd known from the very beginning that that was where all of this would end up. The whiskey and flowers hadn't meant all that much to her. As for the clothes and luggage, hell, she'd been more offended by his purchases than pleased.

Why he'd ever thought there could be something between them was anybody's guess.

From the corner of his eye he saw the flash of a pronghorn dashing across the highway. He touched the brakes lightly, and the truck swerved, then straightened. Sam's knuckles had turned white as her grip tightened; her shoulders were stiff, her eyes wide.

"Don't worry," he told her. "I've driven this road in worse weather."

"The weather gets worse than this?" she asked incredulously.

"This is mild."

She sighed, staring out the window at nothing more than snow. "Maybe we should pull off the road and wait till the weather's better."

"That could be an hour from now, or a week. It's better if we keep on driving."

"Was the weather like this when you had the accident Fay mentioned?"

"Same time of year, but the morning was beautiful. Not a cloud in the sky."

Everyone in town knew about the accident.

He should have known Sam would want to know more.

"Were you hurt?"

"A few scrapes and bruises. Nothing more."

She looked relieved. "No one else was hurt, I hope."

"My girlfriend," he told her, every single word hurting him inside. "She died because I couldn't get her out of the car before it . . . before it blew up."

Sam's eyes were red when he looked at her. "I'm sorry."

"It was a long time ago. I don't talk about it."

He stared at the road again. The only person he'd ever talked with about Beth's death was Mike—and that had been sixteen years ago. He'd never talked to his father, to Lauren, or Arabella. He didn't think he could ever tell Beau.

Yet he'd easily told Sam, a woman who planned to be out of his life in a few days, which made no sense to him at all.

From the farside of the truck, Sam watched the play of emotions on Jack's face. Anguish, guilt, heartache. His jaw tensed. His Adam's apple rose and fell as he swallowed his grief, and all she could do was sit there and watch, and wish she could take away his pain.

It seemed as if he stared at the road forever,

but finally he tilted his head and looked at her fingers wrapped around the edge of the seat. "We've got a good two hours before we reach the ranch. Do you plan on holding on tight all the way?"

"I did it for nearly six hours on two different planes. I'm getting kind of used to it."

"I don't get into wrecks every day, Sam. I don't plan on getting into one today."

"I'm not worried."

He raised his brow. "You might be a good actress, Sam. But I know real fright when I see it."

"Okay, so I'm a little nervous. I'm not used to all this snow."

"Don't worry. I won't let you get hurt."

With that said, he concentrated on the road again, but his words reverberated through her mind. *I won't let you get hurt.*

Unfortunately, he'd already hurt her last night, when he'd asked her to continue the charade.

She stared at the falling snow, mesmerized by the never-ending flakes crashing into the windshield and the steady swish of the windshield wipers.

Fifteen minutes must have gone by before she broke the silence. "Fay seems nice."

"Yeah."

"Do you see her and John very much?"

"Occasionally."

"Have you known them long?"

"Yes."

"Are you going to talk in one-word sentences all the way to the ranch?"

Sam could see a smile just barely form on his lips. "Maybe."

She turned in the seat, preferring the view of his handsome, slightly rugged profile to the hypnotizing snow. "Is Fay the local gossip?"

"One of them. She runs a beauty shop in town. Don't know why, since John makes more than enough to support them."

"Do you think a woman's place is in the home?"

He looked at her out of the corner of his eye. His smile turned to a grin. "I kind of like the idea of a husband and wife working side by side, together, to build a dream. The first Remingtons in Wyoming did it when they homesteaded here. So did every generation after that—until my mom and dad."

He was talking, finally. She could listen all day to the deep timbre of his voice, filled with affection when he spoke about his home. "Why did things change with your parents?"

"They had different dreams. She liked the glamour of Palm Beach, he liked women—too many of them—and they could each have whatever they wanted because there was a plentiful supply of Remington money."

"What about you? Are you like your folks, or your ancestors?"

"There were a few years when I wasn't content with life on the ranch. I went away to college, learned I had a knack for making money, and spent some time building a business that even today keeps on growing. One day I woke up and decided I wasn't happy, and realized I could work just as easily from my home in Wyoming as I could in an office in Manhattan. Lauren thinks I'm out of my mind living out here. She says I should at least buy a place in Palm Beach for the winter. But I've got my own dream."

"What is it?"

"Taking care of the ranch and my family. Being happy with my lot in life. Simple things like that."

He glanced toward her. "What about you, Sam? What's your dream?"

"It's pretty simple, too. I just want to figure out where I belong."

Jack spent the next hour navigating mainly by watching the plow markers along the right side of the road, and just when he thought he should follow Sam's suggestion of pulling over and waiting out the storm, the sun slipped through a hole in the clouds and shone down on the snow.

Although the prairie was blanketed in white, tomorrow brown grass and dirt would probably peek through the snow, and in a month or two the land would be green again. There'd be wildflowers and blue skies overhead. He looked at the wide-eyed awe on Sam's face, and wondered if she'd like seeing the changes from day to day, from season to season.

A hawk soared through the sky, landing atop a wooden post. Jack rarely took nature for granted, but Sam's delight gave him a newfound appreciation for the country.

"Is that a bald eagle?" she asked.

"A red-tailed hawk. Watching for a meal, I imagine."

She leaned forward, folding her arms on top the dash as she watched the scenery passing by. She had an endless number of questions about the sprinkler irrigation wheels stretching out across endless fields, a broken-down wagon and a leaning one-room cabin that had been abandoned sixty or seventy years ago. She asked about crops, and feed for the cows, and how deep the snow got in the middle of winter.

"Is that an Appaloosa?" she asked, her gaze aimed at a leopard-spotted mare.

He nodded, and pointed out another standing on a distant rise. "The brown one over there with spots only on its rump is an Appaloosa, too."

"They're wonderful." She leaned back in the seat and smiled. "I can see why you love it here, Jack."

"Can you?"

"Of course. It's beautiful."

"An awful lot of people come to Wyoming thinking they'll love it, but the winters and the isolation usually drive them away. I've heard people complain that it's too damn flat, that there's nothing to see."

"They've got their eyes closed then."

"I feel that way, too. Of course, I didn't always appreciate the wide-open spaces. I remember wondering why no one ever planted trees around our place. When I got a little older I figured it out."

"Care to tell me?"

"All trees do is block your view of the sunrises and sunsets. As for the mountains, they keep you from seeing forever."

"You sound like a poet."

He laughed. "I just know what I like."

She grew quiet once more, but it wasn't the kind of silence that builds walls between two people. Instead they seemed to grow closer.

She smiled, and he couldn't help but smile back.

When she shivered, he reached across the seat and turned up the collar on her coat. "You know, Sam, you'd be a lot warmer if you'd sit next to me."

"I'm just fine over here."

"The wind and snow's been beating against that side of the truck for the past two hours. Your nose is red and so are your cheeks. I'm not asking you to go to bed with me, Sam. I'm just asking you to sit close and get warm."

She bit her lip as if contemplating his offer. Finally, she popped her seat belt, moved her tote bag from the center of the seat, scooted close, and buckled up again. For the longest time she held her hands in her lap or in front of the heater, but when he put an arm around her shoulders, he watched the fingers of her left hand hesitantly inch across his thigh.

It amazed him how such a simple gesture could make him feel so damn good.

They weren't quite half an hour from the house when the wind picked up again, harder and faster than before. Jack could feel it slamming against the truck, trying to take control. The snow lifted from the ground and shifted and swirled across the road.

Sam's hand tightened on his thigh. He wanted nothing more than to hold her and let her know everything was going to be all right, but he needed both hands on the wheel.

"We aren't going to die, are we?"

"Not today."

"Good, because my life flashed before me on the plane, and there's some stuff I don't want to revisit again, not this soon, anyway."

He laughed, and tried to take her mind off her fear. "Have you ever ridden a horse?"

"No. I auditioned for a part in a Western once. The casting director told me I didn't get the job because I tried mounting the horse from the wrong side, but I think he was just being nice." She turned toward him. "Mind if I tell you something I've never told anyone before?"

"You're gonna tell me a secret?"

She nodded. "I was a lousy actress, Jack. I tried, but too many people told me I tried too hard. I could play a corpse without any trouble because I didn't have any lines, but stick somebody else's words in my mouth, and they'd come out all wrong."

He glanced quickly at her mouth. It was perfect, and so were the words she spoke. He was glad she wasn't an actress any longer. Glad she hadn't been in Hollywood when he'd been in Palm Beach. Glad she'd tried tailoring for a few months, and needed money so desperately that she'd agreed to play along with his foolish charade.

When he got home, he thought he might send a letter to the airline thanking them for losing his luggage a few weeks ago.

Right now, he wanted to protect her from harm, and he was so damn afraid he wasn't going to be able to.

A wall of solid white slipped in front of the truck without warning, and visibility dropped to zero. Jack touched the brakes slowly, evenly, but he'd already hit black ice and the truck spun out of control. Beside him he heard Sam's gasp. He felt her fingers dig into the side of his leg. And he threw an arm in front of her, instinctively needing to keep her safe.

An instant later he felt a jarring impact, and heard Sam's deafening scream.

thirteen

The truck rested at a precarious angle, forcing Sam's body against Jack's. He could feel her heart beat, could hear her breathing, and relief flooded through him. "Are you okay?" he asked, dragging her into his arms, feeling her shaking inside.

"I think so." She drew in a deep, tremulous breath, and clamped a hand above her breasts. "I feel like something hit me."

"My arm. I was afraid you'd fly through the windshield."

She smiled softly, gently massaging her chest. "Thank you."

"You're welcome."

"What about you?" she asked. "Are you okay?"

"Yeah." Except for being scared for her safety and mad at himself for attempting the drive home in bad weather, although he kept those thoughts to himself.

He wiped a gloved hand over the driver's side window, but all he could see was snow. He saw nothing but white through the other windows, too. "I think we might have run into a ditch, but I'm not sure."

"Are we going to be okay?"

"I told you I'd take care of you. I try to keep my promises."

It was far too cold to be outside, and he knew they should stay in the truck until the blizzard cleared, but he had to get Sam away from the pickup until he was sure it was safe.

He pulled the handle on his door and it jerked from his hand, smashing against a bank of snow, leaving an opening of not much more than eighteen inches.

"You're not getting out of the truck, are you?" Sam asked.

"We're both getting out."

"We'll freeze outside."

And if there was a gas leak, if the truck caught on fire, she could die. That's what had happened to Beth, and he couldn't bear the thought of living through something like that again.

"I've got to check out the truck, make sure everything's all right."

"Okay, you do that. I'll stay right here and keep warm."

He didn't want to frighten her, but he had to get her out of the cab. He uncinched her seat belt, and she slid even closer to his body—if that was possible. "You're getting out, Sam. Whether you want to or not."

She sighed, but she didn't argue.

Holding on to the steering wheel and bracing one boot against the door so he wouldn't slide completely off the seat, he popped his shoulder harness. His torso slipped a few inches and Sam moved right along with him, as if they were connected.

He managed to get his feet and legs out of the truck and onto the snow-covered bank, and then he maneuvered the rest of the way through the tight opening. With one arm around Sam's waist, he pulled her out behind him, holding her close when they were on firm ground. Then he scooped her up in his arms.

"What are you doing?"

"Getting you away from the truck."

"I can walk," she protested

"I know. I've watched you." He winked. "You've got a great walk, Sam."

Slowly her frown transformed into a smile. "Thanks."

They were a good thirty feet from the truck when the pelting wind and snow gentled, and a hazy sunlight appeared through the clouds. For the past five minutes he'd been repeating a silent prayer for the snow to stop, and it looked like God had been listening. The reprieve wasn't something he could take for granted, though. He'd lived on the prairie all his life and knew the storm could kick up again without warning.

He set Sam down in the base of the ditch. "Are you sure you're okay?"

"I'm fine. A little cold, that's all."

"I've got to go back and see if I can figure out what we hit, then I'm going to see if I can get the truck out of the ditch. Wait here."

"I'd rather go with you."

"I'd feel better if you'd stay. Please."

"Okay, but don't be long."

He took a few steps, then turned back. Her red hair was nearly white with snow. The freckles bridging her nose and cheeks blended with the redness of her skin. Her teeth were chattering—and she had to be the most beautiful creature he'd ever seen.

"Is something wrong?" she asked.

"No. I just forgot something important."

"What?"

He curled a gloved hand around the back of her head, and then he kissed her, hard, real hard. He could have lingered, he could have spent the next few hours kissing her, but, unfortunately, he had other things to deal with now. He tore his lips away and pressed his cheek against hers. "I'm glad you're okay," he whispered into her ear. "Real glad."

He brushed a quick kiss across her mouth, then rushed toward the truck.

Jack's kiss had stunned her. She hadn't expected it at all. Sam had been storing memories of Jack's kisses so she could think about them in the future. They weren't leading to anything lasting, but the best parts of her life— her mama and Syd—had been short-lived, too. Still, she kept memories of them close to her heart.

She watched Jack near the truck. He got down on his hands and knees and looked underneath, he walked to the front, disappeared from sight for a minute, and finally she saw him reappear on the other side.

"It's okay," he called out to her. "You can get back inside now, if you want."

Walking toward him, she maneuvered cautiously through the mud and snow, with Jack watching her every move. There'd been so much fear in his eyes when he'd hurried her out of the truck. She knew he was thinking about his girlfriend, and the accident that had happened long ago. *She died because I couldn't get her out of the car*, he'd told her. And he'd made sure the same thing didn't happen to her.

She tucked that memory away, too. Jack Remington didn't know it, but gestures like that were redeeming him in her eyes. She still didn't think the charade was right, but he was doing it for what he thought were all the right reasons.

How could she fault him for that?

"Did you figure out what we hit?" she asked, when she neared the bed of the truck.

"A cow."

"Is she dead?"

He nodded. "Her calf's okay. Half-frozen, but she'll live." He brushed a strand of damp, windblown hair from her cheek, and she felt her toes tingle from the gentleness of his touch. "Feel like playing mother for a while?"

"What?"

"I have to mend the fence before another cow wanders onto the road, and I need you to take care of the calf."

Sam was uncomfortable with the idea, until the bedraggled black calf walked around the side of the truck. The wobbly-legged baby headed straight toward her, and some kind of motherly instinct Sam didn't even know she possessed took over. Bending down, she wrapped her arms around the calf. "Don't worry, little one. We'll take care of you."

If there'd been time, Jack would have stood forever watching Sam cuddling that calf, but right now he had to get the truck out of the ditch, had to get Sam inside where it was warm, and head for home before Lauren got worried and sent someone out to search for them.

Leading Sam to higher ground, he left her there with the calf while he carefully backed the truck away from the dead heifer and out of the ditch. Five minutes later he was on the icy road. He pulled over to the shoulder, left the truck running with the heat turned on full blast, and went back for Sam.

He lifted the calf in his arms and followed Sam back to the truck, unable to take his eyes off the seductive sway she maintained even through the snow.

"There's a blanket under the backseat," he told her, when they reached the truck. "Can you get it?"

She climbed into the cab and, kneeling on the passenger seat, leaned over the back. Jack's heart slammed against his chest as he watched her skirt slide up her thighs. God, her legs were long. And shapely. And he wanted to run his hands over every sexy inch.

"I've got it," she hollered, grabbing the back of her skirt and pulling it down as she twisted around in the seat. She covered her curves and bare legs with the blanket. Probably just as well, he decided. She'd told him she was heading for home in a few days, and he didn't doubt her words. But he had plans to change her mind. He had to do it slowly though. The last thing he wanted to do was scare her off.

He slipped the calf into Sam's outstretched arms, and she wrapped the edges of the blanket around the struggling calf. "Do you have anything else we can put around her?"

He stripped out of his coat.

"You can't do that, Jack. You'll freeze."

"It's not that cold out here," he lied, spreading his jacket over wet fur. "Besides, the coat will just get in the way while I fix the fence."

"Will it take long?" she asked.

"A few minutes. I'll go as fast as I can."

She smiled. "Don't worry about us. My mama used to sing me lullabies. I thought this little one might enjoy one or two."

A lump formed in his throat as he closed the door, and through the window watched Sam stroke the newborn's head and neck, looking like she'd spent a lifetime on a ranch. In spite of the snow, in spite of the cold and wind, she seemed happy to be sitting in the middle of nowhere with a motherless calf in her arms.

He didn't think it was possible, not after

years of failed relationships, but he thought he might have just fallen in love.

As promised, Jack didn't take long fixing the fence. When he climbed into the cab, Sam thought for sure the temperature warmed a good ten degrees. That was a dangerous feeling, and she knew it.

Oh, Mama. I'm starting to like him far too much, and I don't know how to stop.

They were on the road in minutes, the tires whining on the icy pavement. Except for Jack calling Crosby to tell him they were on the way, he drove quietly, obviously deep in thought. She continued to hum, stroking the calf's soft, cool fur, and wished she knew what Jack was thinking.

"Are we almost there?" she asked, when they turned off the highway onto a slushy road.

"Another fifteen minutes or so."

"Your ranch is in the middle of nowhere, isn't it?"

"We've been on the ranch for over an hour," he stated. "The house is in the middle of nowhere." He looked at her and winked. "That's the way I like it."

"Pretty big place, huh?"

"Big enough."

"Do you ever get lonely?"

"Not often. I've got family and friends who keep that from happening."

Family. It was important to him, so important that he'd concocted a charade to keep his sister happy.

She stared out the window at the first hint of moonlight shining on the snow, at the long shadows cast by fence posts and scrub grass. She wasn't part of his family. She was someone he'd hired. Oh, he might be enjoying their kisses, but that rich man in Palm Beach had enjoyed her mama's kisses, too, right before he told her she didn't fit into his world—and left her in tears.

She looked at Jack, at his ruggedly handsome profile, and she knew she had to get away soon, before he broke her heart.

fourteen

Sam *had never* lived in a house before, and she couldn't picture herself living in the big, beautiful one she saw when Jack pointed his out. She'd expected a millionaire to live in a stone mansion the size of Fort Knox. She'd imagined formal gardens, although they'd be brown and nearly lifeless now, sprawling patios, and a swimming pool. What she saw was little more than a three-story white farmhouse with black trim, a wide front porch, an old red barn, some corrals, and half a dozen outbuildings. She saw nothing fancy, only something comfortable and well loved.

She saw a home, a real honest-to-goodness home.

A black-and-white dog came bounding out to meet the truck, spinning in circles and barking as they drove up the road.

"That's Rufus," Jack told her. "He pretends

he's protecting the place, but he's never seen a stranger he didn't like."

"I had a dog like that once," Sam told him, remembering the dog she'd called Princess. "She had to have been the ugliest mutt ever conceived—half-dachshund, half-boxer, I think. One ear was gone, and she had a scar across her nose, but that didn't matter to me. She kept me company when I was alone."

"Were you alone a lot?"

"Too much." She faced him and smiled. "My mama worked at night and couldn't afford a baby-sitter. We had an old black-and-white TV that I'd watch until I couldn't keep my eyes open any longer. Sometimes it would still be on when I woke up in the morning. That's when I'd know that Mama hadn't gotten home yet, and I'd have to fix my own breakfast before heading off to school. I didn't like those mornings very much."

"I wouldn't have liked it either."

"It wasn't being alone that I hated so much, it was being afraid that something had happened to Mama, and . . . I hated leaving without a kiss good-bye."

"What about your dad?"

"I never knew him."

Jack frowned as he brought the truck to a stop right next to the barn, and she wondered if she'd said too much. She'd never told anyone about her past. Not the good times, especially not the bad. But the words had spilled so easily today. Somehow she'd known that Jack wouldn't laugh, wouldn't condemn, or even ask for explanations.

But why should he? Their relationship was temporary.

Sam's door was yanked open before Jack shut off the engine. The man standing beside the truck had at least a week's worth of gray stubble on his face. He was stooped, wiry, and stood as if he had an invisible horse between his legs. "I take it you're Arabella," he croaked. He scooped the calf, the blanket, and Jack's coat from Sam's lap and offered her a marginal smile. "I'm Crosby, Cros for short. Don't matter which one you use. You'll find I ain't too particular about things, least of all formality."

"It's nice to meet you, Crosby."

He looked her up and down and shook his head. "You ain't a bit like I expected."

"What were you expecting?"

"Someone a damn sight more finicky. Someone who sure as hell wouldn't hold a wet critter in her lap." He leaned forward and looked at Jack. "You done good this time, boy."

"I think so."

The masquerade had begun again. It was time for Jack to make necessary comments like that. Time for her to put on an act and hope she could stifle the fluttery feelings that crept into her heart every time he uttered something nice.

Crosby boosted the calf higher in his arms, aiming his next words at Sam. "Hope you can cook. I already served supper, so you're gonna have to fend for yourself. Lauren's upstairs primpin' and cryin'. Been doin' that most of the day."

"What about Beau?" Jack asked.

"He's had a bee up his butt all afternoon. He slammed out of the kitchen soon as the blizzard went through. I imagine he's around somewhere. Sulkin' more than likely. Don't think he's too anxious to meet his future ma." Without another word, Crosby turned and walked away.

"I don't want to cause any problems between you and your son," Sam said, realizing that they hadn't talked about the boy at all on their drive.

"Beau and I have a whole hell of a lot of things to work out between us. You're just one of them, so don't worry about it."

"What about Crosby? How does he feel about me being here?"

"That's the nicest greeting I've ever heard him give anyone." Jack smiled. "I think he likes you."

Sam laughed, as she attempted to rub the circulation back into her legs. "Is he family?"

"Closest thing to it. He came to the ranch in the early thirties and hasn't left since. My grandpa told me once that Cros had killed a man in a barroom brawl and came here looking for a place to hide."

"Do you believe it?"

Jack nodded. "He's never told a soul about what he did before he became a cowboy. If he killed someone, I imagine they had it coming. If he's felt any guilt, he's kept it to himself. I only care about what he is now, and I'd trust him with my life."

Those were some of the nicest words Sam had ever heard. Jack didn't care about Crosby's past. Maybe hers wouldn't bother him either—if they had a real relationship, which they didn't.

Climbing out of the truck, Jack came around to the passenger side to help Sam out. A gust of wind stung her cheeks as she stepped onto the dirt and gravel, and without warning her legs gave out beneath her.

Jack swept her up in his arms and carried her toward the house.

"Put me down, Jack. I can't have you carrying me everywhere."

"If I put you down, you'll fall flat on your face."

"My legs fell asleep while I was holding the calf. That's all."

"I think there's more to it than that." His brow narrowed into a frown as he pushed through a side door. "When was the last time you ate a decent meal?"

"I had biscuits and gravy at Denny's right after you called, and I ate on the plane. You're not my mother, Jack. Don't worry about my eating habits."

"Okay, let's talk about your sleeping habits. Had more than a few hours lately?"

She hesitated, trying to remember.

"You work too hard, Sam. That's gonna change while you're here."

"Don't bet on it. And you'd better start calling me Arabella before you foul up your little game."

He raised an eyebrow, his look quelling her words. "I'm taking you upstairs. I'm going to run you a bath, and you're going to soak in it. It's about time someone made you relax."

She liked the sound of a bath. She'd spent too many months cleaning up in the bathroom at Antonio's, or in the institutional-like showers at the KOA. The thought of lazing away in a tub, one filled with bubbles, maybe, sounded delightful.

Better yet, she liked the thought that Jack cared. Of course, there was always the possibility that he didn't want anyone seeing his fiancée looking unkempt and definitely unrefined. That seemed the most logical explanation. Still, she wove her arms about his neck and enjoyed the moment.

He was the only man who'd ever carried her, and she had to admit she liked the feeling.

As he walked through the house, she tried to take in the layout and decorations, but she got lost in Jack's even breathing, the steadiness of his heartbeat, the warmth of his lips brushing her cheek when he turned to her and smiled, and the sound of his boots on the hardwood floors and stairs.

He opened a door and carried her into a room that boasted little more than a big brick fireplace with an old, overstuffed tweed chair positioned in front of the hearth. A large, oval braided rug covered the floor between the fireplace and an antique oak dresser. A matching highboy sat on the other side of the room, and against the far wall, with windows on either side, was the bed.

She shivered.

"Are you cold?" he asked.

"A little."

"I'll start a fire for you. Get this place warmed up."

She wasn't cold at all. She was nervous. She

didn't like the idea of being in his bedroom—
so close to his bed.

"Is this your room?" she asked, hoping he'd
say no, because she wanted to sleep in that big
old four-poster bed.

"Yeah. I've been sleeping in here for thirty-
two years."

"Well, I'm not going to sleep in here," she
said bluntly. "No way."

"This isn't a hotel, Sam. It's not some big
fancy mansion, either, and I'm afraid I'm fresh
out of guest bedrooms."

"Then I'll sleep in the living room."

"No you won't. You'll sleep here. You're my
fiancée, remember? In case you've forgotten, I
paid you to make this look real between you
and me."

"You didn't pay me to sleep with you."

"I didn't ask you to sleep *with* me, did I?"

"You implied it. You've been doing that all
afternoon."

"I kissed you, damn it! Since when does that
mean I want anything more?"

She felt her jaws tighten as she turned away
from his heated gaze. "Maybe I was making
too many assumptions."

"You sure as hell were."

He set her down on the floor, and she
fought the weakness in her legs. She wasn't
about to collapse and have to suffer through

his picking her up again. He'd just made his intentions perfectly clear. She was here for one reason and one reason only. And that meant when they were alone—she didn't have to put up with his touches.

"Just so neither one of us assumes anything more while I'm here, let me make something clear."

He folded his arms over his chest. "I'm listening."

"You can touch me when your family and friends are present. You can say nice things to me, and I'll do the same to you—*when* we're in someone else's presence. But when we're by ourselves—I want to be left alone, no touching, no kissing, no nice words. That's the only way I'm going to go through with the rest of this charade."

"If that's the way you want to play it, be my guest."

He stormed across the room and grabbed the doorknob. "There's some kind of bubble bath under the sink in the bathroom. Lauren sent it to me a long time ago, and it's never been opened. Take a bath. A long one." He took a deep breath. "I'll bring up your luggage later."

"Fine!" she threw back. "Just knock before you come in."

"That's going to look odd."

"This whole thing's odd, in case you haven't realized it."

She could see his chest rise and fall. Could see the angry set of his jaw as he opened the door. "What about dinner?"

"I'm not hungry."

"Doesn't matter. I'll bring up a tray."

If he said or tried to do one more nice thing, she was going to throw something at him. She had her mind set on being mad—that was the only way she could survive this craziness.

"It's been a long day, Jack. I'm wet. I'm tired. And I'd like to be alone."

He looked as if he was going to throw back some retort, but he didn't. Instead, he shook his head and left the room, closing the door behind him.

A tear slid from her eye. The very first tear she'd ever shed from a breaking heart.

Lauren came bursting out of her room a moment after Jack walked into the hall, but at the moment, he didn't want to talk to her. What he wanted was to get on his horse and ride off some of the steam that had built up inside of him.

Sam Jones was driving him mad. He didn't imagine his sister would help the situation.

"I'm so glad you're home, Jack," Lauren

said, blowing on what looked like freshly painted fingernails. "I was worried sick." She started to throw her arms around Jack, then came to a screeching halt. "What on earth happened to you? You're filthy."

"A slight altercation with a cow."

"Is Arabella all right?"

"She's fine. A little sore from the accident—"

"Accident!"

"It wasn't anything serious," he said, continuing his journey down the stairs with Lauren hot on his heels. "She's upstairs getting ready to soak in the tub. I thought she might like resting a bit."

"What she needs is some wine," Lauren said.

"What she needs is quiet."

"Don't worry, Jack, I'm not going to monopolize her time." Lauren stopped in the doorway leading to the kitchen, turned around, and smiled at Jack. "I just want to say hello, take her a nice glass of that Chablis you keep for special occasions, and maybe some cheese and crackers."

It was no use arguing with his sister. It was no use arguing with any woman because they always won.

He left the house through the living room instead of following Lauren into the kitchen, went to the truck, and started grabbing suitcases out of the backseat.

"Need some help with those things?" Beau walked toward the truck, adjusting the new black Stetson on his head.

"Thanks." Jack handed two of the smaller bags to Beau, shoved the brown, duct-taped suitcase under his arm, and latched on to the two bigger ones.

"I hear you've been in a foul mood all day. Care to talk about it?"

Beau shrugged. "It's no big deal."

"Does it have anything to do with Arabella?"

"Like I said, it's no big deal."

Jack hated noncommittal answers and didn't care for Beau's sulking, either. "If you've got concerns about me having a woman in my life, you'd better tell me now."

Beau was silent a moment, and finally asked, "Have you had a lot of women in your life?"

"Enough. Haven't found too many who liked the ranching part of my life."

"What about Arabella. Is she going to like it here?"

He already knew Sam liked the country— even if she didn't care much for him. He answered as honestly as he could. "I think so."

"Are you two getting married soon?"

"Haven't really decided."

"Are you going to have kids?"

Jack shoved the bags on the front seat and leaned against the cab. "We haven't decided that, either."

Beau swung the suitcases he was holding over the side of the truck, set them in the bed, and stood next to Jack. He stared at the side of the barn, focused on nothing more than his thoughts, Jack imagined. "I could go back home if you want me to."

"Is that what you want?"

"Does what I want matter?"

"Does to me."

"I want to stay, but I don't want to be in the way."

"You're not."

"What if Arabella doesn't want me here?"

Jack put an arm around the boy. The real Arabella might have kicked up a fuss. The woman upstairs in his bedroom seemed to run hot and cold about what she wanted, but on sheer instinct alone, he knew damn good and well she would leave before she'd let anything come between Jack and his son.

"I want you here, Beau. That's the only thing that matters."

He saw a smile on Beau's mouth and fought the lump in his throat. "Come on. Help me take these things inside."

* * *

Sam lounged in a bathtub filled with sweetly scented bubbles. Her hair was pinned on top of her head, and she rested against the back of the tub, trying her hardest to relax when all she could think of was Jack coming upstairs to deliver her luggage or a tray of food.

She didn't want to see him right now.

Then again, she did, but under totally different circumstances.

With her eyes closed, she imagined the charade was over, that she was back in West Palm Beach in a little apartment she'd rented with her own money. She pretended that Jack had flown to Florida with no other thought in mind but seeing her. They'd had dinner together. They'd gone dancing, and she'd invited him in because neither of them wanted the night to end.

By then she was feeling kind of dreamy, letting her imagination run wild. What could it hurt to pretend? It seemed the closest she would ever get to having any more wonderful memories.

She dragged a big sponge over her stomach, across her breasts, and suddenly a make-believe Jack was in the tub with her. She'd never shared a bath with a man. Never stood naked in the shower with a lover who was doing erotic things to her body, but her imagination was running wild.

Would it be so awful if she gave in to the feelings she had for him? Would it be so horrible if they made love, if she left this charade with a few wonderful memories?

When she heard the creak of the bathroom door, she made a foolish, absolutely insane and spur of the moment decision. She wanted Jack—even if her heart broke in the end.

"Want to join me?" she asked softly.

"Not today, thank you."

"Oh, God!"

She slid down in the tub till her chin touched the bubbles, and wished she could hide completely. She opened her eyes to see Lauren standing in the doorway with a tray holding two glasses of wine.

"I thought you were Jack."

"I assumed as much." Lauren set the tray on the far end of the tub, and took a seat on the toilet. "Hope you don't mind me barging in. I told Jack I wouldn't take up too much of your time, but he's talking to Beau, and I thought you might like some company."

She handed a glass of wine to Sam and took one for herself. "I brought crackers and cheese, too. I was hoping there were truffles in the house, or something else decadently chocolate, but when you see that kitchen, you'll know this place is inhabited by nothing but men."

Lauren took a sip of her wine. "Now, this is wonderful. Jack says it's from some special reserve in California. I prefer French wines myself, but Jack's more the all-American kind of guy."

Sam tasted the pale pink wine. She didn't know a Bordeaux from a pinot noir, but Lauren was right. It tasted delicious. "Thank you for bringing the wine."

"Oh, it's no problem at all." Lauren took a piece of cheese from the tray and nibbled at the edge. "I know you just got here, and I'm sure you're awfully tired, but I was hoping we could talk."

"About Peter?"

Lauren nodded, and Sam saw a tear slide down her cheek before she wiped it away.

"You'd think after two failed marriages I'd know when a man isn't right for me."

"Peter's gorgeous. He's charming." Sam was looking for the right words to say but found it difficult. "He's—"

"Out of my life for good," Lauren stated.

"You're sure?"

"Positive."

Sam heard Jack's boots and his distinctive walk before he stuck his head into the bathroom. "Am I interrupting something."

"No," Lauren said. "I was just starting to

cry again, but I can do it by myself."

Lauren started to get up, but Sam reached out of the tub and caught her hand. She'd been saved from doing something totally insane, and she didn't want Lauren walking out now, leaving her alone with Jack, who was staring at the bubbles that hid her naked body.

"Don't leave, Lauren."

"No, don't leave," Jack repeated. "I just wanted to tell Arabella I'd brought up her luggage. Thought I might take a ride with Beau," Jack stated. "You two take your time."

"You don't mind?" Lauren asked, looking from Sam to Jack, then back again.

"We don't mind at all," Sam said. "Do we, Jack?"

"Well—"

He had an odd look on his face, a sly smile that made her feel uncomfortable. He walked into the bathroom, right up to the tub. Bending down, he planted a kiss smack on her lips.

He moved back an inch or two, and winked. "I'll see you later, Whiskey." He stood, but continued to stare at the bubbles that were disappearing far too fast.

"Whiskey," Lauren repeated. "What a lovely nickname."

"It's the color of her eyes," Jack informed his sister. "You may not notice it, but they're damned intoxicating."

Sam could hear Lauren sigh as Jack turned and walked out of the room.

She rolled her eyes. This entire situation was crazy.

Lauren crossed her legs and drummed nervous fingers atop her knee. "Peter never called me anything other than Lauren," she said. "It's obvious now that he didn't have any real feelings for me."

There was so much more behind feelings than a special name, Sam thought, but she didn't say that to Lauren. Instead, she took a sip of wine, and held the glass close to her lips. "Tell me what happened with Peter."

"Remember that special present he was going to give me after dinner the other night?"

Sam nodded, remembering the dinner and the way Peter picked on Lauren most of the evening. She'd chosen the wrong wine with her steak. She should eat steamed vegetables instead of buttery potatoes. Sam recalled thinking that although the sex might have been good between those two, there wasn't anything closely resembling love coming from Peter.

"Well," Lauren said with another sigh, "he kept the secret all the way to London. I was dying to know, but he wouldn't tell me. He said it was something we were both going to love. A car met us at Heathrow and we had the nicest drive out to the country. You've been there before, haven't you?"

"No. I'm a lot like Jack. Pretty much all-American."

"No wonder you're so suited for each other. Anyway, Peter took me to this beautiful old castle. A gorgeous place with swans on the lake and a hedgerow maze that was centuries old. I knew Peter had won a lot of money playing polo, but I knew he couldn't possibly afford to *buy* me a country home in England."

"Had he?"

"Oh, no. We were ushered inside by this very tall, very svelte woman who looked me up one end and down the other and pronounced me the perfect candidate for her *spa*." Lauren popped a slice of cheese into her mouth, chewed it slowly, and swallowed. She looked down at the floor. "The castle was a fat farm."

"*For you*?"

"For *me*." Lauren dabbed at her eyes with a napkin. "Maybe I do have fifteen or twenty pounds I could lose, but Peter told me *and* the woman who ran the spa that I had an eating disorder that needed to be controlled. He said our lovemaking was wonderful, but . . . but that I was getting a little too thick around the middle. I just couldn't understand a man giving me something like that as a present."

Sam was aghast. Lauren was radiant, and a decent human would never notice a few extra pounds. They wouldn't even notice fifty or a hundred, because the woman beneath the body was lovely, warm, and generous.

But Peter was only slightly human, and Sam could easily picture him presenting Lauren with a cruel and tasteless present.

Sam took a sip of wine, and tried to think of something to say. "Was Peter going to stay there with you?"

"Oh, no. Not Peter. He'd already planned to go back to London. He had reservations at the Ritz, and had accepted half a dozen invitations to parties with his friends. The fat farm was his gift to me and me alone. He told me it was highly recommended, that I could relax for two entire weeks, sit around eating gourmet cucumber slices and getting wrapped in plastic wrap—in all the right places—so I could be slim and trim for our wedding. He said he'd treat me to a new necklace when I got out. Something that would look wonderful on my new and improved body."

"And what did you tell him?"

"Before or after I pushed him into the lake?"

"You didn't!"

"I most certainly did. I told him if he liked the idea of plastic wrap so much, he should stay and have his head done to take away some of the swelling. As for muscle tone, I suggested he try some of the spa's workouts on his dick, because it was sorely lacking in strength and endurance."

Sam choked on her sip of wine.

"Are you all right?" Lauren asked, jumping up and grabbing the glass from Sam.

"I'm fine." And then she started to laugh.

Lauren joined in.

Finally, Lauren took a deep breath and sighed. "I did the right thing, didn't I?"

"Do you miss him?"

"No."

"Then you did the right thing."

Lauren looked at Sam through tear-dampened eyelashes. "What if no one else wants me?"

"I can't imagine that ever happening, but would being alone be so bad?"

"I don't know. I've tried not to be alone since I was a child."

"First off, you'll never be alone. You've got friends all over the world. You've got Jack, and Beau, and Crosby. You've got me," she said, reaching out through the bubbles and holding Lauren's hand. "Isn't there anything you've wanted to do, but didn't have the time because you were too busy with a husband or boyfriend?"

"I've never given it much thought."

"Is there something you do better than anyone else you know?"

Lauren took a sip of wine while pondering the question. "I throw the best parties in Palm Beach."

Sam smiled at the unexpected answer. "Have you ever thought of going into business?"

"I don't need any money."

"You could always donate what you make to, oh, maybe the homeless people in West Palm Beach."

"I like that idea," Lauren said, as she tapped a perfectly manicured index finger against her lips. "I wonder how much Jack would pay me to plan your wedding?"

Sam let her head fall back against the tub. "We haven't given much thought to a wedding."

"Oh, but you should." Lauren stood up and lifted the tray from the edge of the tub. "Thanks for making me feel a little better about Peter." She sighed. "I'm afraid I've made him sound absolutely horrid, but he does have some wonderful qualities."

"I'm sure he does," Sam fibbed. "But you deserve so much more."

"Someday I hope to have something close to what you and Jack have. Think I ever will?"

Sam nodded as Lauren walked slowly to the

doorway. She stepped over the threshold, then turned around. A smile radiated on her face. "Do you like ice sculptures?"

"Doesn't everyone?"

"Well, I have the perfect one in mind for your wedding."

"You do?"

"Of course. You and Jack on top of a stallion. It'll be perfect. Absolutely perfect."

Absolutely perfect? Sam laughed to herself as she downed the rest of her wine. Absolutely perfect would be if they were really engaged, if Jack loved her and she loved him, but the whole thing was a farce. A sham. An out-and-out lie.

And none of her crazy dreams, none of her wishful imaginings, could make it be something different.

fifteen

The clouds had gone, and the stars and a full moon brightened the night. It was nearly eight, but not too late for a ride.

Jack led Diablo and Pecos, the horse he'd ridden for half his life, out of the barn. "I'm going out to the west pasture to bring in an Appaloosa for Arabella," Jack told Beau, tearing the boy's attention away from the fence post he was lassoing. "Want to go with me?"

"Wouldn't you prefer being with Arabella?"

A simple yes or no answer would have been fine, but Jack had already learned that wasn't the kind of response a teenage boy liked to give. "What I want is to go for a ride. Besides, Lauren's got Arabella cornered in the bathroom."

"Is she crying again?"

"Off and on."

"Probably a good thing you split. I always

250

hated it when my grandma would cry. She'd do it when she was watching TV, or fixing dinner, or reading a birthday card. It's kind of embarrassing."

"Yeah, but it's kind of nice when the woman you love starts to cry and all she wants is for you to hold her. Just remember one thing."

"What's that?"

"Don't try to offer solutions. Don't say things will get better. Do that and those tears will turn to anger."

"What do you do when they get angry?"

A grin touched Jack's face. "Kiss them."

"That's it?"

"For starters." It didn't always work, but it sometimes left them so dumbfounded—like when he'd kissed Sam in the bathtub—that they couldn't utter another word.

Jack grabbed the rope from Beau's hands. "So, are you gonna go ridin' with me?"

"Yeah."

Beau swung up on the back of Diablo and Jack wasted no time riding away from the ranch. He liked the feel of Pecos's steady lope through the snow and the brisk night air burning his face. In the distance he could hear the coyotes, and when they passed a stream lined with cottonwood, he heard the faint hoot of an owl.

They'd been riding nearly half an hour

when Beau slowed his horse and Pecos matched Diablo's pace.

"I like it here at night," Beau said, resting his hands on the saddle horn. "In LA all we could hear was traffic and sirens. Sometimes you couldn't even hear yourself think." He was silent a moment, listening to the sounds around him. "I never could understand why my grandpa didn't like it here."

"He liked it once," Jack said. "I remember when he first opened his practice in town. A bunch of us made bets on how long he'd stay."

"Why?"

"One winter's about all most greenhorns can stand, then they hightail it back to where they came from. Your grandpa didn't seem to mind the cold all that much.

"So why did he leave?"

He took a moment to answer. "I guess he figured LA would be a better place to raise you."

"Did he leave before or after my mom died?"

"After."

"Grandpa never wanted to talk about my mom. You don't either," Beau said, turning slightly in his saddle and looking at Jack. "Why?"

Jack sighed, and watched his breath fog the

air. "Some memories are better left alone."

"Is that fair to me?"

Jack reined his horse to a stop. "I suppose not." He stared at the stars for the longest time, then looked at his son. "I loved your mother."

"That's not the impression I got from my grandpa. I thought you were a one-night stand."

He shook his head. "I was young and wild and she was the prettiest thing I'd ever seen. We used to talk about our future together. I wanted to rodeo, travel from town to town— as long as Beth would go with me. That kind of life sounded glamorous at the time, at least to me. Your mom had other ideas, though. She wanted me to build a cabin somewhere on the ranch. She wanted a white picket fence, and she wanted to plant flowers. On top of that, she wanted us to have lots of kids." Jack laughed. "The last thing I was thinking about at sixteen was being a father. That's when I first learned how big a difference there is between girls and guys."

"I think I figured it out when I was about eight."

Jack chuckled low, and when he spotted the Appaloosa he'd been searching for, he galloped across the prairie with Beau following behind. Jack slipped a bridle and a lead rein on Belle, gave her an apple, then headed back for the ranch.

"Think you'd like to run a spread like this someday?" Jack asked Beau.

"I have a lot to learn before I could do something like that."

"I hadn't planned on giving it to you in the next day or two. I was thinking more like twenty years from now, when I'm ready to sit on the sidelines and let someone else do most of the work."

Beau was silent for far too long. "Why would you want to give the place to me?"

"You're the only son I've got. This place has always belonged to a Remington, and you're the only one in my will."

"My name's Morris, not Remington."

Jack aimed his gaze at his son. "You're a Remington. I don't much care what your last name is."

Beau seemed to mull that over for a while. If Jack had his way, he'd have Beau's name changed tomorrow. But that was a decision the boy would have to make, not him.

"What if you have other kids?"

"Doesn't matter. You'll always be my first."

Beau grew silent again, but Jack watched him from the corner of his eye, and in the moonlight he could see the muscles tensing in his jaw.

Jack reined Pecos in front of Diablo and came to a stop. "Something troubling you?"

Beau nodded. "You didn't put me in your will thinking that would make up for getting rid of me, did you?"

"No." Jack laughed uncomfortably, took off his Stetson, and ran his fingers through his hair. After readjusting his hat, he scuffed his hand across the day's growth of beard on his chin. "Well, maybe," he said, keeping his eyes on Beau's face, "I never did feel right about what I did."

"Why didn't you make an attempt to see me?"

"I did."

"When?"

Jack remembered that day full well. He remembered the sweat on his palms, the tightness in his chest, and his desperate need to hold his little boy. "It was your fourth birthday," he told Beau. "Your grandparents were having a party for you at the LA Zoo."

"I remember that. Sort of. But I don't remember you."

"I don't imagine you would. I stood under a tree watching you open your presents."

"Why didn't you come to the party? Why didn't you come to see me any other time?"

"I made a promise to your grandparents that I wouldn't."

"Why?"

"Because I wouldn't have made a very good dad."

"That's it? No other explanation?"

Jack shook his head. "That's it."

"Well, that's one hell of a reason."

Beau kicked Diablo's flanks and took off across the pasture.

He hated to see the boy so angry, but if he knew the truth, that his grandfather had refused to let Jack see the boy, that he'd promised a messy court battle if Jack tried to get custody, Beau would resent his grandparents, and Jack didn't want that. They'd done their best for Beau, and they'd done enough suffering after Beth was killed.

If Beau had anyone to resent, it was his dad.

Jack showered and shaved in the bathroom downstairs. He always kept a set of clothes in the room off the kitchen because he never knew when he might be too dirty to walk through the house. It was tough enough keeping the place clean without trailing mud from room to room.

The house had been quiet when he and Beau returned from their ride. The lights were off in his bedroom and bath, and he figured Sam had already gone to sleep. He wondered if she was in his bed or if she'd curled up in the big chair in front of the fireplace. Hell, he'd never even built the fire he'd promised.

He'd sure been making a mess of things. Beau was angry with him, too, and after their ride, he'd gone storming up to his room, silent and hurt.

He tried not to think about Beau's justified anger. Instead, he tried to put that anger into perspective. Beau was learning about the past and accepting it one piece at a time.

Jack closed the bathroom door and went to his office. He told himself that he'd neglected his work far too long.

Ah, hell, that was just an excuse. He didn't want to go to his bedroom and see Sam lying in bed. He didn't want to think about his feelings for her, especially when she stomped on them every time he turned around.

He pulled a stack of faxes from the machine and quickly scanned their contents. His partner had sent details for a new advertising campaign. An architect had sent interior sketches for the five new restaurants in Houston and Dallas, and . . .

Jack rested his hip against the edge of the desk and stared at the fax from Wes Haskins, the investigator he'd asked to check on Samantha Jones.

Damn! He'd meant to call Wes and tell him to forget the whole thing. If there was something more to know about Sam, something not so good, he didn't want to find out.

He crumpled the fax and tossed it into the trash, then thumbed through the rest of the correspondence.

Sitting down at his desk, he ripped open the mail that had arrived earlier in the day. He studied a profit and loss statement, then thumbed through the pages of *Horse & Rider* magazine, but the wadded piece of paper stared up at him from the trash.

He'd wondered for weeks if Sam was in some kind of trouble. Maybe Wes's report shed some light on why she'd needed so much money, and why she'd gone to a loan shark to get it.

Grabbing the paper, he smoothed out the wrinkles, and read the contents. Sam Jones had worked as a waitress in at least a dozen restaurants in West Palm Beach before she and her mother had moved to West Hollywood five years ago. She worked for two and a half years in five different dinner theaters in the Los Angeles area, doing everything from waitressing to set and wardrobe design. Acting hadn't played too much of a part in her employment history in any of those theaters. She'd worked for a movie studio as a seamstress, and spent time behind the counter at Taco Bell, Burger King, and McDonald's. She'd rented a small apartment in West Hol-

WIFE FOR A DAY *~* 259

lywood with her mother, and six months ago buried the woman, Felicity Jones—age forty. Friends and acquaintances said she was a nice kid who kept to herself.

Jack scanned the rest of the page and learned nothing new, except that he owed Wes money.

He ripped a piece of Remington Ranch stationery from his desk drawer and hastily scribbled a note to Wes. "Stop searching for info on Samantha Jones. Services no longer required."

The things he wanted to know from Sam he was learning little by little. She'd had a one-eared dog. She'd been lonely and poor, her mother worked at night, and for some reason she'd gone from job to job.

Those were the kinds of things he wanted to know about Sam. The little things that had shaped her, and made him want her more than he'd wanted any woman.

But he needed to know so much more. He wanted to know about her father and why her mother, who had given her so many words of wisdom, had died so young. He wanted to know why Sam was twenty-five, worked harder than any woman he'd ever known, yet lived in a Volkswagen bug.

He also wanted to know why she'd borrowed money from a loan shark. He could just ask her, but she'd looked so damn uncomfortable telling him anything that he'd left it alone.

He tossed the fax on top of his desk and got up from the chair. It was late, he was tired, and sitting in his room watching Sam sleep sounded a hell of a lot better than sitting in his office going crazy thinking about her.

When he reached his bedroom, he knocked softly. Sam didn't answer, so he stepped inside and locked the door behind him.

Moonlight shone through the window, glancing off the empty bed. The bathroom door was open, and it was dark inside. He walked across the room and saw Sam curled up in the chair in front of the cold, empty fireplace, where he sat sometimes at night to read.

She was dressed in one of his white shirts and a pair of his thick wool socks. With her legs drawn up beneath her he could see her thigh, her bare hip. God, she was beautiful.

Her eyes fluttered open and she smiled. "I waited up for you."

"Looks to me like you had trouble keeping awake."

She yawned, and her breasts rose and fell beneath his shirt. "The wine made me sleepy. The bubble bath didn't help, either."

"Why didn't you go to bed?"

"I couldn't, not until we figured out who was going to sleep where."

He laughed. "You can have the bed."

"Good. This chair isn't all that comfortable."

"So you don't mind if *I'm* miserable all night?" he asked, as she straightened her legs, and rose from the chair.

"It was your decision to take the chair." A faint smile touched her lips. "We never had much company when I was little, but my mama used to tell me that guests should always be treated special." She climbed onto the bed and pulled the covers over her. "Mama would have liked the fact that you gave me your bed—and let me sleep here—all alone."

Jack grinned as she taunted him, tested him, and he knew she was enjoying every moment. "Is there anything else your mama would have liked about me?" he asked, taking her place in the chair, extending his legs in front of him, and crossing them at the ankles.

"She would have liked your family," she said sleepily, turning on her side and tucking her hands under her cheek.

"What about me—personally."

"She would have liked the way you gave me your coat today, and the way you carried me into the house and worried that I don't eat or sleep enough."

Jack watched her eyelids flutter, then close. "What about you, Sam? What do *you* like about me?"

She yawned, burrowing her head into the pillow. "That's a tough question, Jack. If you don't mind, I'll sleep on it and get back to you tomorrow or the next day."

He chuckled to himself as he watched her fall asleep. Sam Jones didn't plan to cut him any slack at all. Hell, that was one of the things that endeared her to him. She didn't pull any punches. She didn't fall all over him, either.

She'd gotten all the money she needed and as far as she was concerned, that's all she wanted from him—except the comfort of his bed, which she firmly planned to sleep in alone. She'd carry out her end of their bargain and she'd hightail it back home.

But he had other plans. He wanted to make her dream come true, wanted to make her believe she belonged someplace.

And where he wanted her to belong was exactly where she was right now, with one difference. He wanted her to believe that he belonged next to her.

sixteen

$\mathcal{S}$am woke to the smell of woodsmoke and the crackling of a fire. At first she thought she was caught in the middle of a dream, one she'd had so many times as a child about waking up on Christmas morning in a house where a fireplace blazed and stockings hung from a mantel.

This wasn't a dream, though. Jack stood before the hearth, moving a log with a long-handled poker.

"Can't you sleep?" she asked, turning on her side and pulling the comforter around her shoulders.

"No." He gave the log a shove, and it settled in between two others on the fire. Sparks flew up the chimney, and a gentle flame skittered over the wood. Jack put the poker in its stand, went back to his chair, and sat. "That bed seems to suit you," he said. "You weren't having any trouble sleeping at all."

"It's not quite as cozy as the passenger seat of a VW," she said, smiling, "but I know it's the best you have to offer."

"When was the last time you slept in a real bed, Sam?" he asked in that warm, concerned-sounding voice that constantly caught her off guard.

"Six months ago, I guess. Why?"

"Is that when your mother died?"

"Yes."

"Tell me about her."

"It's the middle of the night," she said, taking a quick peek at the clock beside the bed. It was just past 3:00 A.M., she wasn't tired any longer, but she'd never talked about her personal life with anyone. "Wouldn't you rather go to sleep?"

"I'd rather talk. Arabella and I never talked about personal things until it was too late. Besides," he said with a grin, "I can't sleep, so why should you."

She'd never asked him about Arabella, never really wanted to know about the woman he'd loved. Now seemed the perfect opportunity to ask. "Why did the two of you call it quits?"

"We didn't have enough in common." He folded his arms behind his head and stared at the fire. "Do you know anything about the stock market?"

"Me?" She laughed. "I know that stocks go up one day, down the next, but what that means is beyond me."

"Do you know about mergers and acquisitions?"

Couldn't he ask her something simple, like whether or not she knew how to clean the grill at Denny's, make a hot fudge sundae, or drive a stick shift? She didn't want to look simple in his eyes, undereducated, but she couldn't hide what she was. "You already know I'm not too savvy when it comes to business, Jack. I'm the one who went to a loan shark for money, remember?"

"I remember."

He closed his eyes, and she wondered if her inability to converse about business had bored him enough to put him to sleep.

"Do you like opera and the ballet?" he asked, his voice sounding relaxed, tired.

"I went to see *Phantom of the Opera* once and loved it, but I don't think true opera buffs consider that much of an opera."

"No, they don't."

"As for ballet, I once watched the *Nutcracker* on television at Christmastime. I liked that, too."

"What about camping, Sam. Do you like

sleeping out under the stars at night?"

Rolling onto her back, she looked at the play of the firelight on the ceiling. "Mama and I lived outside one summer. We even stayed in the park a few times, until the police ran us off. But I remember looking up at the stars and thinking how pretty they were, that I wished I could reach out and touch them. That was an awfully nice summer."

She'd revealed too much. She tilted her head to see if Jack was laughing, but he was standing beside the bed, looking down, smiling. "The stars are awfully big out here, Sam. They might be easier to touch than the ones in the city."

"You think so?"

Nodding, he sat on the edge of the bed. "Do you feel like learning to ride tomorrow?"

"Think I can learn the right side to mount on?"

"Just remember that the right side is the left side, and you'll have it made."

"Seems simple enough."

He lifted one of her curls, wrapping the spiral around his finger. He watched her, and she could see the warmth of the fire mirrored in his eyes. She was afraid he was going to kiss her. Afraid he wouldn't—because she'd told him earlier that when they were alone he couldn't touch her.

Oh, why had she said such a crazy thing? She wanted him so darn much she ached.

He leaned toward her, resting an arm on the pillow beside her head. "This bed's big enough for two, Sam. You wouldn't reconsider sharing it, would you?"

"No." She'd thought about saying "yes," but her common sense stepped in and rescued her.

He grinned, her negative answer obviously not surprising him at all. "Could you at least give me a good-night kiss?"

That would be a very foolish thing to do, and she knew it, but her common sense had already retreated. She touched his cheek, feeling the stubble on his face as he moved toward her. His lips touched hers lightly. They lingered only a moment, long enough for her to smell the scent of soap on his skin, to hear him draw in a deep breath before he drew away, long enough for the beat of her heart to quicken.

"Good night, Sam," he whispered.

She watched his back as he went to the chair. He didn't look at her again, but seemed to relax as he watched the fire. Slowly, his eyes closed, his breathing deepened, and she hoped she wasn't imagining it, but it seemed as if he'd fallen asleep with a smile on his face.

*   *   *

Sam bounded down the stairs at five minutes until ten the next morning, shocked that she'd slept so late, upset with herself that she'd missed the sunrise and most of the morning. She wasn't going to have much time at the ranch, and she fully planned to take advantage of every moment she could.

The black cowboy boots she'd found in one of the suitcases fit her like a glove, and they clomped on the wooden stairs, echoing throughout the house. Jack had done a good job picking out jeans, too, but she'd ignored the suitcase full of pretty blouses and sweaters, opting for one of Jack's big flannel shirts instead. It felt comfy, secure, and was the next best thing to being swallowed up in his embrace.

She found Crosby in the kitchen, stooped over the sink slowly washing pots and pans. "Good morning."

"Mornin'." He looked at her over his shoulder. "Coffee's on the stove. There's eggs, bacon, and biscuits warming in the oven."

Leaning over the coffeepot, she savored the scent of Crosby's brew. "Smells like you doubled the amount of beans."

"I did. You want it different, you gotta make it yourself."

"My mama always told me strong coffee's good for the soul."

"I don't know much about souls, but I do know coffee, and I like it strong. Of course, ain't no one else around here feels that way."

Sam poured herself a cup and leaned against the kitchen cabinet, taking slow sips of the scalding liquid. "Where's Jack?"

"He left right after breakfast—a good three hours ago. Went huntin' coyotes."

"Will he be gone long?"

"No tellin'. Said he would have taken you with him, but you was out like a light."

"I don't know what possessed me to sleep so late." She opened the oven door and plucked a piece of bacon from the plate. "It's not like me at all."

"You ain't late. Miss Lauren won't be out of bed till at least noon, maybe later. Pampered socialite is what she is, but it sure does make me feel good seein' her here."

"Did you spend much time with Jack and Lauren when they were little?"

"Yep."

"What were they like?"

"Trouble. Both of them."

"That's it?"

"You want to know more, you gotta ask them. I ain't never been one to tell tales about others."

"I knew there was a good reason to like you."

Crosby looked away from the sink and grinned. "You ain't so bad, either."

Sam rolled up the sleeves of her shirt. "Want some help?"

"Almost done here."

"Then tell me where you keep the cleaning supplies."

"Jack would have my hide if he knew I was lettin' you work around here. Besides, we got a maid who comes once a week to do the cleaning. Course, he don't like her touchin' his office. Don't trust her, I guess. If you're so all-fired ready to do somethin', s'pose you could tackle that room since you're gonna be family."

"If Jack gives you any grief, you tell him to see me. I know how to handle him."

How's that for a big, whopping fib? she asked herself. If she knew how to handle Jack, she wouldn't be here in his house preparing to have her heart broken. He was too darn gentlemanly, too nice, too anxious to make her happy. The men in her life didn't act that way—maybe that's why none of them had ever come close to even touching her heart.

Grabbing a napkin from the table, she took a few more pieces of bacon and headed off to explore the house. It didn't take long to discover that the entire place, not just Jack's bedroom, was devoid of frills. The furniture in the living room was leather and tweed, the tables heavy oak. A moose head hung over the fireplace mantel, and the other walls bore the trophies of pronghorn, elk, and deer.

The entire place needed a woman's touch. The animals could stay, but the rooms needed sprucing up. Throw pillows, rugs to warm the hardwood floors, a vase or two brimming with flowers. If she lived here . . . She let the thought slide right on through her head. *This is temporary, Sam. Only temporary.*

She wandered down a hallway off the living room. Through one of the doors she found a library with floor-to-ceiling shelves, and knew she could get lost in a room like this. She'd never had time to read, but she could easily imagine curling up in one of the big leather chairs set on either side of the brick fireplace.

After thoroughly perusing the books on the shelves, she left what could easily become her favorite room in the house. She crossed the hall and went through the closed but unlocked door. Definitely Jack's office.

The familiar fragrance of cigars and aftershave wrapped around her. Closing her eyes, she inhaled the scents, picturing Jack in front of her. His smile, the lift of his brow. She could almost feel him tugging her toward him, lowering his mouth, and kissing her slow and gentle.

Leaving his home—and leaving Jack— would be one of the most difficult things she'd ever had to do. But she'd been through tough times before, she'd known heartache, and she'd always bounced back.

Of course, this time it might be different. This time she might not recover.

She leaned against the bookshelves, studying Jack's office. It was neat, organized, and unadorned, but it seemed to match the rest of the house, not to mention his personality. He didn't go for frills, for the trappings most rich people seemed to love. He liked the wide-open prairies and the small, sometimes under-appreciated things in life like sunrises and sunsets.

Her mama definitely would have liked Jack Remington—even with his faults.

Sweeping her fingers over the bookcase, checking out the titles on the shelves, she found a brown-leather photo album with a gold-leaf border wedged in the far bottom corner. She knew she was snooping, but she couldn't resist taking a peek. After all, it was only a photo album. Jack might not approve of her looking at something personal, but it seemed an easy way to get to know a man who was short on words.

She opened the album, and the first thing she saw was a wildflower pressed beneath the plastic page, with the photo of a pretty young girl above it. She couldn't have been more than fifteen or sixteen, with straight blond hair and a wide smile.

Turning the page, she was treated to even more pictures of the same girl, but a boy was in the photos with her, and in most every one they were hand in hand. He was tall, broad-shouldered, and thin. He had a cowboy hat tilted low on his brow and even though Sam couldn't see the eyes, she could see the off-kilter smile, and knew it was Jack.

He was good looking in a boyish way. He was obviously in love, she could see it in every picture. He had that special smile, that warm gleam in his eyes—the same look she'd seen on his face during the night.

No, no. That wasn't true. That was the look she'd wanted to see, nothing more.

Once more she flipped a page. The young girl was leaning against a tree, her hands resting on her swollen belly. She must have been eight or nine months pregnant, and even though she was far too young to be a mother, her face held a certain glow. On the bottom of the same page, the girl held a bundle in her arms. Jack knelt beside her, looking down at the baby, smiling.

There were no more pictures of the girl after that. No more photos of Jack. Instead, there were fifteen pages, each with one, single photo centered beneath the plastic sheets. They showed the steady progression of a baby growing into a toddler, a child, a teen. They were nothing more than wallet-sized school portraits, the kind kids exchange with friends. They weren't personal. There were no snapshots taken when the boy took his first step, when he blew out the candles on his birthday cakes, when he opened presents at Christmas.

But the pages were worn, the corners dog-eared, as if Jack had looked at the collection nearly every day for sixteen years.

She closed the album and held it against her. Suddenly, she felt as if she'd trespassed on Jack's heartache, and it became clear to her that he'd wanted to be a father—but for some reason, he'd never been given the chance.

Shoving the book back into its place in a far corner of the shelf, she wiped the tears from her eyes and walked across the room. She stood beside the window that looked out toward the barn. A chair had been dragged across the floor, as if Jack had been in here recently but wanted to look outside rather than concentrate on work. She wondered what he looked at—and then she knew.

Beau stood in the middle of the yard, with a rope in his hands. Rufus ran around, barking and kicking up dust, as Beau tried his hardest to lasso the creature.

She must have watched him for nearly five minutes, and when he looked toward the window, as if he knew she was there, she waved. Like the cowboys she'd seen in black-and-white Westerns, he touched the brim of his Stetson in greeting, then went back to his roping.

She liked him instantly. Leaving the office, she walked out of the house. The cool air seeped through the flannel shirt she wore and stung her chest and arms, but the sun was shining, and it felt warm when she tilted her face to drink in the clear blue sky.

Rufus jumped up and pawed at her knees and she knelt, taking a moment to run her fingers through silken fur.

"Do you like dogs?" Beau asked, walking toward her.

"Friendly ones. I've never been all that keen on the ones that growl when I walk by."

She stood, and held out her hand. "I'm Sam."

Beau's eyes narrowed. "Sam?"

Somehow she laughed, but inside she was berating herself for making the slip. "I wanted to be an actress once and my stage name was Samantha." Telling something close to the truth was easier than telling another lie. "Your dad calls me Sam sometimes, too."

"Yeah, I imagine he would."

"Why do you say that?"

"He doesn't talk all that much, and Arabella's got too many syllables," he said, tossing the rope again.

She smiled at his words, at his typical teenage no-nonsense attitude. She picked up a stick and threw it out for Rufus to chase, all the while watching Beau's movements. He and Jack had been apart for sixteen years, but Beau had the same long-legged gait, the same swing to his arms. He even twisted around and stared at her like Jack.

"Dad's not around, if you came out here looking for him."

"I came out here to meet you. Thought it would be nice if we got to know each other."

"Yeah," he said. "Probably."

Rufus ran back with the stick in his mouth and Sam tugged it from between his teeth, then threw it again. "If you're worried about me coming between you and your dad, that's not going to happen."

"I'm not." He looked her up and down. "You're not going to want me to call you mom, are you?"

"I'd rather you just called me Sam."

She saw the first hint of a smile on his face. She walked toward the corral and turned, watching Beau's perfect rhythm as he tossed the rope. "You're awfully good with that."

"Gettin' to be. Takes a lot of practice."

"Think you can teach me?"

Beau laughed, sounding so much like his dad. "Women aren't good ropers."

"And who gave you that piece of misinformation?"

"Crosby."

"Well, Crosby's full of it."

He grinned, nodding slowly. "What do you want to learn to rope for? You're not going out on any cattle drives, and I doubt you'll be branding calves in a few weeks."

"Is there some unwritten code out here that says I can't do those things?"

"I suppose not, but why would you want to?"

"I imagine for the same reasons as you. First, I've never done it, and I like to try new things. Second, I want to be with your dad."

The revelation hit her smack in the face. She wanted to be with Jack more than anything, and when it was time to leave, she wasn't going to bounce back easily.

"As for you teaching me how to rope," she said, "it's an opportunity for us to get to know each other. On top of that, if I don't do something constructive, I'll go stir-crazy."

"You mean my dad didn't give you an

endless amount of chores to do while you're here?"

"No. How about you?"

"I've shoveled shit till I'm blue in the face. I've curried horses, trimmed hooves, learned how to shoe, and polished every piece of leather in that whole blasted barn."

Sam laughed as the somber kid she'd been talking to loosened up and became the boy she really wanted to know. "Did your dad teach you how to do all those things?"

"Yeah." Beau tossed the lasso over Sam's shoulders and pulled it tight. "He can shovel shit better than anyone I've ever seen."

"He's not what you expected, is he?"

"Why do you say that?"

"Because he's nothing like I expected, either. When I met your dad, I expected some snooty millionaire with half a dozen attendants following in his wake. I thought he'd have an attitude, you know, sort of holier than thou."

Beau loosened the rope and pulled it over her head. "I didn't know what to expect. I spent nearly sixteen years wondering what kind of man would ditch his kid."

"So, you came here hoping to find out that he wasn't worth thinking about anymore?"

"Yeah."

"And what do you think?"

Beau shrugged, then worked the rope into

another big circle and tossed it over Sam's shoulders again. "I don't know if he's worth too much trouble or not."

"But you haven't left."

"I like it here. Shoveling shit isn't all that bad."

Smiling, she worked the rope loose and pushed it over her head. She went to Beau and took the lasso from his hands. "Care to show me how to throw this?"

She tried making a circle like she'd seen him do, but she ended up smacking her head and shoulders with the unwieldy piece of rope. "First you've got to learn how to build a loop," he told her. "Hope you aren't in any big hurry."

I've only got a few days, she could have told him, hating the fact that she was going to leave heaven when she liked it so well. Instead, she said, "I've got all the time in the world."

They went into the barn to find a rope. Beau told her there were different lengths, different widths, different stiffnesses and materials, and every cowboy had to have a rope that worked just right for him. Then they got down to serious business.

At noon, with blisters rising on her palms and sore arms and shoulders, she begged Beau to take a break. Lauren appeared fresh and alert from a good night's sleep, and hopped into the Explorer. She'd decided to take advantage of the pretty day to drive the two hours into Sheridan to shop. Sam had declined the invitation to go along, and went to make steak sandwiches and fried potatoes for Beau and Crosby.

They ate at the kitchen table and talked about the cows, about rodeoing, about the changes Crosby had seen on the ranch in sixty-some-odd years, and horses. Beau talked endlessly about the black gelding named Diablo that Jack had given him when he'd first come to the ranch, and Pecos, the dun-colored stallion Jack always rode, who liked the mares and Jack but nothing and no one else.

By one, she'd bundled up in the wonderful coat Jack had given her, and she and Beau were roping again.

At two, several ranch hands came by to introduce themselves, and Sam was beginning to feel more and more uncomfortable with the charade. When Mike Flynn rode into the yard on a white stallion, and she saw the gold cross hanging around his neck, she wanted to run and hide. He looked like the Almighty arriving on a cloud of dust to chastise her for her sins.

"Afternoon," he said. Dismounting, he took off his hat, slapped it against his knee, and walked toward her with his hand extended. "I'm Mike Flynn. Jack's ranch manager and confidant, the man he shares *everything* with."

Sam timidly shook his hand, then shoved it into her pocket. "It's *Pastor* Flynn, isn't it?"

He laughed. "It's Mike." He looked over Sam's shoulder toward the house. "Hey, Cros. You got any coffee on?"

"Yep, but I ain't gettin' it for you."

Mike slid his arm through hers as if it was the most commonplace thing in the world to do and led her toward the kitchen door. "Mind if we have a little chat?"

"About something in particular?"

A slow grin touched his face. "I imagine you already know what I want to talk about, but I'll save it till we're inside, in private."

Oh, good. She'd never been chewed out by a minister before, definitely not by one with jet-black hair, drop-dead-gorgeous green eyes, and the physique of a god. She hoped she wouldn't be struck down by lightning for noticing those things about him, but he didn't fit the classic holy-man mode.

"How do you like your coffee?" he asked her when they entered the kitchen.

"Black."

He set two mugs on the table and filled them to the brim with Crosby's thick brew. "Have a seat."

His simple statement sounded very much like an order, and Sam plopped 'down in the chair and picked up the steaming mug, hoping she could hide her discomfort.

"I'm not here to preach," he said, sitting next to her. He rested his elbows on the table and fingered the cross around his neck. "I take that back. I *am* here to preach."

"You don't have to."

"Someone's got to tell you what you're doing is wrong. Lauren isn't the only one whose feelings are at stake here. There's Crosby, the ranch hands, the people in town who are already talking about you, and then there's Beau. Did either one of you think about the effect this would have on others before you put this scheme in motion?"

Right about now, she felt as small as an ant. "I can't speak for Jack, only for myself. I knew it was wrong, but I did it anyway. I'm not going to lie to you about that. I'd like for it to end, but—"

"Jack's the only one who can stop it," Mike interrupted. "And you're the only one who can make him."

"Me?"

"You could leave. You could go back home and make Jack face the issue."

Sam pushed up from the table and walked to the kitchen window. She looked at Beau currying one of the horses. At Rufus barking at his heels. At the barn and the prairie that seemed to go on forever.

The touch of Mike's hand on her shoulder surprised her. "You don't want to leave, do you?"

Sam shook her head.

"Are you in love with Jack?"

"No . . . I'm not sure."

"A lie's the thing keeping the two of you together, but it's also keeping you apart."

She wiped a tear from her face. "Couldn't you tell Lauren the truth. You're a minister. You could break it to her easily."

"It's not up to me. It's up to Jack, but I haven't been able to convince him."

Sam turned around. "I've tried, too."

"Try harder, Samantha. I meant what I said. You're the only one who can make him stop the charade."

He smiled gently, and put his hat back on. "It was nice meeting you. Hopefully, next time we can be a little more sociable."

Sam sank down into the kitchen chair and sipped at the coffee. Mike was right. Jack did have to tell the truth, and he had to do it soon. She drew in a deep, shaky breath. What they were doing was wrong, very wrong, and if her leaving was the only way to make things right, then that's what she'd have to do.

She only hoped that God and Mike and everyone else would forgive her, because she wanted one more day and night with Jack, one more chance for memories that would be better than any she'd ever had.

seventeen

Sam wandered through the house, capturing memories of Jack's home to store away with one day's worth of delightful experiences. There were the hours she'd spent laughing with Beau, listening to his tales of school, his friends, and most importantly his dad, talk that was underscored by a hint of pride and a certain amount of animosity, not unlike other kids his age. She'd stored away Crosby's cantankerous talk, and Lauren's own special brand of joy and tear-filled woe. These people, in a matter of hours, had become a family she could love.

Tomorrow, they'd be gone—but at least she would have wonderful things to remember.

She touched her lips. They'd never forget the feel of Jack's kiss, nor would her arms forget his embrace. Those two precious things should be enough, but she wanted more. She wanted to know how it would feel to lie with him in his big old bed all night and wake up with him beside her in the morning. She wanted to know what flavor of ice cream he liked, if he preferred Pepsi or Coke, if he wore boxers or Jockeys when he wasn't wearing a skimpy thong.

But those were the kinds of intimate details that could take weeks, months, even years of togetherness to learn, and her time was running out.

She went into his office and stared out the window, sitting finally in the chair where she could watch life going on outside. Mike sat atop his horse, talking to Beau. When he rode off, Beau went back to roping a fence post, which seemed to be his favorite pastime. Rufus chased the rope's shadow, and farther away, high on a snow-dusted rise, she saw Jack riding slowly back to the ranch.

Behind her she heard the phone ring twice before the answering machine clicked on. "Jack, pick up if you're there." Sam's first thought was that the woman on the line might be Arabella. Instead it was someone calling about fabric for the chairs and booths in the Houston restaurant.

Jack didn't seem the kind of man who'd be interested in the colors or design of a restaurant. He seemed more interested in spring roundup and how many head of cattle he could ship to market. But whether or not he enjoyed the nitty-gritty details of his business was something more she wouldn't have the time to learn.

She followed the sway of Jack's body in the saddle as Pecos carried him toward the corral. He dismounted and patted his horse's rump, sending the gelding toward the clumps of grass growing on the farside of the barn.

Beau walked toward him. Father and son laughed together, their body language so similar. They shared a few words, then Jack took the rope in his hands and built a loop so fast and easy that it seemed a natural part of his movements.

She tucked the moment away, along with Jack and Beau going into the barn and bringing out an Appaloosa that looked exactly like the one she'd seen yesterday, grazing in a far-off pasture. Could it possibly be the same? she wondered.

Again the phone rang. Again the answering machine picked up. "Hey, Jack. It's Wes Haskins. Call me. I want to talk about Samantha Jones."

She twisted around, staring at the phone, at the answering machine. Had she heard the man correctly? Had he mentioned her name? Getting up from the chair, she played back the message. The man on the phone, Wes Haskins, was someone she'd never heard of, but it was definitely *her* he wanted to talk with Jack about.

Why?

She laughed at her sudden anxiety. She had nothing to worry about. Nothing to fear. She wasn't in trouble with the law. She hadn't done anything wrong. All she had to do was ask Jack about it when she went outside.

She grabbed a blank piece of paper from his desk and rummaged around for a pen so she could write down the man's name. It wasn't common, and she didn't want to forget. She lifted a wrinkled sheet of paper and a sparkling shoe glistened atop a stack of folders.

Why on earth had Jack kept that one rhinestone shoe? Had he been holding on to a reminder of their first night together? *That's silly,* she thought. *Men aren't sentimental that way.* Still, it brought a smile to her lips.

And then the smile faded.

The words *Wes Haskins—Investigator* glared at her from the wrinkled paper in her hand. They were printed in bold block letters. Beneath them were the words: *Subject, Samantha Jones.*

Her fingers trembled as she read the report. Wes Haskins had found out very little about her past, because there was little to tell. But that didn't make her feel any better.

Jack had had her investigated.

That hurt, more than him wanting her to come to Wyoming for Lauren's sake and no other reason.

She leaned against the desk, wondering what she'd done so wrong in her life to deserve this on top of everything else.

Jack tightened the cinch on the Appaloosa's saddle and adjusted the stirrups. He tied a bedroll on the back, not that he planned to keep Sam out all night, because it was far too cold. But he thought it might be nice to find a quiet spot where they could sit together and watch the stars.

Teaching Sam to ride was something he'd been looking forward to all day. He'd spent sixteen years enjoying the solitude of his rides on the prairie, yet today he'd felt alone, like part of him was missing.

When he heard the screen door he looked over the saddle and watched Sam walk toward him, already bundled up and ready to ride. She had a smile on her face, but it didn't quite reach her eyes. They normally sparkled. Right now, they looked as if she'd been crying.

"Did you find the coyotes?" she asked, standing a good ten feet away from the horse as if she was afraid to get too close.

"Only their trail," Jack answered. "I plan on

going back out tomorrow. Care to go with me?"

"We'll have to see what tomorrow brings."

He folded his arms atop the saddle. "Something troubling you?"

She shook her head.

Jack never had been able to figure out a woman. If you didn't ask what was wrong, they'd get upset. If you asked, they'd say nothing. Why the hell they couldn't give you a straight answer was anybody's guess.

"Beau tells me you spent the day learning to rope."

"Not too well, I'm afraid."

"She's okay, Dad," Beau said, walking out of the barn. "Given a little time she might even be a good cowboy."

A real smile touched her lips when she looked at Beau. She'd obviously taken a liking to his son during the day; but he, himself, seemed to have fallen out of favor. "I'm afraid a good cowboy has to be able to get the rope over a cow's head," she said, laughing while she spoke to his son. "I haven't even figured out the basics of making a decent loop."

"Do you know how to dally?" Jack asked.

"We didn't get that far," Beau told his dad.

"Wanna learn?" he asked Sam.

"Sure. Why not."

Jack ignored her noncommittal attitude, figuring he'd pry the reason for her gloomy mood out of her when they went on their ride. He whistled, and Pecos lifted his head and came toward him. He mounted, the saddle leather creaking beneath him, and untied his rope. "You mind playing the part of a cow?" he asked his son.

"You gotta be kidding."

Jack swung a loop over his head as he and Pecos circled Beau. "Seems to me I did it for you a time or two."

"Can't you use Rufus?"

"He'll just bark at my heels. You, on the other hand, will give me a hard time."

Within minutes, Beau was trying to evade his rope, laughing as he ran, even when the lasso sailed over his shoulders. Jack showed Sam the basics of dallying the rope around the saddle horn, showing her how easily the line could be turned loose if the roped animal or rider got into trouble. Then he showed her how to tie hard and fast, a maneuver he didn't recommend because the rope couldn't be untied quickly—and that could easily spell danger.

Jack circled his horse around Sam and came to a stop. He rested his hands on his saddle horn and looked down at her pretty face. "Are you ready for your riding lesson?"

She avoided his eyes, but nodded.

"Can I ride with you?" Beau asked.

Jack angled his head toward his son. "I'd rather you rode out to the south pasture to check the fence."

"Can't that be done tomorrow?"

"No. And when you get back, you've got homework to do."

"I don't see why that can't wait."

"Because I promised your grandparents I'd make sure it got done. Because you've got a straight-A average to keep up. Because you might decide one of these days that cowboying's too damn hard and you'll want to be a doctor again."

"Fine!" Beau stomped off, disappearing into the barn.

"Do you have to be so hard on him?" Sam asked, anger in her eyes. It wasn't the emotion he longed to see, but it was a hell of a lot better than the blank glare she'd aimed at him for the past fifteen minutes.

"I'm not being hard, I'm being a good father."

"He thinks you're too hard sometimes. He thinks you should lighten up."

"Did he tell you that?"

"Not in so many words."

"Living out here isn't easy, Sam. I'm not going to coddle him."

"No one says you have to, but where does

love fit into the picture? Have you ever come flat out and told him how you feel?"

"That's my business."

"If you haven't told him, Jack, you'd better."

"You're the one who told me actions speak louder than words."

"Sometimes they send mixed signals. If you love Beau, you'd better tell him—because I don't think your actions are getting the message across."

She was right. Too damn right. His actions didn't seem to be making any sense to her, either.

Beau led his horse out of the barn, and he looked over the saddle at Jack. "Since I've got to do everyone else's job while you're out having fun, mind if I borrow the truck tonight?"

"You know the rules," Jack told him. "No license, no driving."

"I don't want to go all that far."

"No."

Beau's jaw tightened. "Fine!" He jumped on his horse and took off at a gallop.

Jack swung down from his saddle, crossed his arms over his chest, and watched Beau head halfway up the rise toward the old twisted cottonwood tree. When Beau stopped, he laughed.

"What's so funny?" Sam asked.

"You'll see."

Beau had a scowl on his face when he galloped back to the barn.

"Forget something?" Jack asked.

"Gloves!"

Beau stormed into the barn, came back out pulling rawhide onto his hands, swung up in the saddle again, and took off.

"What was all that about?" Sam asked.

Pride swelled inside his chest. He might be hard, but Beau was learning fast. "It's about a boy growing into a man."

"Ready for your riding lesson?" Jack asked. He walked toward the Appaloosa and held out a stirrup.

Until that very second Sam hadn't given a moment's thought to being frightened, but the horse looked so big, the saddle looked so high off the ground, and she had no idea how to control the beast once she got on top. She'd nearly forgotten her one and only experience with a horse, nearly forgotten that the beast had tried to take a hunk out of her arm when she'd attempted to mount from the wrong side, nearly forgotten that the casting director at the audition she'd gone to had made her feel like a fool.

Suddenly her hurt feelings about being investigated were eclipsed by her fear of the horse.

"Maybe we shouldn't go riding today," she said, backing away.

"Scared?" The rise of Jack's brow and the cocky manner in which he'd asked the question made her mad at him all over again.

"I'm not scared of anything."

"Then grab on to the saddle horn and put your left foot in the stirrup."

"What if the horse tries to bite me."

"Belle doesn't bite. She's gentle, that's why I picked her for you." Jack took hold of her hand and pulled her toward the horse. "Here, pet her," he said, guiding her fingers over the horse's neck. "Show her you like her. This is one of those moments when actions speak louder than words."

She smoothed her hand over the mare's sleek coat. Belle twisted her head, and Sam started to move away, but Jack's arms folded around her, keeping her from going anywhere. "Don't let her see that you're afraid." His fingers pressed against her belly and she felt the strength of his chest against her back. His whispered words were warm against her ear. "Let her know you're the boss."

He kissed her neck, his lips tender and feeling oh so good against her skin. "I missed you today."

It would have been easy to rest her head against his shoulder and fall under his spell, but she was confused about what he wanted from her, and until she was certain, she wasn't going to let him get the best of her.

"What do I do next?" she asked, pulling his hand away from her stomach and dropping it off to her side.

"You put your *left* foot in the stirrup," he said gruffly.

She did just as he told her, not liking the fact that one foot was pretty much tied to the side of the horse. If Belle took off—she'd probably die.

Jack's hands slid over her hips.

"What do you think you're doing?" she snapped, jerking around to stare at him.

"I'm teaching you how to ride."

"With your hands on my butt?"

She could feel the expelled air from Jack's sigh hitting her temple. "I'm helping you into the saddle, Sam. That's all."

"Well, don't get any other ideas."

She could feel his thumbs on her bottom, and even though he said he was helping, she imagined there was more behind his touch than mere teaching.

"Now," he said, "pull yourself up and throw your right leg over the saddle."

She took a deep breath and did exactly what

Jack told her. Strangely enough, once she was on Belle's back and had her hands firmly gripped around the saddle horn, things didn't look so ominous.

"This isn't so bad," she said, smiling at Jack as she fumbled to put her right foot in the other stirrup.

"You surprise me, Sam."

"Why?"

"I didn't think you were afraid of anything—except flying."

She was afraid of so much more, especially of losing Jack. "It's easy to get hurt if people know your weaknesses. I try my hardest not to show mine."

He leaned against Belle's side. His fingers worked their way over her leg, making small, lazy circles as he studied her face. "You keep people from getting to know you that way, too. Is that what you want?"

"Where I grew up, it was better if people didn't know too much about you. Our worlds are different, Jack, but you and I are an awful lot alike."

"What do you mean?"

"You don't open up much. You hide things from Lauren, from Beau, and who knows who else. I may be open about superficial things, I might joke a lot and tease, but I prefer keeping feelings inside where no one can trounce on them. You do the same thing. That's probably the biggest reason we're both still alone."

"Do you want to be alone?"

She shrugged, wanting to end a conversation that was leading nowhere. There would be time for more talk later, talk about her leaving, talk about him having her investigated, but right now she wanted to gather more memories of life on the prairie, of riding under a big blue sky, because all too soon she'd be alone again.

They rode for nearly an hour through snow, dirt, and prairie grass, catching sight of an occasional jackrabbit, the lone hawk that soared overhead looking for a meal, and the pronghorn that seemed more plentiful than the cows. Jack taught her the difference between a walk, a trot, a lope, gallop, and run, and showed her how to guide Belle not just with the reins, but with the nudge of her knee. She was far from an expert, but she soon felt comfortable sitting astride the beautiful Appaloosa.

But dusk was drawing near, and it was time to talk.

"I want to go home tomorrow," she said, when they reached a rise that looked out on forever.

Jack circled around her and stopped. His lower leg brushed against hers.

"Why?"

"I'm tired of the charade. You don't need me here for Lauren any longer."

"You can't leave until she knows the truth."

Those weren't the words she'd wanted to hear. She'd wanted him to say he needed her here for him—but he'd gone right back to being an employer again. He'd paid her; he wanted his money's worth.

"Tell her the truth, Jack. If you don't, I will."

He looked away, staring off toward the faint line of mountains to the west. "I spent half the day trying to figure out how to tell her. No matter what I say, neither one of us come out looking too good."

"I don't care how I look anymore, Jack. If you want to put all the blame on me, go right ahead. I don't have to live with Lauren, so it doesn't matter."

He looked back at her, his eyes blazing. "I'm not going to put any blame on you. This whole thing's my fault, not yours, and you sure as hell don't have to go because of it."

"The only reason I'm here is because of this charade."

"You're here because I want you here."

"Yeah, to make your sister feel good."

"You think I didn't have any ulterior motives?"

"Everything you do is surrounded by ulterior motives."

"Such as?"

"Such as having me investigated."

"What?"

"I saw the report in your office. I heard Wes Haskins calling to talk to you about me. You tell me why I should stay, when you hired a private investigator to check me out."

"You should stay because I care for you."

"Well, someone ought to teach you how to show it."

"I've shown you every time I've turned around. I've bought you clothes that I handpicked, and I hate to shop. I rode out last night in the cold and brought back an Appaloosa because you said you'd love to have a horse like the one you saw as we drove to the ranch. I've done dozens of things for you, but you keep pushing me away."

"You *paid* me to be here, Jack. You told me you wanted me to come here because of Lauren. A few minutes ago you told me I couldn't leave because of Lauren. Where do I fit into this picture?"

"Ah, hell!"

"Don't ah hell! me, Jack. I think I deserve more than that."

He jerked on Pecos's reins and spun the horse around, riding across the top of the rise at a full run. Suddenly he brought the horse to a halt. He sat there for the longest time, staring at the horizon. Finally, he turned Pecos around and rode slowly back.

Even from a distance Sam could see the heat in Jack's eyes, the anger, and she didn't want to look.

She grabbed the rope from her saddle, needing something to do to keep from going out of her mind. She started building a loop as Beau had shown her, doing her best to circle the rope over her head.

"You won't find much use for your lassoing skills in West Palm Beach," he told her when he neared.

"Nothing says I have to go back to Florida. I might go to Montana or Colorado instead. I hear they need cowboys there."

"I could always use a good hand here," he said, forcing a wink.

"I don't want you to joke about this. I want your promise that you're going to tell Lauren the truth. Once you do, I'm leaving."

"I'll tell her tonight," he stated flatly. "Tomorrow morning at the latest. But there's no telling when I can drive you back to town."

"Don't worry about me. I can find my own way."

He took off his Stetson and plowed his hands through his hair. "Your arm's gonna be sore if you keep that up," he said, staring at the loop circling over her head. "I could probably stir up a calf if you want something to rope besides blue sky."

"I was hoping for something more your size."

"Anything my size would pull you right off Belle and drag you half a mile."

"Should we find out?"

He shook his head in total frustration. "Why don't we just head back to the ranch?"

"Lead the way, Jack. I'll follow."

Yanking on the reins, he dug his heels into the horse's flanks and headed off at a nice steady lope.

Sam let go of the lasso.

It was a fluke. Sheer luck. The rope sailed over Jack's hat and shimmied down his chest. Sam jerked the line to tighten it and dallied fast, holding on to the rope with all her might.

Jack slid over Pecos's rump and landed with a thud in snow, dirt, and clumps of grass. "What the—"

She slipped off Belle, ran across the short stretch of prairie, and pounced on Jack. She straddled his stomach before he came to his senses, took the loose end of the rope and quickly wrapped it around his wrists, again and again and again.

"What the hell do you think you're doing?"

"You were the biggest thing around, and I thought you'd look good flat on your back."

"Let me up."

"Not until I make something clear."

He could have struggled. He could have escaped, but he didn't move. Instead, his jaws ground together as she tied knots around his wrists.

"Make your point."

"I've been hurt in my life, Jack. More than you can imagine. But you've hurt me more than all those other hurts put together."

"How have I done that?"

"You paid me to come here for your sister, but you figure you might as well have a little something for yourself, too. Well, I'm not cheap. I'm not a whore, and I'm not going to give you something just because you think you've paid for it."

"Is that what you think?"

"I don't know what to think, Jack. You tell me you want me to come here and then you say you don't know why the hell you do want me to come here. You tell me you trust me, and then you have me investigated."

"If you'd read the damned report, you would have noticed that it didn't say a thing. You're pure as the driven snow as far as the investigator's concerned."

"I don't care what the report says. I want to

know why you had me investigated in the first place."

"*Why*? You charged nearly nine thousand dollars to one of my accounts. You stole a sewing machine, you masqueraded as my fiancée at Lauren's country club when I wasn't even there. I didn't know where to find you—and believe you me, I wanted to find you. You looked like you were in some kind of trouble. *That*, Samantha, is why I had you investigated."

"Once you found me, once you learned that I wasn't some two-bit crook, you should have called off your investigator."

"I did!"

"When?"

"Last night. Right after the fax came in."

"Last night!" She wrapped another length of rope around his wrists. "You should have done it right after you learned the truth."

"Believe it or not, I've had other things on my mind!"

"Well, I'm going to walk out of your life again, and then you don't have to worry about my past or my present or my future. That will give you a few less things on your mind."

She pushed up from his chest.

"Untie my hands, Sam!"

"You're a cowboy," she shouted, climbing onto Belle's back and grabbing the reins. "You know all about knots and ropes. Get out of them yourself."

Damn fool woman!

Jack struggled to his feet as soon as Sam rode off. He managed to step out of the loop she'd thrown over his shoulders, but his hands were another matter. She'd knotted a good ten feet of rope around his wrists and arms as she'd sat on his chest and berated him.

When he got his hands on her . . .

Ah, hell!

He whistled for Pecos—and waited.

He whistled again, but the horse didn't come.

"Damn fool horse!" he mumbled, bending over and doing his best to pick up his Stetson off the ground. "See if I ever give you a lump of sugar again."

He managed to get his hat on his head and started to walk. Once more he whistled, then blew out a frustrated sigh, watching a cloud form in the chilly air.

"Damn fool woman! You're gonna pay for this."

He put his hands up to his mouth and started gnawing at the knots as he walked. He was a good hour from the ranch, one solid hour he could spend thinking up a long list of ways to get even. Tying Sam up sounded good for starters.

Within the first two miles or so he'd worked the knots free with his teeth and in the last two or three miles, with his feet aching something awful, he decided what to do to Sam.

He was going to murder her.

It was dark when he reached the ranch. Pecos was unsaddled and in the corral with Belle and Diablo. "Just you wait till tomorrow," he told the horse when it tried to make amends by coming to the railing and whinnying softly. "No carrots, no apples, no sugar. As far as I'm concerned, you're dog meat."

Pecos kicked up his heels and galloped to the farside of the corral.

Sam Jones, on the other hand, wasn't going to have the chance to run away.

He went into the barn, found a good strong rope, and headed for the house.

He slammed through the kitchen door. Beau was at the table tending a cut on his hand, and looked up. "You made it back."

"Yeah."

"Arabella said you might be gone a while."

"She did, did she?"

"Yeah."

Jack grabbed a beer from the refrigerator, twisted off the cap, and took a swig.

"I rode about two miles of fence," Beau told him. "Didn't see anything down."

"Good."

"Have you given any more thought to me using the truck tonight?"

"The answer was no. That hasn't changed."

He took another swallow of beer, watching the way Beau gritted his teeth, but he ignored the anger. It would go away shortly. "Where's Arabella?" he asked.

"Upstairs," Beau spat out. "She said she was going to take a bath."

Jack unconsciously looked up at the ceiling, as if he could see the object of his rage through the wood. "Tell Crosby not to expect Arabella and me for dinner."

"Why?"

"We've got some talkin' to do."

Jack caught the shrug of Beau's shoulders from the corner of his eye as he stormed from the kitchen.

When he reached the living room, Lauren rose regally from her perch on the couch, a thick magazine in her hands. "Jack. I'm so glad you're back. Do you have a moment to look at—"

"No!"

"But I found this wedding cake, and I thought it would be perfect for you and Arabella. Of course, I'd have to make a few—"

Lauren stopped talking when Jack aimed his glare at her.

"My goodness, you look upset."

"I'm going to kill my fiancée."

"Oh, dear."

"If you hear screams, don't bother coming up. There's a strong possibility something might get aimed at you."

"I don't suppose you need a referee?"

"No!"

Jack took the stairs two and three at a time. His bedroom door was locked, which added to his anger, but it didn't stop him. He simply reached above the door, took down the key, and a moment later stepped into the room, slammed the door behind him, and locked it.

He pocketed the key.

Sam stood in front of the closet wearing nothing more than a pair of panties and a matching bra.

She looked good. Damn good! And right then he could picture her lying in her coffin wearing nothing else.

She grabbed the white shirt she'd worn last night and held it in front of her. "You look upset."

"Upset? What gives you that idea?"

"I haven't seen you frown like that since I dropped your tuxedo outside your hotel-room door."

He took a long, cool swallow of beer and sat down in his chair. "Took me half an hour to get the knots untied. Do you have any idea how mad you get walking across a prairie in thirty-degree weather, trying to work knots loose with your teeth?"

"I imagine a person could get a little upset. But do *you* have any idea how mad you get when you find out someone is investigating your background?"

"The only reason you should be upset is if you have something to hide. Do you?"

"No, and even if I did, I wouldn't tell you."

"Why not?"

"Because you wouldn't believe me any-way."

"Try me."

"No!"

"I'll get it out of you if it's the last thing I do."

"How?"

He grinned as he worked the loop over his head, watching her every move, wondering which way she'd go.

"What are you doing?" she asked.

"Same thing you did to me."

"That was a fluke. I couldn't do it again in a million years, even if I tried."

"It didn't feel like a fluke when my butt hit the ground. Didn't feel like a fluke when you landed on my stomach and started tying my hands."

"I'm sorry."

"You don't sound sorry."

"Okay, so I'm not. That doesn't give you any reason to rope me, now."

"I've got a hell of a lot of reasons to lasso you."

"Name one."

He shook his head. "I'm not in the mood for games. Make your move, Whiskey. Let's see if you can get away."

eighteen

Jack watched Sam's gaze dart from the bedroom door, to the bathroom, to the loop circling over his head. It was just the perfect size, the lasso was the perfect length, and she was the perfect target. Once he roped her, he planned a slow revenge.

"You'll regret doing this," she said, clutching his white shirt tightly to her chest.

"I have very few regrets in life. I won't be adding this one to the list."

"Couldn't we call a truce?"

"You've got something white in your hands," he told her, looking at the shirt clutched in her fingers. "If you want to wave it over your head in surrender, be my guest. I'll enjoy the view—but I still plan on roping you."

"Then do it and get it over."

"There's no fun in roping a stationary target. I want you to run."

He could almost hear her teeth grinding as she looked from right to left. She thought she was being clever when she took a step toward the bedroom door, but he could see in her eyes that she was planning to bolt the other way. And he was ready.

The moment she moved, he threw the rope, and it slipped perfectly over her shoulders and her full, luscious breasts. He pulled it taut when it reached her waist.

She was trapped.

"Let me go." She struggled against the rope, but he could hear a hint of laughter behind her words.

"Not yet."

He pulled her toward him, right between his widespread knees, and slid his fist up to the honda to keep the rope from slipping loose. He didn't want her to run. Not this time.

Her hot brown eyes stared down at him. The anger in her expression was mixed with a touch of fear and a hint of excitement, and all those things made him rethink his plan of revenge. He'd hurt her. Not intentionally, but he'd hurt her just the same, and she deserved better than that from him—from everyone.

But that didn't mean he planned to loosen the rope.

"What are you going to do?" she asked softly.

"For starters—" He grinned, lightly caressing her cheek. "I'm going to apologize for the investigation. If I'd known as much about you then as I know about you now, I would have known you weren't a con."

"Do you mean that?"

"Every word. As for the charade—it's over."

"You told Lauren?"

"I haven't had time, but I will first thing tomorrow. I know that doesn't make us exactly even, but I'm gonna look at it that way."

She stared at the rope, at his fist holding the knot against her belly. "I'm all tied up. That doesn't seem too even to me."

"I didn't say you were out of trouble. I just said that there's no money standing between us. No charade. No job. I want *you*, Sam, for purely selfish reasons."

"As far as apologies go, that one's somewhat acceptable. So what are you going to do now? Let me go?" she asked, struggling far too passively to make her efforts look real.

"Actually, Sam, I'm going to drive you out of your mind. Slowly. Very slowly. I'm going to make you forget about leaving. I'm going to make you beg me to stop at the same time you're begging me not to stop."

Sam dragged in a deep breath and willed herself not to cry. He wanted her even though she'd lassoed him and pulled him off his horse. Even though she'd left him stranded out in the cold.

This wonderfully erotic thing going on between them wasn't a charade. It wasn't a job— he wanted her, really and truly wanted her.

And she wanted Jack Remington.

"You know, Jack," she said, enjoying the feel of his fingers toying with the elastic on her panties, "this is a little, well, awkward. Wouldn't you like to just go to bed."

He shook his head slowly. "We'll get to bed eventually, unless you holler stop. Right now, I want you right where you are."

He hauled her a little closer, and she made no attempt to struggle. Telling him to stop was the furthest thing from her mind. Pulling the white shirt from her hands, he tugged it from under the rope and threw it behind him. His gaze blazed over her body and she felt herself begin to tremble.

Reaching out, he hooked a finger under one bra strap and she could feel the heat of his knuckle as it slid over her skin, all the way down to the cup.

She swallowed hard as he stared at the silk covering her breasts, at the pale white skin of her stomach, and the tiny triangle of diaphanous green fabric that masqueraded as intimate lingerie.

"Are those the panties and bra you swore I'd never see you in?" he asked.

She nodded slowly, and smiled. "All three hundred and twenty dollars' worth."

His gaze trailed back up to her eyes. "Do they only come in green?"

"I remember seeing them in pink. They were in yellow and lavender, too."

He traced the plunging top of the bra, his rough fingertip burning her tender, oh-so-sensitive flesh. "Call the store tomorrow," he ordered. "Tell them to send you a set of each—overnight FedEx—and charge them to me."

"Why?"

"Because I like them. I like looking at you in them."

He let the rope drop between them and slipped his hands over the soft curve of her bottom. His head lowered, and he slid the tip of his tongue along the top edge of the panties. Her insides throbbed, and she reached out and wrapped her hands around his neck to keep from crumpling.

He caressed her thighs from the outside to the inside, his fingers tantalizing her senses, making her throb with desire as they reached between her legs and skimmed slowly over the silk that was so thin he might as well have been touching her skin.

Gooseflesh rose on her arms and her legs quivered. A deep, pulsing need rumbled inside her.

"Make love to me," she begged.

"That's what we're doing, Sam. Very slowly." He leaned back in the chair, casually watching her breasts rise and fall. "Now, why don't you take off your bra."

"Wouldn't you like to do it for me?"

One eyebrow rose as he shook his head. "I want to watch."

Breathing became difficult. She'd never done a striptease before, never let a man study her body—but she was enjoying every moment.

She took one step away from the intense heat of his body, but not so far that he couldn't reach out and grab her if she succumbed to the euphoria that was making her weak. Her eyes trailed down his dusty shirt, to the big silver buckle he wore, and even lower. She could see that he was more than ready, yet he was trying to look cool and in control.

He'd started this little game. But it was one she could play just as well.

Slowly, she drew one bra strap over her shoulder until it dangled at her elbow. She did the same with the second, watching the way his eyes burned as they traveled from her face, to her shoulders, to her breasts. His Adam's apple rose and fell in time with his chest. She circled her silk-covered nipple with her index and middle finger, and listened to his sudden intake of breath.

She couldn't believe she was doing these things, but she wanted to do them—for Jack.

For herself.

Seduction was much more fun than she'd ever imagined.

She stuck two fingers in her mouth and drew them out slowly, then ran them over her chin, along her neck, between her breasts and all the way down to the top of her panties. "Want more?" she asked, swirling them around her navel.

A slow smile touched his lips as he nodded.

She reached behind her and released the hook on her bra, then let the silk drift down to the floor. Heat rushed through her face when he looked at her like a man ready to consume every ounce of her flesh. He reached out, and she stepped back. "No touching, Jack. Not yet."

"I thought this was my little game."

"This isn't a game," she said, cupping her breasts in her hands, swirling her thumbs over her nipples. "It's foreplay." She licked her lips. "Stand up, Jack."

He rose slowly, his eyes following the movement of her fingers.

"Take off your shirt," she instructed. "It's my turn to watch."

With agonizingly slow movements, his fingers moved down the buttons, releasing each one, then tugging the shirt from his body. The light from the fire she'd lit in the hearth glimmered on his skin. Muscles rippled on a hard, flat stomach. They bulged in his arms, recounting years of wrestling bulls, roping steers, and working from sunup until sundown.

Game playing ceased to be fun once her body began to ache with need. She wanted him to wrap her up in his arms. Wanted him to carry her to bed.

She beckoned him with the curl of her finger.

But he didn't move. He just stood there, staring at her, his eyes growing hotter by the moment. It was her turn to swallow, and she knew she'd just lost all control of the game.

"Come here," he said, his voice deep and raw.

Like a woman in a trance she moved toward him. His big, rough hands spread over her belly and wrapped around her waist, and before she knew what had happened he swept her up in his arms.

"Is this what you want, Sam?"

She nodded, as he laid her down on the bed

and straddled her thighs. She could feel the leather of his boots at her calves, could feel his jeans brushing her skin. His big silver belt buckle gleamed in the light from the bed lamp.

He caressed her breasts and lowered his body over hers. The instant their lips touched, sparks flew. Great, huge soaring bolts of electricity that could easily set the room on fire.

Cold silver rubbed against her belly, while Jack's warm hands swept down her sides and whispered over her legs. In one swift movement he spread them apart and pulled them over his shoulders.

He looked up at her and grinned. "Hold on tight, Sam. You're in for the ride of your life."

Even if she'd wanted to protest, she couldn't. She lost all control the moment his fingers pushed her panties aside and his dangerously hot tongue swirled over the very center of her being.

She latched on to his hair like a pair of reins, but instead of pulling him to a stop, she gave him leeway to do whatever he wanted.

What he wanted, apparently, was to drive her out of her mind as his teeth nipped gently, and his tongue circled her over, and over, and over again.

"Make love to me," she begged for the second time, but he looked up at her and laughed.

"We've been making love since you pulled me off Pecos's back today." He licked her again. "Keep begging, Sam. I'll know when it's time to stop."

She could feel the pad of his thumb against her, rubbing, teasing, while his mouth ravaged her and made her buck.

A moan escaped from down deep in her throat, and he looked up at her. "You like that?" he asked, watching her eyes.

She nodded.

He did it again and again and when he didn't think she could take any more, he rose, pulled her panties from her legs, and released his belt buckle.

She was gasping for breath when she raised up on her elbows and watched him unzipping his jeans. "Oh, God, Jack. Have I died and gone to heaven?"

"Not yet."

He swung his legs over the side of the bed and rid himself of his boots and every last stitch of clothing. He'd thought about dragging her into the shower with him, but he was about ready to burst, and all he wanted was to press her into the bed and bury himself inside of her.

Jerking open the drawer in the bedside table, he searched for a foil pouch. He found a cigar, a lighter, and a set of keys, but the damned condoms were missing.

"Hell!"

"What's wrong?" she asked, sitting up in bed beside him.

"No condoms."

"Never fear." She slipped off the bed and strolled slowly across the room as if he could hold on forever. She had him so turned on he was afraid he was going to explode just watching her.

The moonlight flooding the room glistened on her body, over every silken curve as she bent over and fumbled through that damn black tote she always carried around. Finally, she turned and smiled. "I got these on the way to the airport—just in case."

She held a black box in her hands, and when she dumped it upside down condoms rained onto the floor. She scooped one up and tossed it to him, then walked with that sexy and provocative sway toward him. Her breasts bounced, her thighs rubbed together, and he drew in a deep breath.

She plucked the pouch from his hands. "May I?"

He chuckled low. "Be my guest." He tried not to lose himself in the feel of her fingers working the condom over every hard inch of him, cupping him, squeezing him, rubbing her hand up and down over him while her naked hips gyrated right in front of his eyes.

When she was done, she crawled ever so slowly onto the bed and held out her arms. "I'm ready, Jack."

He loved her.

All doubts had just flown out of his mind.

Stretching over her, he captured her mouth, tasting her sweetness, and nudged her legs apart. He felt her wrap them around his waist, felt her fingers nestling into his hair as he eased himself into her, and with a rhythm as old as time, he began a leisurely, gentle love-making.

This was more than lust and desire, it was the need to hold on to someone who made him feel so damn good that she pushed sanity and reason and everything else right out of his head.

"What are you thinking?" she asked, cupping his face in her hands as she lay beneath him with a smile on her face.

"I was just thinking how good it feels being inside of you."

She drew in a deep breath and let it out slowly. "Drive me crazy, Jack. Think later, okay?"

He laughed, and rolled over so she was straddling him. "Why don't you show me how well you learned to ride today."

With a grin that touched his heart and made him feel as if he'd swelled a good inch or two more, she moved up and down on top of him in the most graceful, fluid motion he'd ever seen, while waving one arm in the air like she was queen of the rodeo.

Damn!

He grabbed hold of her, flipped her onto her back, and plunged into her body. Every nerve ending screamed with pleasure as he moved in and out, faster and faster and faster.

Her fingernails dug into his back, scraping his skin.

"Don't stop!" she begged. "Oh, God, Jack. Don't stop."

He moved his hand between her thighs and teased her soft, warm wet flesh, finding the spot where the friction and heat of his fingers would drive her crazy.

"Stop, Jack! Oh, God, please. Stop!"

His mouth swept over hers, swallowing her plea.

When her breathing became pants, when her moaning rumbled in his throat, when he felt the scream inside of her, he thrust one more time, and stilled, memorizing the moment, the feel of her throbbing around him, the sensations that were far more fantastic than anything he'd ever known.

*　　*　　*

Jack woke tangled in Sam's hair and legs. The sheet covered her only to the waist, and her soft creamy flesh was right there at his fingertips, ready to explore.

He rolled over on his side, propped his head up with his hand, and played connect the dots with the freckles on her chest.

She purred in her sleep, and he enjoyed the sound. He could see the movement of her eyes beneath the almost transparent skin of her eyelids, and when he lightly swirled his fingertip over her nipple, enjoyed watching it wrinkle and harden under his touch.

"I could lie here and let you do that for hours," she whispered.

"That's what I had in mind. It's Sunday—time to relax. Everyone should be leaving for church when the sun comes up, and the house will be quiet, except for the sound of you moaning."

She smiled. "I've never been to church," she confided, her voice soft, hesitant, as he rested his hand on her belly and watched the play of emotions on her face. "Well, that's not exactly true. I did go once." She opened her eyes and looked up at the ceiling. "Mama didn't come home one Sunday morning. I'd heard what sounded like gunshots during the night, and I was afraid something had happened to her. She'd taught me how to pray when I was little, but I had the feeling that praying in bed wasn't as good as praying in church—and I wanted God to hear my prayers to keep Mama safe. I put on my best dress—one that Mama had gotten for me at the Salvation Army—and walked to the closest church I could find."

She turned on her side, tucked her hands under her cheek, and watched his eyes when she spoke. "An old lady came up to me. I remember everything about her. She had on a pink sweater with a fur collar and a matching pillbox hat. Her skin was dark brown and wrinkled and she had circles of rouge on both her cheeks that was nearly as red as her lipstick. "I don't think you belong here, honey," she said. "This church is for colored people."

Jack swept a curl away from her face, tucking it behind her ear. "Did you stay?"

She shook her head. "They were singing and praising the Lord and shouting hallelujah and I knew the lady was right. I didn't belong there. Besides, my prayers had always been rather quiet, and I decided maybe Mama was right."

"About what?"

"That going to church didn't matter all that much. That being good inside was what really counted."

"I would have liked your mother."

She scooted close and kissed him. "She would have liked you, too."

Jack slid an arm under her waist and pulled her on top of him. He felt himself swell and harden and watched her sit up and lower herself until he was sheathed tight inside. He didn't consider himself a very religious man, but right now he was having a very heavenly experience.

She smiled as she rode him, slow, easy, teasing the hair on his chest and belly with her fingertips. Closing her eyes, her head fell back as her breathing deepened, and she tested different angles, getting the most pleasure out of every up and down stroke.

Rolling her beneath him, he took over, making soft, sweet love with her. This wasn't fiery like before, this was tender, joyous, a time for watching the different degrees of delight sweeping across her face. And then he kissed her, holding her tight as they exploded together, sharing a moment in time that was so phenomenal that he wanted to rise up and shout hallelujah!

nineteen

Jack shot up in bed when he heard the coyote howl. It was close. Too damn close.

"What's wrong?" Sam asked, rolling over in bed, sliding her arms around him.

"Coyotes. Listen."

He heard the howls again, and this time the chickens raised a ruckus. When the horses started kicking at the fence, he rolled out of bed, pulled on his jeans and shirt, and ran down the stairs. He grabbed a rifle from the mudroom, shoved his feet into his boots, and burst through the back door, out toward the corral.

Pecos, Belle, and Diablo were lit by the moonlight. They were restless, their eyes wide with fright as they ran around the enclosure.

"Damned coyotes!" Crosby muttered, pushing open the gate. He closed it behind himself and walked up to Diablo, calming the gelding with gentleness and inbred horse sense.

"Are you going to go after them?" Sam asked, standing at Jack's side, her hands shoved into the pockets of her jeans to keep them warm.

"Yeah. They're getting too damn brave, thinking they can come around here in the middle of the night." He wrapped an arm around her shoulders. "I might be gone for a day or two. Think you can stand it here without me?"

She looked at him and grinned. "I'm going with you."

Jack frowned, and shook his head. "You're not doing any such thing. You barely know how to ride, and you definitely don't know how to shoot."

She rose up on the toes of her boots and looked him in the eye. "I know how to keep you warm, and if you're out all night, you just might need something more than a bedroll."

"Sounds tempting," he said, wishing right now they were back in bed, learning a few more ways to please each other. "But . . . I was thinking about taking Beau."

Crosby closed the corral gate and limped toward Jack. "Beau ain't here."

"What do you mean?"

"He left a good hour ago. Long before sunup. I was in the kitchen fixin' coffee and he told me you'd said he could take the truck."

Jack shoved a hand through his hair. "I didn't do any such thing."

"Well, take it out on him, not me."

What was the kid thinking? Jack had told him no—but he hadn't listened. He shot a scowl at Crosby. "Did he tell you where the hell he was going?"

"No, and I didn't ask."

Anger mixed with fear washed through Jack as the events of sixteen years ago rushed out of his memory. He'd taken a truck, too. It was the middle of the night, and he'd been told to stay at home—but he hadn't listened.

He felt Sam's hand on his arm. "Are you going to look for him?"

"Yeah, for what it's worth."

"What do you mean?"

"Do you think hunting him down and dragging him back to the house, then putting him on restriction for a month will make an irresponsible kid stay put?"

She looked toward the corral, far from his angry eyes. "I suppose not."

"That's right, it won't. As soon as I get my hands on him, he's packing his things."

Sam grabbed his arm. "You can't send him away."

"I can, and I'm going to." Jack looked at the

disgust in Sam's eyes. "I don't want a kid around who can't obey the rules."

"All he did was take the truck. Is that any reason to send him away?"

"It's reason enough."

"Did your dad send you away every time you got in trouble?"

"No, but this is different."

"Why, because Beau hasn't lived here all his life?"

"Drop it, Sam."

"If you think I'm going to let you off the hook where Beau's concerned, you're dead wrong. Someone's got to talk some sense into you, Jack Remington, and it might as well be me."

Jack tossed a brown bag full of sandwiches Crosby had concocted into the backseat of the fancy Dodge pickup he'd bought last year but rarely drove. He preferred his old Ford—but there was no telling what part of the country it was in now.

He had every intention of finding it—and his foolhardy son.

He'd called all the ranch hands he could reach, sent two of them out looking for coyotes, and asked every one to keep an eye out for Beau. If they saw him, they were to make him stay put until they got hold of Jack. He'd give the kid a talking to that he wouldn't soon forget. If his own dad had done that to him a few times, Beth might not have died, and he might have spent the past sixteen years raising his own son.

Now all he could do was worry.

The morning was cold, the ground covered with frost. He thought about black ice on the highway, and a kid driving on roads that weren't familiar. He pounded his fist against the side of the truck and tried to push away the worry of all that could go wrong.

Behind him he heard light footsteps in the gravel and felt Sam pressing her hand against his back. "Want some coffee?"

He turned, took the cup she offered him, and watched her through the steam. Her hair was braided, and a few curls hung over her brow. Her cheeks were red, making the freckles across her nose and cheekbones almost disappear. The dark circles she'd always had beneath her eyes were gone. Wyoming was good for her.

She was good for him. She couldn't take away his fears for Beau's safety, but she could ease them a little, just by being close.

He took a sip of coffee and set the white mug on top of a fence post. "You ready to go?"

She nodded as she slid into the truck. Driving into Sheridan was probably foolish. The boy could have gone toward Cheyenne, or joy-riding on old cattle trails. But he'd exhausted every other possibility he could think of, calling the people he knew in town and on the surrounding ranches. He'd even called the sheriff, but no one had seen Beau or the old familiar Ford. Driving two hours into town seemed his final option.

Jack was just climbing into the truck when Mike turned into the drive and pulled his pickup to a stop next to Jack.

"Mornin'," Jack said.

Mike tipped his best Sunday hat to Sam, and smiled, then aimed his eyes at Jack. "Heard anything from Beau yet?"

"No. Sam and I are driving into Sheridan. Don't know if we'll find him, but I'll go crazy sitting around here waiting for him to show up."

"I got a call from Tom Donovan a little while ago. I don't know if this means anything or not, but he asked me to tell you to keep Beau away from his daughter."

"What's Beau done to Tynna?"

"Probably nothing—but Tom's protective. He told me Tynna and Beau have been on the phone most every night—all night—and Tynna wasn't around this morning. He's afraid Beau's going to get her in trouble."

Jack closed his eyes, and all he could see was Beth's father delivering similar words to Jack's dad. "If you see Tom at church, tell him not to worry. Beau's leaving—probably tomorrow."

Mike frowned. "That's a message I won't deliver, Jack. You've been wanting that kid for sixteen years; don't let one incident blow the chance you've got to finally be together."

"Save your preaching for church. I've already made up my mind."

Jack jumped into the truck and slammed the door. He rolled down the window. "If you see Beau..." Jack shook his head. "Make him come home with you, okay? He doesn't have a license, and I don't feel comfortable with him driving all alone."

Mike smiled, fingering the cross around his neck. "He'll be okay, Jack. Put this in God's hands. Please. And don't worry."

Worrying about Beau came easy. He'd been doing it for sixteen years. Even if he did put it in God's hands, he'd still go crazy until he found his son.

Gunning the pickup's engine, Jack drove away from the ranch and headed toward the highway. Sam moved to the middle of the seat, fastened her lap belt, and put a comforting hand on his thigh.

They drove in silence for the longest time.

It was nearly 8:00 A.M. and sunrise had long ago come and gone. The sky was cloudless, beautiful, the same perfect kind of morning when Beth had died. He couldn't bear to go through another day like that.

"Penny for your thoughts," Sam said.

They were too grim to repeat. "You don't want to know."

She squeezed his leg. "Mike's right, Jack. Beau *will* be okay. I know it."

"Life doesn't come with any guarantees."

"I didn't think it did." She stared silently at the road ahead, watching the sights, watching for the truck. Out of the corner of his eye he could see her look toward him again.

"Do you really want to send Beau away?"

He shrugged. "I don't want him getting Tynna pregnant and screwing up both their lives. I've been there before, and I know what trouble it causes."

"He could get a girl pregnant just as easily in LA."

"He could, I suppose, but at least in LA he'll have other distractions besides girls. He could play sports again. Go to a good school."

"That's not what he wants, and you know it. He came here because of you. All he wants is your attention—and love."

Jack laughed. "I've been trying like hell to

figure out why he'd want to be with me, especially after I abandoned him."

"Because there's a special connection between the two of you. Probably the same kind of connection there was between me and my mother."

"You *lived* with your mother. There's a big difference."

"Is there? My mother was a drug addict with a very expensive habit. She may have had a heart of gold, but she sold herself for whatever she could get on the street." She sighed and looked away. "I never knew my dad because Mama didn't know which one of her clients had gotten her pregnant."

He could see her biting her lip, and when she turned toward him her eyes were red. "I'll tell you what real abandonment is, Jack. It's when your mother is too high on drugs to remember which hooker friend she left you with. It's when your mother goes out with a rich john and forgets for two or three days that she even has a daughter. Don't tell me you abandoned Beau, because you didn't. You gave him up to people you felt could give him the best home."

"Because I didn't have the guts to care for him myself."

"You were sixteen, Jack. Give yourself a break."

"Did anyone give your mother a break?"

"No, but she didn't have a good family to give me to, either. She did what she thought was right. Just as you did. She wasn't always around for me, Jack. When she was, it was wonderful. When she wasn't, well, I still knew she loved me. Beau knows you love him, too. I imagine he's always known."

"So why did he take off with the truck?"

"Because he's a teenage boy who wants to see just how far he can push you."

"I think he's reached my limit."

Sam smiled. "He'll push further, Jack. Just wait."

Put it in God's hands, he told himself, and prayed God would hear his pleas.

Sam spent the next half hour counting hawks on the fence posts and the myriad herds of pronghorn scattered across the prairie. Hardly a car had passed them, but Jack continued to hope.

"What's that over there?" Sam asked, pointing east of the highway.

Jack saw the downed fence posts, the old lean-to that had been knocked over, and then he saw the sun hit the chrome bumper of his old Ford.

He slammed on the brakes as he pulled off the road, set the emergency brake, and shoved out of the truck. He jumped the ditch, the downed barbed wire, and ran toward the overturned truck. The cab was flat, and all Jack could see were torn jeans and a bloody leg.

Twisting around, he shouted at Sam, "Call nine-one-one. Oh, God. Tell them to hurry."

twenty

$\mathcal{T}he$ _waiting room_ smelled like alcohol and pine-scented disinfectant, and the occasional people walking through spoke in hushed tones. Rooms like this were a horrible place to wait, Sam thought, as she stood silently against a wall. They made you worry instead of cheering you up and giving you hope.

That's what she was existing on now—pure hope.

Jack paced, just as he'd been doing for the past hour, while waiting for a doctor, a nurse, for anyone to come out of the operating room and tell him that Beau would be okay. He hadn't sat down. He'd refused the coffee and sandwich she'd brought him. He didn't want to be comforted or given any kind of false cheer.

He didn't want or need anyone now—except his son.

Lauren sat next to Mike on a sofa, staring at the swinging doors and the empty hallway beyond. Mike's head was bent, and he was holding his cross. Praying.

The sheriff had come by the hospital an hour after Beau went into surgery and told Jack that it looked like the truck had gone off the highway at somewhere close to eighty miles an hour. There were two dead pronghorn on the road, and until he could talk with Beau, all he could assume was that Beau had swerved to keep from hitting a herd running across the highway. The pickup had torn through barbed wire and struck an old log line shack that should have been ripped down years ago. The truck rolled three times—at least—before it came to a stop upside down.

Beau wasn't wearing his seat belt. If he had been . . . no one wanted to venture a guess.

Tynna Donovan hadn't been with Beau, Mike had learned from her dad. She'd sneaked out of the house and gone to a girlfriend's during the night, sometime after she and Beau had had a fight on the phone. Tynna told her dad that Beau wanted to talk, and all anyone could figure out was Beau had taken the truck so he could see his girlfriend face-to-face.

The story was all too familiar. All too tragic.

Now Beau was in the hospital—paying for being young.

It seemed an eternity before a doctor came through the doors. He smiled as he walked toward Jack, and put his hand on his arm. Sam could hear some of his words. "He got banged up pretty bad, Jack. He came through surgery okay. Now all we can do is wait—and watch."

Sam listened, trying to absorb all the information. Beau's legs were broken, and they'd had to set one with a pin. Four broken ribs, some internal bleeding, a head injury—but no brain damage. A lot of scrapes and cuts would leave him black-and-blue.

Sam watched Jack stare at the doctor, looking for words of encouragement, but he heard nothing more than "wait."

Jack came toward her, his red and swollen eyes attempting a smile. He ran his hand through his hair, and for the first time Sam noticed it bore traces of Beau's blood. "Are you okay?" he asked, as if she was the one who needed consoling.

She wanted to be there for *him*, not the other way around, but her tears fell. "I'm scared, Jack. So darn scared."

He pulled her into his arms, and she rested her head against his chest, listening to the steady beat of his heart beneath her cheek. She didn't know how long they stood that way. Five minutes, maybe ten, but slowly she raised her head, and he gently kissed her brow.

"Is there anything we can do?" Mike asked.

"Call Crosby," Jack answered. "He'll pretend disinterest, but he's probably worried sick."

"I'll call him," Lauren said, rising from the sofa. Sam stepped away and Lauren hugged her brother. Wiping a few silent tears from her eyes, she smiled at Sam, then walked down the hall.

"Is she all right?" Jack asked Mike, showing more concern for his sister, for everyone else, than he was for himself at the moment.

"She's worried about you. We all are."

"I'm fine," Jack said. "Tired. Frightened."

"Do you want to talk?" Mike asked.

"No. Not now."

Jack slumped down on a sofa, leaned his head against the back, and closed his eyes.

Sam sat on the chair across from him and watched the movement beneath his eyelids. He wasn't asleep. He was thinking, praying, the same thing he'd done since morning. The hours passed by slowly, and finally he slept.

It was nearly eight when he woke.

"I didn't miss the doctors, did I?" he asked almost frantically. "They haven't given you an update, have they?"

"No," Sam said. "Not yet."

He paced again, and picked at the cold sandwich Mike and Lauren had brought back from their own dinner two hours before. He took a drink of lukewarm coffee, looking at his sister and friend. "Why don't you go back to the ranch," he told them. "We'll call you if there's any change."

"I'd rather stay," Lauren said, but Jack shook his head.

"You're tired, and you'll sleep better in bed. Go on home and get some rest. If you want to come back tomorrow, bring some things to spruce up Beau's room. I imagine it'll look like a dungeon."

"Are you sure you want us to leave?" Mike asked.

Jack nodded. "Sam's here. She's all I need right now."

Lauren frowned, staring from Sam to Jack and back again. Jack seemed to know that he'd made a mistake, but he didn't bother correcting himself, and Lauren didn't question what must have seemed like an obvious error.

Five minutes later, Sam and Jack were alone.

"How are you doing?" he asked, putting an arm around her shoulder as they sat together on the couch.

"I've been better. I've been worse, too. I don't remember ever praying so much."

"The last time I remember praying, *really* praying, was the day Beau's mom died." He leaned forward, resting his elbows on his widespread knees, and stared at the floor. "I hadn't seen Beth for nearly two weeks, since she'd taken Beau home from the hospital."

"Why?" she asked, encouraging him to talk about that day, about the memories that had haunted him so long.

He laughed lightly. "Her father didn't want his little girl messing around with a cowboy. Didn't matter that I was the father of his grandchild."

"What about Beth? Didn't she have anything to say about it?"

"We were sixteen, Sam. How do you tell your parents when you're that age to stay out of your life?"

"Kids do it all the time."

"Not Beth. Not at first." He smiled, as if remembering a good memory amidst the bad. "I showed up at her bedroom window one morning and talked her into running away. She looked so darn pretty when she handed Beau and a bag full of his things to me through the window. Then she jumped down to the ground and gave me a kiss. We weren't thinking much about what we were doing, we were just thinking about being together, the three of us."

"Beau was with you during the accident?"

Jack nodded. "I'd bought a car seat a week before he was born. I'd bought a crib and a high chair and a pair of fancy cowboy boots that were big enough for a five-year-old. I had so many plans for the three of us. I was going to build a cabin, put up the white picket fence Beth had wanted, and even plant flowers. That's what we were talking about that morning. We were laughing and having a good time, and I wasn't paying the least bit of attention to the road."

He got up from the sofa and walked across the room, going to the window to stare out at the starry sky. Sam stood behind him, resting her cheek against his back, feeling so much of his pain.

"I heard the big rig's air horn just before I saw the grille bearing down on us. I jerked the steering wheel—probably the same thing Beau did when he saw the pronghorn this morning. My pickup rolled. I don't know how many times. I don't remember much of anything except lying on the ground and seeing the truck a good thirty feet away from me.

"Beau was crying. Beth was screaming for help." He dragged in a deep, trembling breath. "My leg was broken, but I don't remember any pain. All I remember was getting to the pickup, smelling the fuel, and seeing the blood and tears on Beth's face. Her legs were trapped beneath the dashboard, and she couldn't get loose. I needed to help her, but I had to get Beau to safety before I could do anything else. She begged me not to leave her, and I promised I'd be right back.

"I remember the truck driver running toward me, asking if there was anything he could do. I just gave him the baby to hold, and started to run back. But it was too late. Too damn late."

There were tears in his eyes when he turned toward her. He wiped them away with the back of his hand. "I'm not going to lose Beau," he told her. "I'm not going to lose you, either, Sam."

He cupped her cheeks in his palms and kissed her softly. "It's been a long time since I've been in love. I'd almost forgotten what it felt like," he said. His gaze was warm. The sorrow was gone from his eyes, and they were filled with other things now. Hope—which she knew all about, tenderness, and something wonderful that she hadn't seen from a man before.

"I love you, Sam. God, how I love you."

"I love you, too," she whispered, sliding her arms around his neck and holding him close.

"Remember me telling you about my dream, about being happy with what I had?"

"Of course I remember. I thought it was the best dream in the entire world."

"Something was missing from that dream,

though. Something I hadn't been able to find, you know, like a missing puzzle piece. But I've found it now. You're the missing piece, Sam, and you fit perfectly."

"I do?" she asked, unable to keep her tears from falling.

"You do," he said softly. "Marry me, Sam."

It didn't seem possible. It didn't seem real, but Jack Remington had just made all her hopes and dreams come true.

"I always wanted to fit in somewhere, to be part of someone's dream," she said. "I can't imagine a better one to marry into."

Jack's eyebrow rose. "I take it that's a yes?"

She nodded, and tried to smile through all her tears. "I love you, Jack."

He wrapped her in his arms and kissed her, softly, sweetly, warm, and oh so very tenderly. For the first time in her life she was in love, really and truly in love, and it felt heavenly.

"Mr. Remington." A woman's voice startled both of them.

"Is it Beau?" Jack asked, worry lining his brow as he stared at the lady in pale green scrubs.

"His vital signs are good. He's not awake yet, but you could have a few minutes with him if you'd like." She looked at Sam. "Just one of you—for now."

Jack looked in Sam's eyes. "This has turned

out to be a pretty great day after all." He brushed a kiss across her lips, and Sam watched him talking with the doctor as they went down the hall.

Sam went to the window and stared out at the sky. She remembered a night like this six months ago. She'd been in a hospital then, too, holding her mother's nearly lifeless hand. "Is it cloudy outside, honey?" she'd asked, using every last ounce of strength to talk to her daughter.

"No, Mama. The stars are shining big and bright."

Sam remembered the gentle squeeze her mother gave her hand. "Since the clouds aren't in the way anymore, maybe I can touch a star."

"You can, Mama. I know you can."

"I want the stars for you, too, honey. I just never knew how to give them to you."

She'd gasped for breath, but she never finished. She closed her eyes as if she were falling asleep.

And then she was gone.

Sam wiped a tear from her cheek. "I've touched the stars, Mama," she whispered. "Thanks for leading me to them."

Somehow Sam slept. She'd wanted to stay awake for Jack, for Beau, but sometime in the middle of the night, when Jack made one of his brief but frequent trips to Beau's room, she closed her eyes. When she felt the cushion shift beside her on the sofa, she opened her eyes. Jack wrapped an arm around her. "I didn't mean to wake you up."

"What time is it?"

"Not quite two."

"Is Beau awake yet?"

He shook his head, weaving his fingers through hers. "It could be hours. Why don't you try to sleep again."

"You don't mind?"

He kissed her temple and shook his head.

She rested against his shoulder and with one hand pressed against his chest felt the steady rhythm of his heart, a heart that would always beat next to hers. She closed her eyes, and when she opened them again, Jack was gone. It was six-thirty. More doctors and nurses bustled through the halls now.

Rising, she went to the nurse's station and asked where she could find Beau's room. "Could I see him?"

"I suppose it wouldn't hurt to have two of you in there, but don't stay long."

She walked down the hall, stepped through the open door, and saw Jack sitting in a chair next to Beau's bed. His legs were widespread and he rested his elbows on his knees. He watched his son.

"Mind if I come in?"

He looked up and smiled.

She stood behind him, and he rested his head against her chest. "How's he doing?" she asked.

Beau's eyelids fluttered. "I hurt," he mumbled.

A lump froze in Sam's throat as Jack reached for his son's hand. "You had us worried for a while."

Beau opened his swollen eyes. "I did?"

"Yeah. Pretty nasty accident you got yourself into."

"Are you mad at me?"

Jack shook his head as Beau's eyes closed, then opened again. "I was, but not anymore."

Sam put a hand on Jack's shoulder, squeezing it gently. "I'll be outside."

"You don't have to go," Beau said.

"The two of you have things to talk about." She touched her fingers to her lips and pressed them against Beau's cheek, never more thankful to see anyone awake. Brushing a soft kiss across Jack's mouth, she whispered, "I love you," then left the room.

Jack wished Sam was still at his side. He could use the moral support. He'd kept things from Beau far too long. It was time to tell him everything.

"I'm sorry about the truck," Beau said. "I'll pay you back."

"It's insured. So are you—but you can't be replaced."

A weak smile touched Beau's bruised and swollen lips. "You mean that?"

"Never meant anything more in my life."

"Do my grandparents know about the accident?"

"I called them almost twenty-four hours ago. I imagine they'll be here to see you sometime soon."

Beau looked toward the window. "Are they going to take me back to LA?"

"They want to, but I told them the decision's yours."

"I don't want to make that decision."

"If you leave it up to your grandparents, they'll have you back in LA in a couple of days."

Turning his head on the pillow, Beau looked Jack straight in the eyes. "I want *you* to make the decision."

In sixteen years, he'd made only two decisions for his son. He'd given him a name—he'd picked his grandfather's, a loving man with a generous heart. And he gave his son away—because he'd wanted to forget the best and the worst parts of his life.

This time he prayed he'd make the right decision.

"You're staying with me, Beau."

Beau sniffed back a tear, and Jack leaned over and kissed his son, just below the bandages on his forehead. "I love you, Beau," he whispered. "I always have. I always will."

"Me too, Dad."

twenty-one

Lauren relaxed on the living-room sofa, thankful that Beau was out of danger, relieved that Jack had called her at the ranch to share the wonderful news. Her nephew had to be the most adorable young man on the face of the earth, and she couldn't bear the thought of losing him. As for her brother, he meant more to her than anything or anyone. Seeing Jack in despair had been more painful than either one of her divorces, far more distressing than her breakup with Peter.

Fortunately, Beau was recovering nicely, and now that she didn't have to worry about her nephew or big brother, she could get back to the job at hand: planning a wedding.

Taking a sip of coffee, she flipped through the pages of *Bride* magazine, ripping out pictures of gowns that she knew would look absolutely perfect on Arabella.

Or was her name really Sam?

It had seemed so odd to hear Jack call his fiancée Sam. Whiskey, she could understand. But a man's name? Perhaps the mistake should be forgiven, considering the horrid circumstances he'd been facing in that dreadful waiting room yesterday, but as soon as she and Mike got to the hospital this afternoon, she'd have a talk with her brother about his little slip. Heavens, she'd be mortified if the man she loved called her by the wrong name.

What if Jack accidentally did it on his wedding night or at the altar? No, she couldn't let that happen. It would spoil all her plans for the wedding and reception.

She'd already made out a guest list, then crossed off her ex-husband, Chip. She'd hesitated at Peter Leighton. Should he be invited? Shouldn't he? She'd drawn a thin black line through his name, stared at what she'd done, and rewritten her ex-lover's name at the bottom of the list just in case she changed her mind.

That was a woman's prerogative, after all.

As for where Arabella and Jack would get married, she'd already decided that, too. Her home in Palm Beach was the only place that would do. Arabella would look stunning gliding down the curving, pink-marble staircase. And even though the caterer for her last en-

gagement party had mistakenly hired an ine-
briated ice carver who specialized in
pornographic figures, he was the best in Palm
Beach and the only one who could provide the
cake, the hors d'oeuvres, and wine. Charles,
her butler, had been instructed to have the
house cleaned from top to bottom, and she'd
talked with an aviary about renting doves and
lovebirds to release when Arabella and her
brother said, "I do."

This wedding would be the most glorious
event in Palm Beach history.

Arabella and Jack were both going to be
thrilled.

The phone rang, momentarily pulling her
thoughts away from what color china to use
at the reception. "Charles," she called out.
"Could you—" Oh, dear, she'd nearly forgotten she wasn't at home. Tossing the magazine
onto the coffee table, she crossed the room and
answered on the third ring. "Hello."

"Jack Remington, please."

Lauren didn't like the sound of the woman's
voice. There was a certain rudeness to her
tone, like so many of the women Jack had associated with before meeting Arabella. "I'm
afraid he's not here at the moment. Could I
have him call you back?" she asked, plucking
a pen from the pencil holder next to the phone.

The woman at the other end of the line

heaved a disgruntled sigh. "Tell Jack I'm getting married tomorrow. Tell him I found a man who knows how to treat a real woman."

Lauren stared at the receiver. What a crazy message. Still, she wrote it down word for word. "Is that it?"

"Yes. Of course, you could also tell him that I still think he's a son of a bitch."

Must be an old lover, Lauren thought. "Could I tell him who called?"

"Don't you know?"

"Why should I? You don't know who *I* am."

"I'm Jack's *ex*-fiancée. Arabella."

The pen slipped out of Lauren's fingers and rolled across the desk. "Arabella *Fleming*?"

"As far as I know, I'm the only Arabella Jack has ever been engaged to."

"But I thought—"

"Who is this?" the woman interrupted, her tone sharp.

"Lauren," she said softly, almost too stunned to speak. "Jack's sister."

"Oh." The woman's word was clipped. "Sorry I missed your engagement party. Jack wanted desperately for me to be there, but considering the state of our relationship at the time, I couldn't possibly go. You understand, I'm sure."

"Of course, I do." But there were many *other* things she didn't understand. "I'll make sure

Jack gets your message—Arabella."

Lauren hung up the phone. She walked across the room, absently picked up *Bride*, and sat on the sofa. She stared at the pretty woman on the cover, at the baby's breath and rosebuds, the white satin and lace, and all of it became a blur.

Who was the woman pretending to be Arabella Fleming? she wondered. What was Jack up to and why?

And how could her brother and that woman—Sam, or Whiskey, or whatever her name was—put on such a wonderful act of being in love?

A terrible knot of sadness squeezed her heart. Jack may have thought he had a good reason for his foolish scheme, but in the long run, she felt deceived. Worse yet, for the first time ever, he'd hurt her.

Jack rented a room at the Holiday Inn. He hadn't wanted to leave Beau's side, but his son was resting comfortably, and the doctors and nurses were watching over him, providing the best of care. He'd spirited Sam away from the hospital in the middle of her protest. She hadn't wanted to leave Beau either, but he'd insisted. She needed rest. She needed comfort.

He doubted he could have made it through the past twenty-four hours without her. She'd stood at his side every moment, offering him compassionate support and gentle strength. It seemed second nature to her. The hardships in her life had made her strong. Now, he wanted to spend a lifetime taking care of her, giving her everything she deserved.

Especially his love.

And right now, he desperately needed to love her.

"Are you tired?" he asked her, as she went to the bed and turned back the covers.

"A little." She smiled softly, the kind of smile that had made him want her the very first time he'd seen her, the kind of smile that whispered I love you, I need you, and begged for a response.

"Come here," he whispered.

She didn't ask why, she simply walked toward him. He clutched the bottom of her sweater and drew it over her head, tossing it somewhere across the room. "There's something I need to tell you about myself," he said, releasing the catch at the front of her bra. "I don't need a whole lot of sleep. Never have. Doubt that I ever will." He slipped the bra away and let it fall to the floor, at last cupping her sweet, wonderful breasts in his palms. "I might be keeping you awake a lot at night."

"Is that a promise?"

He nodded, popped the top button on her

jeans, and slid open the zipper. Pushing his hands under her panties, he cupped the soft, smooth flesh on her bottom and pulled her hard against his hips. "I need a promise from you, too, Sam."

"Anything."

She slowly unbuttoned his shirt, pressing soft kisses to each speck of skin as it became exposed. "First, don't ever stop doing just what you're doing," he told her, wanting her to make love to him with her eyes, her lips, her smile every day for the rest of their lives. "Second, don't ever leave me."

The intensity of her frown startled him. "Why would I do something crazy like that?"

"Remember that investigation?"

"*Remember*? There's a possibility I might never forget." She studied his eyes, obviously trying to read what was in them. "You didn't by any chance get another report—"

He kissed her to silence, tasting the sweet lips he knew he'd never get tired of. When she sighed, when he felt her fingers clutch the fabric of his shirt, he went back to his question, one that had bothered him for days. "I didn't get another report. Like I told you before, Wes Haskins isn't working for me any longer. But, that original report made it perfectly clear that you're not big on sticking around any one place too long. I've been worried that you might have a tendency to get bored with everything after a while."

"Do you really think you might bore me?"

"I've been known to bore other women. Arabella, for one."

"Did you ever lasso her?"

"No."

"Did you ever make her do a strip tease for you?"

"No."

"Did you ever hire her to be your fiancée for a night?"

"No."

She smiled that special smile again as she tugged his shirt from his jeans. "Well, Jack, I guess those women weren't as lucky as me." She uncinched his belt buckle and trailed her finger along the edge of his waistband. "I guess they didn't know you as well as I know you, either, because you're the least boring man I've ever met."

"I'm not a son of a bitch?"

"No."

"And you love me?"

"Yes."

"Then promise me one more thing, Sam," he said, dragging her up his body, loving the feel of her breasts rubbing against his chest.

"Anything," she answered, her pretty brown eyes sparkling.

"Don't ever learn about stock, or mergers and acquisitions, because those things are boring as hell."

She smiled. "I promise."

He kissed her, and Sam thought she'd gone to heaven. He had the most delightful way of swirling his tongue around hers, sliding it over her teeth and her lips, then teasing her with feathery kisses and soft nips as he worked his way down her neck.

How he got her to the bed was anyone's guess. How he managed to get her out of her clothes without her feeling anything but his kisses all over her body, and how he managed to strip down to his glorious skin was nothing short of a miracle. But suddenly she was lying on a firm, king-size mattress and he was stretched over her doing all sorts of delicious things with his mouth.

"Make love to me," she begged. "Please."

His blue-eyed smile sent heat rushing through her breasts. They tingled, hot and flaming, and then he nudged her legs apart and entered her in one powerful stroke that took her breath away.

His tempo was masterful, rhythmic. In and out, over and over, he moved with the grace of a cowboy who'd ridden hard and ridden long and never tired, and he seemed to know every time that he was driving her to scream because that's when he kissed the living daylights out of her.

And just when she thought she couldn't take it any longer, he thrust one more time, deep and hard, and the most magnificent skyrockets she'd ever been treated to exploded around them both.

He stilled. His breath was ragged and deep, but a slow smile softened the taut, determined line of his lips. "God," he moaned, resting his head on her chest, "I'm gonna be thanking United Airlines and Mr. Antonio for the rest of my life. If they hadn't screwed up, we wouldn't be here right now. And let me tell you, Sam, being here with you is the best thing ever."

She could think of a thousand things to say, but words wouldn't come. Not now. All she could do at the moment was purr, and when he rolled over and tugged her on top of him, she ran her fingers down his chest, and did her very best to make him want her all over again.

They showered together, made love, dozed off and on, and in between lay together, sharing their love, their secrets, their hopes for the future, even the haunting moments from their pasts.

Jack held her close, drawing lazy circles on

her arm, hesitantly tracing the scar on her jaw. "How'd you get this?" he asked. She didn't want to tell him about that night six months ago, but all of it came pouring out. She couldn't hide anything from him, not now, not ever. She told him about her mother being beaten, about needing money for better doctors, about going to Graham Welles who'd promised to help her if she was ever in need. Anger flared in Jack's eyes, she could feel his muscles tense when she told him Graham had ripped her blouse and slapped her more than once before she'd been able to run away.

"It was so foolish, Jack," she said, a tear sliding down her cheek. "I knew he was no better than the men in my mother's life. I knew what he'd ask of me, and when I went to his house I had every intention of giving him what he wanted—as long as he'd give me the money to save my mother." She looked into his eyes. "Do you hate me for that, Jack?"

"Hate you? God, no, Sam. It makes me love you even more."

"Why?"

"Because you'd do anything for someone you love. *Anything*. There aren't many people who'd do that."

"You would."

He laughed. "I love my sister dearly, and

I'd do anything for her, but my charade wasn't heroic."

"I'm not talking about the charade, Jack. I'm talking about giving up Beau."

"That wasn't heroic, either. That was the most foolish thing I ever did."

"But you did it for what you thought were the right reasons. I believe that. Beau believes it. It's time you start believing it, too."

He lifted her hand and pressed gentle kisses into her palm. "Right or wrong doesn't matter anymore, Sam. All that matters is that I have my son again. I've been given a second chance, and that's something I'll never jeopardize."

She kissed him softly, loving everything about him. "You know what, Jack?"

"What?"

"My mama would have loved you."

A smile tilted his lips as he pulled her on top of him. "I'll make sure she never stops," he said, trailing his hands down her sides and over her bottom. "I'll make sure you never stop—"

The loud knock startled him to silence.

"Jack? Are you in there?"

Hell! What on earth was his sister doing outside the door? "Is that you, Lauren?" he asked, rolling Sam off his chest and onto the bed.

"Oh, it's me all right, and I want to come in."

Hell!

"I don't know who you've got in that room with you, but if you don't open the door in thirty seconds, I'm going to find the house-keeper, have her unlock the door, and I'm coming in."

"Hold your horses, Lauren," he shouted, swinging his legs over the edge of the bed and grabbing his jeans. "I'll open the door in a minute."

"I said thirty seconds, Jack. Not a minute."

"I'm coming!"

"Do you think she found out about the cha-rade?" Sam whispered, scooting off the bed.

"More than likely, and I've got the damned-est feeling she's not happy about it."

"Your thirty seconds are up, Jack," Lauren said, her knuckles knocking not too lightly on the door. "Do I have to get the housekeeper?"

"No. Just let me get my pants on."

Sam tossed aside sheets, blankets, and pil-lows, searching for her sweater, while Jack fumbled with his zipper.

"What are you going to tell her, Jack?"

"The truth." He grabbed Sam around the waist and kissed her hard and fast. "Wish me luck."

Lauren waltzed into the room the moment

he opened the door. Mike followed right behind, a smirk as big as Wyoming plastered on his ugly mug, a smirk Jack might have knocked right off if Mike hadn't been fingering his cross.

"I think I've got some explaining to do," Jack said, hoping his sister would listen.

Lauren spun around. She had a smile on her face. It looked a little fake, but it was definitely a smile. "You have more than explaining to do, brother dear. You and your friend—" She sauntered toward Sam, who smiled nervously as she shoved her bra into the pocket of her jeans. "Hello," Lauren said, holding out her hand. "We haven't been properly introduced. I'm Lauren Remington Chasen Lancaster." Lauren raised an eyebrow. "And *you* are?"

Sam cautiously shook Lauren's hand. "Sam Jones. Samantha, actually."

"Well, I'm glad we've finally got that out in the open."

Lauren sat down on the edge of the bed and gracefully crossed her legs. She aimed a deadly gaze at Jack. "I talked with the real Arabella today. She told me to tell you that you're a son of a bitch. Part of me tends to believe that's true. Part of me . . ."

Jack watched his sister's lips start to tremble. She'd been putting up a good front, but her defenses suddenly crumbled. He went to the bed and sat down beside her. "I never meant to hurt you," he said, and in a rush of words told her everything, about losing his tux, about hiring Sam, about begging her to come to Wyoming when Lauren needed a woman to talk to.

There were tears in her eyes when she looked from Jack to Sam and back again. "You should have told me the truth, Jack. I'm not a little girl anymore, and you can't spend your entire life trying to protect me."

"All I want to do is make you happy."

"I know, and I appreciate it. But I've told you a hundred times before, *your* happiness is what matters the most to me. Hiring a fiancée for a night, even for a day or a week, won't bring you anything but misery."

"You're wrong, Lauren," Jack told her.

"Wrong?"

Sam walked toward him, and he slipped an arm around her waist. He smiled at his wife-to-be. "A month ago I hired Sam to play my fiancée. At the outset it wasn't the proper thing to do, but looking back on it, I never did anything so right."

"What do you mean?"

"Last night I asked her to be my wife—forever."

Another tear slipped down Lauren's face. "You're not making this up, are you?"

"No," Sam said, putting a comforting hand on Lauren's arm. "The masquerade's over."

"Thank God," Mike uttered, speaking for the first time since he and Lauren walked into the room. "I've been praying for this, but I was beginning to wonder if the two of you would ever see the light."

"We saw it," Jack said, looking at the woman he loved. "Problem is, we didn't recognize what it was." And he promised himself he'd never lose sight of it again.

"Well," Lauren said, climbing up from the bed and latching on to Mike's arm. "I'm certainly glad the two of you decided to fall in love. I've got your wedding halfway planned—"

"You what?" Jack blurted out.

Sam tugged on his arm, dragging his attention from his sister and uneasy thoughts of her always grandiose schemes. "I thought Lauren needed something to take her mind off her troubles, and she came up with the wedding idea," Sam said. "I couldn't exactly tell her no."

Jack plowed his fingers through his hair. "I'm not having some big fancy thing—"

Lauren smiled indulgently, knowing full well she could talk him into anything. "It's going to be beautiful, Jack. Doves. Lovebirds. Palm Beach in the spring."

"Doves, fine. Lovebirds"—he shook his head—"whatever! But Palm Beach—absolutely not!"

Lauren sauntered toward the door with Mike in tow. "We'll discuss this later, Jack. Right now, Mike and I are going to visit your son. I'm sure Sam can convince you to see things my way by the time you meet us at the hospital." As she walked out of the room, she smiled at Jack over her shoulder. "I haven't yet forgiven you for the charade, brother dear. You should remember that when you're deciding what kind of wedding you want."

What he wanted was something peaceful and quiet, a small affair with ten or fifteen guests at the most. Hell, going to Las Vegas for a quickie wedding in a brightly lit neon chapel with an Elvis impersonator singing the "Hawaiian Wedding Song" sounded better than a Palm Beach gala. All he wanted to do was get himself firmly hitched to Sam and stay that way for the rest of his life.

Sam smoothed a hand over his back, her soft touch calming him. "I don't mind a Palm Beach wedding," she said softly.

Turning around, he leaned against the door and pulled her against his chest, loving the way she fit perfectly in his arms. "You don't?"

She shook her head. "When I was little I wanted to go to the ball. I wanted to be like

Cinderella and get all dressed up and have everyone watching me as I walked into the room."

He raised an eyebrow. "You still want that?"

"I want *you*, Jack. I honestly don't care where we get married, but . . ." She sighed. "Palm Beach is lovely in the spring and that's where we first met and—"

He kissed her lightly, stifling her words. "If you want to get married in Palm Beach, that's where we'll get married. If you want to spend the winters in Florida, we'll spend the winters in Florida."

"I only want to get married there, Jack. It's pretty and Lauren's home is gorgeous and we'll both be making her happy. But the ranch is my home now. Even though I've been there just a couple of days, I feel like I belong."

"Where you belong is with me," he told her, cupping her face, gazing into warm, fathomless brown eyes. "It doesn't matter if we're at the ranch or in Palm Beach. What matters is that we're together, and I plan on keeping you by my side forever."

She kissed him softly. "Is that a promise?"

"It's a promise, even if I have to lasso you to keep you close."

A gentle smile touched her lips. "You've already done that, Jack. You might not be able to see it, but that rope's good and tight, and it's never going to let go."

epilogue

$\mathcal{F}$_or the_ _fourth_ time in five minutes, Lauren adjusted the circle of baby's breath and white rosebuds atop Sam's head. "This isn't right, Sam. I told the florist I wanted miniature white rosebuds, not regular rosebuds. These are too large and . . . and . . . oh, dear, I wanted everything to be perfect."

Sam smiled, stretching her arms around the woman who'd be her sister-in-law in just a few more minutes. "Everything's beautiful, Lauren, in spite of the rosebuds."

"But it's not, Sam. The ribbons and bows lining the aisles were supposed to be shell pink but they're peach instead. The caterer made crab puffs with imitation crab instead of making crab quiche with the real thing." She sighed. "I don't understand how so many things could go wrong, especially in Palm Beach."

Sam kissed Lauren's cheek. "Wrong would have been no wedding at all."

"That's true."

"Wrong would have been red ribbons and bows lining the aisles, carnations in my hair, and pigs-in-a-blanket for hors d'oeuvres."

"Who would ever plan something like that?"

"Me, more than likely."

"You wouldn't?"

"I would. Never in a million years would I have thought about releasing butterflies at the end of the ceremony, and you know I would have picked a white miniskirt from How Tacky instead of flying to Paris to have a gorgeous gown like this custom made."

"It is beautiful, isn't it?"

"It's *all* beautiful, but I'm afraid I'm going to ruin everything when I pass out halfway down the stairs."

Lauren adjusted the wreath about Sam's head one more time. "There's nothing to be nervous about, Samantha. Trust me. I've been through this twice and I've never passed out." She put her fingers to her lips, deep in thought. "I'll tell you what. If you think you *are* going to faint, give me a sign, like . . . oh . . . fanning your face, and I'll make sure Jack rushes up the stairs to catch

you. That would make everything perfect—
and oh-so-romantic."

Suddenly the music started. The time had
come. After two months of preparation, two
months of falling ever more deeply in love,
she was finally going to be Mrs. Jack Remington.

"Remember, Sam," Lauren instructed.
"Walk slowly, and don't go until you're sure
I'm at the end of the aisle. This is your wedding, and I don't want anyone looking at me
when they should be looking at you. And one
last thing. When you meet my mother after the
ceremony, don't feel intimidated and whatever you do—don't call her Lady. She's a little
upset with the Lord right now and doesn't
want anyone reminding her that she married
the little twit. As for my dad, he brought two
big-chested blondes with him because he
couldn't decide who he could be without for
a few days."

Sam caught Lauren's fingers and squeezed
them. "There's one more thing, Lauren."

"Oh, no. Did I forget something?"

"No, I just want to say I love you."

Tears glistened in Lauren's eyes. "Me too."

Without another word, Lauren swirled her
gown around her, positioned her bouquet at
exactly the proper angle, and transformed
from wedding planner to elegant matron of

honor, gracefully walking down a pink-marble staircase. Sam studied every move she made, until she caught sight of Beau, leaning on crutches, proudly watching his dad.

Jack stood out in the crowd, tall, handsome, and beaming like he'd never been happier. His gaze traveled from his son, to his sister, to the top of the stairs. Sam stood in a shadowy alcove, but he found her. She watched his chest rise and fall as he smiled, and she blew him a kiss as the "Wedding March" began.

Taking a deep breath, she clutched the bouquet of white rosebuds in front of her. "Break a leg," she whispered, and stepped into the light.

The guests rose from their chairs and turned. All eyes, all smiles were on her.

She belonged here, and she felt wonderful.

Most of the faces she passed were nothing but a blur of strangers, and then she saw Tyrone, giving her two thumbs-up. Maryanne clutched the arm of the man next to her and pointed excitedly at the diamond ring on her finger. Fay and John Atkinson had flown from their ranch to Palm Beach for the occasion, and both of them were in tears. Finally, she saw Crosby. He stood in the very front row, looking curmudgeonly dapper in a tux. When she smiled at him, he pulled a red-and-white bandanna from his pants pocket and put it to his eyes.

No one could have asked for a more perfect wedding.

The most perfect part came when Jack stepped forward and tucked her hand around his arm. His smile warmed her heart, and calmed all her fears. "I love you," he whispered, and when they knelt in front of Mike, who stood just beyond an archway of ivy and white roses, Jack pressed something cool into her hand.

With Mike looking down at them, with a room full of people hushed and waiting for the ceremony to begin, she opened her palm and found a sparkling crystal star. There were tears in her eyes when she looked at Jack, and he caressed one away from her cheek. "You told me once you wanted to touch the stars," he whispered. "I'm going to give them to you every day of your life."

Her lips trembled. "I love you."

He kissed her, long before he was supposed to. "Forever."

Mike grinned, opened his Bible, and began. "Dearly beloved, we are gathered today, in the sight of God . . ."

Through the haze of words, laughter, and tears, the only things clear to Sam were the smile in Jack's eyes, the touch of their hands as they exchanged simple gold bands, and the sweetness of Jack's lips when he lifted her from the floor and kissed her, giving her a memory she would never forget as long as she lived.

The applause rang out all around them as Mike introduced them as husband and wife. And when the butterflies fluttered about, Sam turned to the opened doors that looked toward the ocean and the cloudless sky. There were millions of stars out, but one seemed to shine brighter than all the rest.

Sam couldn't help but smile. *Oh, Mama, I can just imagine what you would say right now.*

Dear Reader,

So many of you have been patiently waiting for Lori Copeland's next Avon Romantic Treasure, so I'm thrilled to say you don't have to wait any longer! Next month, don't miss *The Bride of Johnny McAllister*—it's filled with all the wonderful, warm, western romance that you expect from this spectacular writer. Johnny McAllister is on the shady side of the law, and never in a million years would he believe he'd fall for the local judge's daughter. But fall he does—and hard. You will not want to miss this terrific love story.

Contemporary readers, be on the look out—Eboni Snoe is back, too! Your enthusiastic response to Eboni's last Avon contemporary romance, *Tell Me I'm Dreamin'*, has helped build her into a rising star. Next month don't miss her latest, *A Chance on Lovin' You*. When a stressed-out "city gal" inherits a home in the Florida Keys, she thinks that this is just what she needs to change her life...but the real changes come when she meets a millionaire with more than friendship on his mind.

Gayle Callen is fast becoming a new favorite for Avon readers, and her debut Avon Romance, *The Darkest Knight*, received raves. Now don't miss the follow-up *A Knight's Vow*. And sparks fly in Linda O'Brien's latest western *Courting Claire*—as an unlikely knight in shining armor comes to our heroine's rescue.

Don't miss any of these fantastic love stories!

Lucia Macro
Lucia Macro
Senior Editor

ael 0899

Discover Contemporary Romances at Their Sizzling Hot Best from Avon Books